The Hymn Tune Mystery

George A. Birmingham

First published: UK: Methuen, 1930; US: Bobbs-Merrill, 1931

This edition published 2022 by

OREON

an imprint of

The Oleander Press
16 Orchard Street
Cambridge
CB1 1JT

www.oleanderpress.com

A CIP catalogue record for the book
is available from the British Library.

ISBN: 9781915475091

Cover design, typesetting & ebook: neorelix

The Hymn Tune Mystery

For first news of
titles, give-aways and
discounts, sign up to our
infrequent newsletter at:
oleanderpress.com

1

OF THE SMALLER CATHEDRALS in England none is more
beautiful than Carminster, and none, surely, more felicitously
peaceful. For many centuries, indeed since the days of Bishop
Feda, who flourished in the Renaissance period, Carminster
has been almost without a history. The Reformation and the
Elizabethan settlement of Church affairs descended quietly on
Carminster, scarcely disturbing the placid life of the place. The
Civil War passed it by, and it may fairly claim the singular dis-
tinction of being the only church of any size in England in
which Cromwell's troopers did not stable their horses, whose
stained glass was not shattered by iconoclastic Puritans. Dean
has succeeded dean, and dwelt for his allotted span, usually
a very long span, in the fine old Deanery, pacing in scholarly
leisure the wide slope down to the river, passing morning and
evening through the gateway which leads into the cloisters and
thence to the cathedral itself.

Canons residentiary, four of them, have succeeded each other,
inheriting pleasant houses in the Close, the claustrum canonicorum of the ancient charter. The Bishop lives some miles away
in the splendid seclusion of Calverton Castle, and this fact does
much to secure the peace of Carminster. A bishop is a potentate
whose rights and privileges sometimes clash with those of deans

1

and chapters. But a bishop who lives miles away is seldom trou-blesome. Even now, when motor transport is swift and cheap, it is difficult for disputants who live ten miles apart to keep up a quarrel with any vigour.

The little town of Carminster has been almost as fortunate as its mother church. The men of the industrial revolution never discovered it. There is no coal within many miles of it, and therefore no one ever thought of establishing a factory in it. It huddles, or perhaps one should say nestles, in a little maze of narrow streets at a respectful distance from the cathedral, separated from the venerable walls by the pleasant quadrangle of the Canons' Close and the lawns of the Deanery. The town seems to exist – indeed really does exist – solely for the sake of the cathedral. No one who has ever been there would suppose for a moment that the cathedral exists to serve the town. Yet, nowa-days, when travellers in search of the picturesque have taken the place of the old pilgrims, the town does benefit greatly by the existence of the cathedral. The Mitre Inn, owned and managed by Mr. Powell, would be a place of slender profit if it were not for the Americans who come in hired Daimler cars to remark on the 'cunningness' of both cathedral and town. Powell, a wise man, has not wasted money in modernising his inn. He realises that though Americans like baths and central heating they prefer atmosphere; and atmosphere, since the Mitre dates from the reign of Queen Elizabeth, is easily supplied, and is much cheaper than either baths or heating.

There are, jostling each other in the narrow streets, eight dealers in antique furniture. Neither the dean nor any of the four canons is likely to buy antique furniture, having as much of such stuff as their houses will hold. These dealers, like Mr. Powell, depend for their trade on Americans and other visitors who come to see the cathedral. There are other shops, a grocer or two, a modest though old-established wine merchant, a bookseller, and a butcher (who inhabits a small side street well out of sight) to supply the wants of the dean, the four canons, several minor canons, some lay vicars, a band of vergers, the visitors to the Mitre and – there is considerable eagerness to secure this trade – the great new house in Carminster Park.

The house in the Park, Carminster Chase, was built in 1923 by Lord Carminster, one of the new men of immense wealth, whom the tempest of the war period flung up, precious flotsam and jetsam, on the beach of English society. A puzzled monarch, acting constitutionally on the advice of a grateful and hopeful Prime Minister, made Tom Lyon an earl. Tom, having paid heavily for his title, felt that he was free to choose his new name. He chose Carminster, because he had once been a choirboy in the cathedral and had received the education of which he made such good use in the cathedral school. Whenever he made a speech in Carminster or the neighbourhood, he used to say that he was not in the least ashamed of having been a choirboy and was very proud of 'the old school'. This spirit, a pride which aped humility, made the earl very popular. The newness of the mansion he built in place of an old, greatly-dilapidated manor house, was forgiven him, even in Carminster, where newness is an almost unpardonable sin.

The earl gained further popularity by his generosity to the cathedral. He established, one after the other, three valuable scholarships in the school, and on each occasion the dean made a speech of thanks, saying that the fortunate boys who held the scholarships ought to take Lord Carminster for their example and inspiration in life, using opportunity – on one occasion the dean said redeeming the time – as the pious donor had used his.

Dean Grosvenor did not like making this kind of speech, and in his heart believed that the boys would be better and happier if they did not follow in the steps of Lord Carminster. But the dean was largely under the control of his daughter, and

Miss Grosvenor realised that nice things ought to be said about generous benefactors. It was Miss Grosvenor who wrote out these speeches for the dean. She submitted them for approval to the archdeacon, who was chief of the four residentiary canons. He agreed with Miss Grosvenor about the speeches, so the dean, only daring to modify them very slightly, delivered them.

Lord Carminster's next gift was an enormous processional cross, a standard of pure silver, richly jewelled, designed by a member of the Royal Academy. It turned out to be so heavy that the aged lay clerk who usually headed the cathedral processions staggered under the weight of it. A young man of very sturdy form, who had no previous connection with the choir, was specially hired to carry it, and even he was damp with the sweat of exhaustion when a procession came to an end.

Benefactions fell on the cathedral like heavy rain. Lord Carminster next offered to bear the entire expense of moving the tomb of Bishop Feda from its place in the very middle of the choir to — He did not much care where it was moved to so long as it was taken from its old position. There is no doubt that this transference of the bones of the great bishop was suggested by the archdeacon, who was, as usual, warmly supported by Miss Grosvenor. The tomb is a very large one and is enclosed in a shrine of highly ornamented renaissance work of purely pagan spirit. The archdeacon complained that it completely obscured the view of the high altar from the nave of the cathedral, and the humble worshipper – so the archdeacon said feelingly – ought to be able to see the high altar. Miss Grosvenor agreed with the archdeacon, and added on her own account that the shrine, overloaded with ornament, and decked with Cupids and Venuses, was quite out of place in a Christian church of the Early English period. Here the archdeacon agreed with Miss Grosvenor. They were also at one in their dislike of Bishop Feda. He had, so tradition said, designed his own tomb, shrine and all, and had fixed on its site in the middle of the choir. If he did design it the Cupids and Venuses were accounted for. There had been several ladies in the life story of Bishop Feda, especially a tawny-haired Chloe to whom he actually wrote a poem. The poem was in Latin, but even that did not excuse the bishop. The archdeacon felt, and Miss Grosvenor felt even more strongly, that there ought not to have been a tawny-haired Chloe, and that on her account, even if for no other reason, the bishop's tomb and shrine ought to occupy a less prominent position.

The tomb and shrine were duly moved, with some ceremony, and the bill was paid by Lord Carminster. The dean gave his consent most unwillingly. He hated moving anything in the cathedral, and had, besides, a private liking for Bishop Feda. The dean was a student of medieval Latin lyrics. He admired the poem about Chloe as a piece of literature, though he disapproved, as he was officially bound to disapprove, of the lady. The archdeacon and Miss Grosvenor wanted to deposit the offensive tomb in the crypt, where it would seldom or never be seen. But about this the dean suddenly and obstinately asserted himself. He refused to consent to the total banishment of Bishop Feda. In the end, after an acute controversy, the tomb, shrine and all, was set up in the aisle at the south end of the high altar.

The removal, transference or translation took place in 1924, and in the same year there was another event which excited the dean, chapter, and staff of the cathedral even more than the removal of the tomb.

Scarcely any benefactor is entirely disinterested. There is generally something looked for in return even by the most generous donor. Lord Carminster, who did so much for the dean and chapter, wanted the dean and chapter to do something for him. It was a small thing. In 1923, shortly after the presentation of the processional cross and while the discussion about Bishop Feda's tomb was going on, the oldest and most venerable of the cathedral vergers died. The immediate result was that Carson, a slightly younger man but almost equally venerable, became the dean's verger. Every other verger gained a step upwards in the hierarchy of vergerdom, and there was a vacant place at the bottom of the scale. Lord Carminster put forward a man called Hill for the post. No one knew exactly why Hill wanted it, for he was Lord Carminster's valet, and that surely is a position of more honour and profit than a junior vergery. It was whispered that Lord Carminster wanted to get rid of the man because he was too clever and too energetic to be a comfortable valet. Brains, a disadvantage in a valet, who might easily come to understand his master's affairs too well, are no drawback to a cathedral verger. In that profession there is little or no opportunity for the use of brains, which are therefore of no disadvantage to their possessor.

The dean and chapter without hesitation appointed Hill to the vacant post. The other vergers, especially Carson, resented the intrusion of an outsider. But nobody paid any attention to them. Whether there is a strong trade union among vergers or whether they ought to hold diplomas from some college of ecclesiastical procedure is not known. All that is certain is that the appointment of an unqualified non-unionist is resented by vergers everywhere, and was felt bitterly in Carminster.

The opposition to the appointment was soon and dramatically justified. There was a sensational burglary at the Chase and Lady Carminster's emeralds were stolen. They were immensely valuable but of no sentimental interest. Lord Carminster was not the kind of earl who possesses family jewels, and the stolen emeralds had been bought only a few years before. They were fully insured, so the only people deeply interested in the matter were the unfortunate insurers. It was at their urgent request that Sergeant Hodson was brought down from Scotland Yard to investigate the crime. He succeeded in catching the criminals, among them – indeed the ringleader of the gang – was Hill, the lately-appointed cathedral verger. Hodson was an able man, who knew his business as a detective, but it is doubtful whether he could have discovered Hill's share in the burglary if he had not had the help of Carson and the other vergers. They had, so Carson said, suspected him of iniquity from the very first moment they saw him. They had watched him, indeed spied on him. They joyfully gave Hodson information which led to the arrest of Hill and the capture of his associates. The judge imposed sentences which were described in the newspapers as 'exemplary'. Hill got seven years' penal servitude. His friends got five years each.

Hodson went back to London highly pleased with his success. The insurance company was less pleased. The criminals were arrested and punished, which was satisfactory; but not even Hodson could discover what had happened to the jewels. Lord Carminster received his money and bought more emeralds. The insurance company suffered a severe loss.

The dean and chapter, after the first excitement had worn off, began to feel acutely the disgrace which had tarnished the reputation of their cathedral, spotless since Bishop Feda was laid in his tomb and the tawny-haired Chloe in hers. The archdeacon, who had an almost morbid horror of what he called scandal, suffered more than anyone else, except perhaps Miss Grosvenor. A cathedral verger very seldom turns out to be a burglar. There is a certain rather piquant antithesis between the two professions. The newspapers, alive to anything likely to tickle the palate of the public, seized on the burglar-verger as a heaven-sent subject for headlines. The archdeacon quivered with disgust every time that he saw the words 'cathedral convict', 'crime in the Church', 'verger-burglar condemned'. One 'detestable rag' – the words were the archdeacon's – even published an article headed, 'Are the Movies Responsible for All the Crime? What about Cathedrals?' Miss Grosvenor, like the archdeacon, suffered severely, and it was noticed by her friends that two wrinkles appeared on her neck during the trial. The dean, who was getting very old, shut himself up more and more with his books and began a translation, into English verse, of some of the less-known medieval lyrics.

The public interest in the affair did not last long. Public interest never lasts long. The Carminster scandal died out of memory; but the archdeacon, Miss Grosvenor, and perhaps Carson, the dean's verger, could not wholly forget it. There remained in them a soreness, a scar, a sense of disgrace which not even the passing of many years would wholly obliterate.

2

potatores exquisiti,
Licet sites sine siti...

THE DEAN STARED AT the words, stroking his upper lip gently with the end of his pen. 'Consummate drinkers'. That was Miss Waddell's translation and the dean appreciated its merits.

To you, consummate drinkers,
Though little be your drought,
Good speed be in your tankards,
And send the wine about.

That was good, very good. Miss Waddell had caught both the spirit and the lilt of it. Yet the dean was not quite satisfied. That word *exquisiti*. It was a delightful epithet and wholly unexpected when applied to roistering drinkers. 'Consummate' was not a satisfying translation. There ought to be a better word, a perfect word, if only it could be found. The dean frowned thoughtfully and rubbed his upper lip across and across with the blunt round end of his fountain pen. 'O rare delicious drinkers.' No. That missed the sense of full-mouthed copiousness. 'Rare' and

9

'delicious' suggested the feelings of a connoisseur with a bottle of vintage port in front of him, not the joyous quaffing of the singers in their tavern. 'Ye reckless, merry topers.' But that would not do either. Exquisite does not mean either reckless or merry. There is something fine about the word, a touch of the spirit of the pagans who held Bacchus to be a god. The dean squeezed his upper lip tightly against his teeth and his frown deepened. What was the word?

The door of the room opened gently and his daughter came in. The dean sighed and quickly turned over the pages of the book in front of him. When his daughter reached him and glanced over his shoulder the book was opened at another Latin poem of quite a different kind: 'O quanta, qualia, sunt illa sabbata.'

That poem has been translated many times, since Neale's version of it found a place in 'Hymns Ancient and Modern'. 'Oh what the joy and the glory must be!' The dean had no particular wish to translate it again. But if he was to be caught by his daughter reading medieval Latin lyrics he preferred to be caught reading a hymn rather than a drinking song. It is not of course wrong for a dean to read a drinking song. It is not even wrong to appreciate the spirit of it and to enjoy the abandoned lilt of the verse. But Dean Grosvenor was aware that his daughter would regard 'consummate drinkers' with serious disapproval. She would think of them as vulgar creatures and the study of their works as – well, a dean is styled 'Very Reverend' and Theodore Grosvenor was Dean of Carminster, one of the most beautiful of our English cathedrals. 'The Very Reverend the Dean of Carminster.' 'To you, consummate drinkers.' The two things do not go together harmoniously. Sybil Grosvenor, the dean's daughter, would be conscious of an unpleasant discord.

And Sybil Grosvenor was capable of forming an opinion of her own on such a subject. She was not a parson's daughter of the meek domestic kind, interested chiefly in house linen and the bad behaviour of Dicky Smiles in Sunday School. After four years at Somerville, Sybil took a brilliant First Class in Classics, a rare achievement for a girl. She could read without the slightest difficulty the book of poems before her father, and was classic enough to despise the medieval latinity as wholeheartedly as she disliked the spirit of the songs.

With the chance, indeed the certainty, of becoming a female don, she deliberately, out of pure sense of duty, left Oxford, cut herself off from the mild delights of scholarly society, and came home to look after her father and to 'run' his deanery for him. She did both with cool efficiency, and, since she was a young woman of abundant energy, took an active and influential part in running the cathedral, with the aid of the archdeacon. Intended by nature to be the head of an institution, she felt that she was rather wasted in Carminster. But that was a feeling to which she never gave expression, and indeed sternly repressed, consoling herself when it came upon her with a repetition of Keble's lines about 'the daily round, the common task'.

Unfortunately for himself, and perhaps a little unfortunately for Sybil, the dean did not like a house which is 'run'. He preferred the kind which ambles quietly, where nothing is very highly polished, and meals are served unpunctually. Nor did he think that his cathedral ought to be 'run'. A cathedral in a great city, St. Paul's, for instance, ought perhaps to be spurred into a perpetual gallop in order to keep well abreast of the swift steeds of modern life, if such a thing is possible. That might be so. Dean Grosvenor had no views about the proper management of such places as St. Paul's. About Carminster Cathedral he had a very clear opinion. It stood in a little town amid a wide expanse of peaceful, rural land. It ought – yes, ought – in his own mind the dean was certain about this – Carminster ought to loiter, lagging a little behind the trampling regiments of progress.

But Sybil thought that Carminster ought to be 'run'. And the archdeacon, by far the most influential member of the chapter, agreed with her. Therefore the cathedral was 'run', though the dean, a dead weight rather than an active force of opposition, delayed the progress.

But chiefly the dean disliked being 'run' himself. Sybil had her way with the house and a good deal of her way with the cathedral, but she never succeeded in making her father what a dean ought to be. Up to a certain point he satisfied her. With his silky white hair and his thin, ascetic face, he was, beyond dispute, the most picturesque dean in England. His attendances at the cathedral services were regular and reverent. No dean ever walked with more gracious dignity behind a verger carrying a silver mace. But Sybil wanted more. She wanted a Dean of Carminster who made influential speeches in the Church Assembly, who carried weight in Convocation, who published from time to time treatises on the Apostolic Succession and the bearing of that doctrine on the validity of sacraments. These things Dean Grosvenor obstinately refused to do. He was growing old – very old. He hated public meetings, and especially hated deliberative assemblies. He had long ago discovered the worthlessness of scholarly treatises. He liked his own study. He liked his medieval lyrics. He refused to recognize – though the thing was clear enough to Sybil and the archdeacon – that his fondness for quiet and for ancient drinking songs, was a sign that his mind was growing feeble and that his feet required guiding along the ways of life.

'I was talking to the archdeacon for a few minutes after evensong,' said Sybil.

The dean was very sorry to hear it, though he did not venture to say so. Sybil's talks with the archdeacon usually meant trouble for him.

Sybil waited a moment before she announced the subject of her conversation. She glanced at the book on the table in front of her father and saw that it was open at Abelard's Vesper Hymn. Sybil was forced to admit that this was a thoroughly suitable subject for a dean's study. Yet she would have been more satisfied if her father had been reading, or, still better, writing, a treatise on Anglican Orders. Abelard's hymn is pious, no doubt, in a wild, mystical way. But then there had been that unpleasant affair with Héloise. If Sybil had been a less refined woman than she was she would have sniffed at the 'O quanta qualia'. Being what she was she only pressed her lips together for a moment before she opened them to speak again.

'We were talking about Mr. Cresswood,' she said.

'Ah,' said the dean. 'Cresswood, poor Cresswood.'

'Mr. Cresswood is becoming a scandal,' said Sybil. 'The archdeacon says so, and I quite agree with him.'

It was scarcely possible even for the dean to disagree with the archdeacon and Sybil about Cresswood. A cathedral organist – that was the post held by Mr. Cresswood – ought to be above reproach. A little eccentricity may perhaps be tolerated, for, after all, an organist is, or ought to be, a musician, and therefore not quite as sane as an archdeacon is. But Cresswood was worse than eccentric. The man drank too much – far too much – and everybody knew it. The thing was as bad as it could be. There were stories, told profanely by choirboys, of empty whisky bottles found in the organ loft. There was no getting away from the fact that Cresswood's life was scandalous.

'Poor fellow! Poor fellow!' said the dean.

Now, the dean ought not to have spoken in that way. No dean ought to. Perhaps no dean would unless he had just been trying to translate a medieval drinking song. Was Cresswood a 'potator exquisitus', a 'consummate drinker'? He could certainly play the organ. Drunk or sober, and perhaps better when drunk, he could make music. Whatever was said and should be said about the empty whisky bottles in the organ loft the music was 'exquisitus'.

And the dean had another reason, a strictly private reason, for feeling tenderly towards Cresswood. The man could not only play the organ; he understood, or showed some signs of understanding, the dean's translations of the medieval Latin lyrics. The dean had once shown him a lyric, done into English verse, the very best thing he had so far accomplished. He showed it to Cresswood in order to find out whether it would be possible to find a tune, a singable melody for such verses. And Cresswood, amazingly, had understood, had promised to do his best, was perhaps actually at that very moment, while Sybil voiced the archdeacon's feelings, composing a tune, conceived in the spirit of the Church's ancient plainsong, but as scurrilous – Sybil would certainly call it scurrilous – as the words were.

'Something will have to be done about Cresswood,' said Sybil firmly, and done at once. 'That was what the archdeacon said this afternoon, and I quite agree with him.'

The dean knew that something must be done, though he hated the idea of doing it. The 'something' thus vaguely indicated by the archdeacon would be very difficult to do. A cathedral organist is not a housemaid, to be dismissed at a month's notice, at the whim of her mistress. He has a certain security of tenure. He holds a position from which it is exceedingly difficult to dislodge him. Even a resolution, passed unanimously by the entire chapter, calling for his resignation, might be ineffective if the organist chose to ignore it. No doubt in the end the Law could be called to the aid of the Church when a man's life is so plainly scandalous as Cresswood's; but proceedings in courts of law are very odious.

'I wish,' said the dean plaintively, 'that you wouldn't attack me about these things after dinner in the evening. I do think,

14

Sybil, that I am entitled to a little peace and quietness after dinner.'

'Poor father,' said Sybil. 'I am sorry for you; but you know that you'd hate it just as much if I spoke to you about Mr. Cresswood after breakfast, or just before luncheon, or at tea.'

The dean was a just man and recognised the truth when he heard it. There was no hour of the day or night at which he would have been willing to talk about Mr. Cresswood's insobriety.

'Why doesn't the archdeacon speak to me about it himself?' he said.

The archdeacon could not get at him between 9 and 10 o'clock at night in the study in the Deanery, where he was pleasantly occupied in finding a translation for 'exquisitus' applied to a heavy drinker. The archdeacon could only tackle him personally at set times, and that would not be nearly so bad as having his evening spoiled.

'The archdeacon is going to speak to you tomorrow,' said Sybil; 'but we both thought it would be better if I had a word with you first.'

'I don't see why,' said the dean. 'I don't see why it's better that my work should be interrupted in this way, just when I had settled down quietly for the evening.'

'I'm so very sorry, father,' said Sybil, 'but it really seemed to be my duty. If I did not speak to you, you might not listen to the archdeacon. Don't you understand that we must try to make you realise how serious the position is?'

The dean, a just man, even when annoyed, saw that. Sybil's clear sense of duty and her ruthless performance of it were admirable things. He even felt, with a humility rare in deans, that he ought to be more faithful to duty than he was.

Yet there it was, the thing he particularly disliked, the assumption that it was necessary for Sybil and the archdeacon

15

to make him see what he could perfectly well see for himself, though he did not like it when he saw it. This was treating him as if his mind was giving way, as if senile decay was creeping up on him. He was perfectly convinced that his mind was not giving way. He could find a better translation for 'exquisitus' than the archdeacon could – if, indeed, the archdeacon could find a translation at all, being a man of affairs and slightly contemptuous of scholarship.

'So you will think it over, father, won't you? Think it over before the archdeacon sees you tomorrow.'

'I'm not the least likely to be able to think of anything else tonight,' said the dean.

Sybil, who knew her father very well, was not at all afraid of his spending a sleepless night, tossing to and fro, tormented by thoughts of a lawsuit with a drunken organist. She hoped, and surely it was a good thing to hope, that he would be prepared the next day to consent to the archdeacon's demand for definite action. With this hope in her heart she gave her father a gentle little kiss and bade him good night.

The dean turned from Abelard's endless Sabbaths back to the drinking song. But he turned back vainly. He could not regain his lost delight in the exquisite drinkers. All he could do was to wish, petulantly and quite vainly, that Sybil would marry and leave him in peace. Unfortunately, an old rhyme – the dean had a taste for such things, Latin or English – came into his mind:

Miss Buss and Miss Beale
Cupid's darts do not feel.

He knew all about Miss Buss and Miss Beale. They were two of the earliest of our great race of schoolmistresses, and Sybil was very like them. There was no chance of her ever feeling Cupid's darts. If she ever married at all she would make a calmly suitable match when she was forty or forty five. By that time the dean would be dead and would gain nothing by it. What a pity it was that the archdeacon had a wife already or – the dean sometimes had queer, unorthodox fancies – what a pity it was that neither Church nor State allows men like the archdeacon to have two wives, one for domestic use, to be loved and cherished, the other purely official, to be respected and admired.

Sybil would make a splendid official wife for an archdeacon. The dean closed his book and got up. On a peg on the door of his study hung a long black cloak, worn over his surplice when, preceded by his verger with a silver mace, he made his progress morning and evening to the cathedral. He slipped on his cloak and went out. He crossed the Deanery lawn and passed through a little gate into the cloisters. The cathedral was locked for the night. The dean let himself in with his own key by a door set in a corner of the south transept, a door of which he and some privileged members of the staff had keys. He felt a longing for the great dark spaces, the solitude, and the utter silence of a vast building at night. There surely, if anywhere, he would find peace from the harassing worries which for some of us are far harder to bear than life's greater evils.

3

THE CATHEDRAL WHEN THE dean entered it was dark, as he expected it to be. A faint glimmer of light, the dim glow of a night in June, showed through the clerestory windows; but down below, among the pillars and arches of the nave, beyond the screen where the choir stalls were, and upwards to the high altar, the darkness was complete.

The cathedral was also cool and empty. No sightseers wandered, staring curiously at tombs or monuments, as they did all day. No congregation was gathered for worship anywhere. After the verger on duty, thankful to get home to tea, turned the key in the door, no one could get into the cathedral except the dean himself and a few members of the staff who possessed keys of the little door which the dean had used.

But the cathedral, though dark and empty, was not silent. Cresswood, one of the favoured few who possessed a key of the door in the south transept, was playing the organ, playing without knowing that he had any audience, and therefore solely for his own delight. Cresswood always played well. Even when, at the instigation of the archdeacon, he played the meretricious tunes of sentimental hymns, he played as few other men can. No one – at all events neither the archdeacon nor Sybil – guessed the contemptuous bitterness of his spirit. He played well too when, also at the instigation of the archdeacon, he gave short recitals after evensong on Sundays. A short organ recital was, according to the archdeacon, a suitable thing to have in a cathedral on Sunday afternoon, after evensong. Sometimes he stopped and listened to it himself, and when he did Cresswood made as much noise as he could on the organ, for he knew that the archdeacon liked noise. But Cresswood played best when he played at night by himself, unaware that he had any audience. Indeed, he never had any audience except the dean, who had a habit of wandering into the cathedral late at night, and counted himself fortunate if he happened to be there when Cresswood was playing.

It was whispered among the cathedral staff, and said aloud by profane people, that Cresswood played best when he was slightly drunk. The dean had for some time suspected that Cresswood only visited the cathedral by himself at night when he had been drinking more than usual. That perhaps, along with the absence of unappreciative audiences, accounted for the exquisiteness of his playing, in the dark, when the dean alone heard him. Exquisite was just the word for the music at these times. The dean, moving softly through the dark, felt that exquisitus did sometimes go harmoniously with potator. Cresswood was, alas, a drinker, but Cresswood's music was exquisite.

The dean, passing under the heavy screen, made his way eastward towards the high altar, and took his seat beside the shrine which held the tomb of Bishop Feda.

He had, when Lord Carminster first made his offer, opposed the moving of the shrine and tomb from their original place in the middle of the choir. He had given way in the end because it seemed ungracious to refuse the offer of so generous a benefactor. But he had stood firmly against the archdeacon's plan of hiding the shrine in the crypt. The dean had a liking for the memory of Bishop Feda, a liking which gathered strength because the archdeacon and Sybil both strongly disapproved of the man. It is not to be supposed that Dean Grosvenor, a man of pious life, approved of the tawny-haired Chloe and the old Bishop's affection for her. He passed no judgment at all on that episode. He simply felt that a bishop, as great as Feda had certainly been, had a right to choose the site of his own tomb, especially when he took the trouble to design the thing himself and to write his own epitaph – a sound piece of Ciceronian Latin, that epitaph of Bishop Feda. It, and the tomb, and the tawny-haired Chloe always brought to the dean's mind that bishop of Browning's who ordered his tomb at St. Praxed's and set it where he could

Hear the blessed mutter of the mass
And see God made and eaten all day long.

That was, apparently, the wish of Bishop Feda when he chose the site of his tomb, and if the coming of a new race of church-men of severer faith had cut him off from these consolations, at least a glimpse of the high altar ought to be preserved for him. And it was preserved, thanks to Dean Grosvenor's firm insistence, that the tomb should be moved no farther than the south aisle.

The dean sat down beside the shrine and listened to Cress-wood's playing. It may have been the music, made by an organist who drank too much, or it may have been the Cupids, the Venuses, and the luxuriant ornament of the shrine, or it may have been the devil. Whatever it was the dean found himself thinking with sympathy of Bishop Feda – a way in which no dean ought to think.

Dean Grosvenor was a product of Oxford scholarship and the chaste piety of the English Church. Bishop Feda belonged to an age when men were intoxicated with the re-discovery of the glory of life and the greatness of the world. Yet, while Cresswood played, the dean thought tenderly of Feda and his shrine. He even remembered without moral indignation the scandalous tale of the bishop's affection for the lady whom he called Chloe. The little song he wrote about her, a song never published, but to be found under lock and key in the cathedral archives, pleased the dean. The bishop had given orders that Chloe should be laid with him in his shrine when he died. But that impiety had, apparently, been too glaring even for the generous ecclesiastics of those days. The bishop lay in his shrine. Chloe's dust, so it was understood, had long ago mingled with common earth in unconsecrated, or very slightly consecrated, ground.

A strange fancy came to the dean, the result no doubt of Cresswood's music. It seemed to him that the old bishop had come to life again, that he was leading Chloe by the hand up the choir towards the high altar, that the pair moved forward in a sort of stately dance, and, still dancing, genuflected to the altar, before they turned aside to enter the shrine. The sound of the organ went rippling among the arches of the long colonnade, soared to the dim windows of the clerestory. Notes followed each other trippingly among the canons' stalls with their pinnacled canopies. Cresswood was, indubitably and most impiously, playing a dance, an ancient dream of a dance, like that toccata of Galuppi's which Browning made immortal:

Dear dead women with such hair too.
What's become of all the gold?

Fulva comes, the gold hair or tawny hair of poor outcast Chloe, outcast but reclaimed at last by her bishop lover.

Ought a dean, a modern English dean with a daughter who has been to Somerville, ought he to enjoy such imaginings? Perhaps not. At all events Dean Grosvenor did not enjoy them for very long. The music, and with it the imaginings, came to a sudden end. There was a crash, wild discord, the shrieking of a hundred notes at once. The notes of a whole keyboard, of three keyboards, had been pressed down at the same moment, and the air rushed through the pipes, wailing, howling, groaning, a storm of violent discord.

Cresswood had apparently fallen forward, arms outstretched, chest pressed forward, head drooped, right across the keyboards of the organ. The dean pressed his fingers into his ears to shut out the horrible sounds. But no stopping of his ears was of much avail against the torrent of noise. The dean stood up and strode down the choir towards the screen. He was angry and bitterly ashamed. His immediate desire was to get out of the cathedral as quickly as possible, away from the hideous sounds and the more hideous cause of them. He shrank from any contact with Cresswood. It was an offence against all decency, against religion itself, that the man should be sprawling drunk and unconscious across the keyboards of the organ.

The dean neither could nor would do anything himself; but through his rage and disgust he realised that something must be done. The wretched man could not be left there all night. The calm cathedral, with its tombs and its monuments, could not be left till morning to be desecrated by the blaring discords of a drunken organist. Even Bishop Feda, even the tawny-haired Chloe, if their spirits lingered in the shrine, might well be shocked by such profanation. Their immoralities had a certain dignity about them. They were never vulgarly, disgustingly drunk.

The dean's mind was quickly made up. His verger, George Carson, lived close at hand. He should be sent to drag the unconscious Cresswood from the organ loft. He must get him somehow through the sleepy streets and home to his bed. George Carson, a tall, strong man, whose dignity of bearing added something to the stateliness of the cathedral processions, might not like the job, but George Carson would have to do it if the dean told him to.

Then, just as the dean was passing under the screen, the noise suddenly stopped. There was a drawn-out shriek of discord, diminishing to a faint wail, and then silence. The switch which controlled the electrically driven blowing apparatus had been touched. No air was any longer being blown through the pipes. The dean knew just what had happened and felt thankful that the miserable Cresswood had retained consciousness enough to put an end to the worst effects of his offending.

The dean passed on. It would still be necessary no doubt to send Carson to the rescue of the organist, but at all events the desecration of the cathedral silence had ceased. Then there reached the dean's ears a fresh noise from the organ loft. There were footsteps, slowly moving, dragging steps. There was a sound of bumping as if someone were moving clumsily, tripping over things and knocking against corners. The dean hurried on. It seemed clear to him that Cresswood had awakened, more or less, to a sense of his position. He was trying to get out of the organ loft down the winding stairs which led to it. The dean hurried to the door in the south transept by which he had entered the cathedral. An encounter with a drunken Cresswood would, he felt, be a horrible experience. Better let the man make his own way home as best he could, tripping and stumbling. It would not be necessary after all to send Carson. Indeed, it would be better not to send Carson. It would be better that no one, except the dean himself, should know what had happened.

The dean reached the door and paused for a moment. The noise of movement in the organ loft was still plainly audible. Cresswood had not yet, apparently, attempted to descend the stairs. The dean passed through the door and shut it behind him. Cresswood might fumble with the lock when he got to it.

23

The dean, his anger now dominating his disgust and shame, felt that Cresswood ought to be left to himself, without help from Carson or anyone else.

The dean went along the cloisters and through the gateway to his own lawn. His mind was fully made up about Cresswood. The archdeacon and the immaculate Sybil were perfectly right. The man must go, and go at once. There might be trouble and publicity. There might conceivably be a lawsuit, if Cresswood were fool enough to fight for his position. At the moment, so angry was he, the dean actually welcomed the thought of publicity. There might be scandal, but he would like, actually like, to tell the story of what had happened in the cathedral so that the utmost shame should come to Cresswood.

The dean reached his study. There on his table lay the book of medieval lyrics, open at the drinking song of the *potatores exquisiti*. The dean shut the book with a slam. There was nothing exquisite about any drinkers. The whole thing was degrading and abominable. At that moment the dean, though ordinarily a man of balanced mind, would have given his assent to a measure of prohibition more drastic than anything conceived by any American Methodist Synod. That, of course, then and there, in the Deanery at 11 p.m. was impossible. It was impossible to take any immediate steps for the removal of Cresswood from his post. But there was something which the dean could do at once.

Earlier in the evening he had been annoyed with Sybil when she interrupted his reading to urge the necessity of dismissing Cresswood. He had snubbed her, so far as Dean Grosvenor ever snubbed anyone. He owed her an apology, and, such was the dean's conscience, he felt that he could not sleep quietly until he had paid the debt, until he had owned to his daughter that she and the archdeacon – yes, even the archdeacon – had been perfectly right, and that he, the dean, had been wrong.

Sybil, though she had kissed her father good night an hour before, had not gone to bed. She was in the little room which she called her office. She was seated at a desk with a pile of papers before her. She was halfway through the heavy task of tabulating the cases which had that day come before the committee responsible for preserving social purity in the diocese. Sybil had a hundred activities, everyone of them to be described as a social service, everyone of them requiring the preparation of tables and statistics. The night before she had sat up late over the figures supplied by the Voluntary County Organisers of Women's Institutes. Tonight it was the turn of the offenders against social purity, the tawny-haired Chloes of these later days. Tomorrow she intended to deal in similar competent fashion with mentally defective children whose existence was reported by schoolteachers, whose homes had been inspected by the harassed and unwilling wives of country clergy, whose lives when they grew up would, it was hoped, be brighter because Sybil Grosvenor completed her tables of statistics.

She looked up from her work as her father entered the room. She disliked being disturbed when she was busy just as much as he did, but with far better reason. The dean merely pottered over medieval lyrics. She plotted graphs which represented the numbers, increasing or diminishing, of social impurities, mentally defective children, and instituted women.

But Sybil, though she had reached a critical calculation when the dean came in, was mistress of herself. She looked up to him with a bright smile of welcome, a well-cultivated smile which she had ready for all emergencies.

'I'm sorry to interrupt you,' said the dean, 'but I thought I'd like to tell you before I go to bed that I entirely agree with you and' – here he swallowed with an effort, for he hated agreeing with the archdeacon about anything – 'and with the archdeacon about Cresswood. We must get rid of him.'

'I'm so glad that you feel that, father, dear,' said Sybil. 'I was sure you would, once you thought the matter over.'

Nothing could have been more dutiful than the tone in which she spoke. There was not the faintest hint in her voice which suggested that she was congratulating herself on her wisdom in speaking firmly to her father earlier in the evening. Yet the dean felt that she and the archdeacon would certainly think that they had insisted and prevailed. He could almost hear the archdeacon saying: 'The poor old dean! One must take a strong line with him nowadays.' It was almost more than he could bear. For one moment he thought of changing his mind again and saying Cresswood must be given another chance.

'All the same,' he said, Cresswood is a musician. 'We're not likely to get anyone else who can play as well as he does.'

He also thought, but did not say: I shall never again find an organist capable of seeing how plainsong melodies can be adapted to drinking songs.

'It's much better – much, much better,' said Sybil, 'to have a man who lives respectably, even if he can't play as well as Mr. Cresswood.'

'I suppose so,' said the dean, with a little sigh.

'And now,' said Sybil, 'I really must say good night. Go to bed at once, father. You look tired. I'll just finish these figures before I go. Tomorrow I'll see the archdeacon and tell him that you'll take immediate steps about Mr. Cresswood.'

The dean's anger was already cooling. Perhaps Sybil's manner helped to cool it. Her entire self-possession and the fact that she was invariably right on every subject had before then cooled many passions in many people. It was an odd thing, but after his few words with Sybil the dean was conscious of an awakening sympathy with the wretched Cresswood. He was certainly less anxious than he had been to plunge into a struggle to dismiss the man.

'I'd much rather,' he said, 'that the archdeacon took any steps that must be taken. You and the archdeacon can manage the matter between you. I'm sure you'll do it far better than I should. Of course I'll sign any papers you bring me and do anything else that's absolutely necessary.'

4

AT 10 A.M. EVERY week day – on Sundays at 10.30 – matins is sung in Carminster Cathedral with due dignity.

At 9.45 the choirboys, having passed through the troubles of morning school and had their breakfasts, clatter along the cloisters to the Song School, a room containing a grand piano, a small harmonium, shelves laden with music, and a number of cupboards in which the surplices and cassocks of the boys are hung in neat rows. At 9.50 George Carson, the dean's verger, wearing a long gown and carrying a heavy silver mace, stands at the door of the Deanery. At 9.55, for things are orderly in Carminster, the dean comes out, his long cloak cast over his surplice and hood. With great solemnity he follows Carson to the Chapter Room. At 9.55 the archdeacon, if in residence at the time, emerges from a door in his house which opens into the cloisters. His college cap is on his head. His surplice falls in chaste folds from his shoulders. He walks gravely to the Chapter House. At 9.50 or 9.55, or perhaps a minute or two later still, the Rev. John Dennis crosses the close with his surplice over his arm. He alone, of all members of the cathedral staff, is a little irregular in his movements. Sometimes he is too early. On such days he strolls across the close and whistles as he goes. The archdeacon dislikes this whistling. It strikes him as unseemly.

Sometimes Dennis is a little late. Then he runs across the close and the surplice over his arm flutters as he goes. The archdeacon dislikes his running. It seems to him even more unseemly than the whistling.

The Rev. John Dennis, precentor and minor canon, is an Irishman, and meticulous punctuality is not natural to him. Nor is dignity. He listens to the archdeacon's slightly petulant rebukes, and promises, meaning to keep his word, that in future he will neither whistle nor run on his way to matins. He never manages to reform his ways for very long. His language is sometimes as undignified as his manners. It is said that he once described the dean as 'a dear old pussy whom nobody could help loving'. And this is a wrong way to talk about a dean, even if the love is sincere, as Dennis's was. He has said, and such things are repeated in cathedral closes, that the archdeacon would be 'a decent enough old josser if he hadn't swallowed a poker when a boy'. That sort of thing, even if true, ought not to be said about an archdeacon, especially by a mere precentor, who, after all, is barely superior to a minor canon.

When the choirboys, who stand in rows, the archdeacon and the canon in residence, who stand together, the dean, who stands apart from the others by himself with Carter beside him, and the Rev. John Dennis, have assembled in the Chapter Room, the cathedral clock strikes ten. That is the duty of the clock, and it performs it as punctually, unhurriedly, and gravely as the choir and clergy – with the exception of Dennis – perform theirs. At the fifth stroke of the clock Dennis intones a preliminary prayer, and the choirboys, their faces like the faces of cherubs in heaven, sing 'Amen'. Exactly as they utter the last note the organ begins to play, and the procession, led by an inferior verger with a silver wand, moves off. At the end of it comes the dean, Carson, with a silver wand, stalking in front of him.

On the morning after the dean's unpleasant experience in the cathedral these things happened just as they always do, always have for the last four hundred years, and, it is to be hoped, always will. Dennis reached his place without running and remembered not to whistle on the way. The clock struck, and at the fifth stroke he intoned the familiar prayer in the beautifully clear voice which won him the position of precentor, and has done much, even in the archdeacon's judgement, to atone for his irreverent habits. The 'Amen' was sung and then – then nothing more happened. The organ did not begin to play.

The choir and clergy stood in embarrassed silence. It was enormously to the credit of the boys that they refrained from giggling. Only Tom Hodson, a leading boy, and the winner of one of Lord Carminster's scholarships, threw a glance full of meaning to his friend Jimmy Bent. Dennis, as precentor, was responsible for the boys' behaviour. He saw the gleam in Tom Hodson's eyes and the answering flicker in Jimmy Bent's. He at once suspected that some mischief was being silently planned. But it is impossible to rebuke a choirboy for the expression of his eyes, and there was no sign of any attempt to whisper.

Carson, the dean's verger, scowled. Dennis looked up out of the corners of his eyes towards the organ loft, and then looked round at the junior verger and winked. Fortunately the archdeacon, who had shut his eyes while he frowned, did not see the wink. The dean gave a shivering little sigh. Every one knew, or suspected, what had happened. Cresswood had been making a night of it, so the choirboys put it in their own minds. Cresswood had exceeded again. So the archdeacon phrased it to himself. Cresswood, however you expressed the cause of it, was plainly unfit to perform his duty. The organ was silent.

'Shall we proceed?' It was the archdeacon who spoke. 'Proceed without the organ?'

The dean nodded.

The procession moved off into a silent, organless cathedral. The dean found himself wondering, as he followed Carson and the mace, whether the exquisite drinkers of the medieval song ever found themselves unable to sing matins next morning. He had a theory that the authors of those songs, the love songs and the drinking songs as well as the hymns, were monks or minor ecclesiastics of some sort. If so they must have had duties, the singing of matins probably among them.

The want of the organ did not interfere with the orderly progress of matins. The Carminster choir was perfectly well able to sing, even to sing a complicated *Te Deum* or an anthem, without an instrument to help them. On certain days of the week, since organists, like housemaids, must have an afternoon off occasionally, the choir was accustomed to find its own notes and to sing without accompaniment. With the help of Dennis, who had a sure sense of pitch, there never was any difficulty about it. There was none that morning. But, though the singing was excellent, the service was not all that it should have been. It is an unpleasant thing to record about a cathedral staff, but the truth ought to be told. Everybody was thinking of something else, not the words of psalms or prayers. The choirboys were agreeably excited. There would, so they anticipated, be a row. Rows usually gathered round them, their behaviour, or their singing. These rows, though exciting, were unpleasant. This time the storm centre of the row would be, not a choirboy, but Cresswood. This promised thrills without unpleasantness.

Dennis, his voice as clear and sweet as ever, was also thinking of Cresswood. He had a natural sympathy with all offenders, a fondness for black sheep as such, which set him wondering whether anything could be done to save Cresswood from the extreme penalty of his evil ways. He doubted whether mercy would any longer be possible.

'Poor old Cresswood,' he murmured, while the archdeacon read the first lesson, 'has just about put the lid on it this time.'

The archdeacon's meditations were less amiable, but he found a certain satisfaction in the thought that it would no longer be possible for the dean to shirk the duty of getting rid of Cresswood. The dean knew that he would at last be forced to take strong action, but he was by no means happy about it. He tried in vain to recapture his angry mood of the night before. Then, as he remembered, he would have been perfectly willing to cover Cresswood with disgrace and to inflict any suffering or loss on the man. Now, in his morning-after temper, he was by no means eager for vengeance. From his stall he faced east and could just see the shrine of Bishop Feda, its gilded ornaments and carved pagan deities. He found himself wondering helplessly how the great bishop would have dealt with Cresswood. The tawny-haired Chloe – the dean felt sure of this – would have pleaded for mercy for the offender. These Chloes are sinners themselves and they are generally inclined to be merciful to other prodigals. This is perhaps their one virtue. Would the bishop have listened to Chloe's pleading? That was doubtful. Of sin Bishop Feda was no doubt tolerant enough, but would he have forgiven an offence against decorum?

Carson, settled in his seat below the dean's stall, his silver mace beside him, his long gown draped round his knees, was thinking. But who can guess at the thoughts of a dean's verger? There are beings so eminent in dignity, so absorbed in their own stateliness, that all human emotions pass them by and no thought of any kind ever troubles them. There are only a few of these men in the world, and they find felicity when they succeed in obtaining the post of dean's verger. Dennis, glancing round him while the choirboys were expressing a wish for the wings of a dove, saw with wonder the unvexed steadfastness of Carson's face. Here was calm, while all round was excitement, trouble, and perplexity.

Matins came to its appointed end at last. Carson, his mace on his shoulder, led the dean from the cathedral. In the cloisters the archdeacon approached him.

'I should like,' he said, 'to have a word with you, dean, if you can spare the time.'

The dean sighed. From the cloisters, as he followed Carson and the mace, he could see his daughter Sybil coming from the south door of the cathedral. She also would want a word with him, and the dean knew what these words would be. Cresswood must go. The dean bowed to the inevitable, but even bowing does not make the inevitable pleasant.

The choirboys returned to their song school and got rid of their cassocks, surplices, and angel faces all at once. They were no longer – for five glorious hours would not again be – cherubs. By a merciful ordinance they had a whole quarter of an hour – sometimes it was twenty minutes, sometimes only ten. That depended on the length of the psalms and the lessons. For a quarter of an hour or thereabouts they might run and shout in their playground before they went back to their schoolroom and the dreary business of learning Latin grammar.

Dennis watched them go. It was his business to see them safe out of the cathedral and to make sure that their progress through the cloisters was orderly and not unduly noisy. After that, when they reached their playground, they passed under the control of another minor canon, the master of the cathedral school. Dennis, himself a young man with a good deal of the spirit of a boy in him, sympathised with the natural desire to shout, whistle, clatter on the stone pavement of the cloister – indeed, make any kind of noise, except singing, which possessed the boys. But Dennis had a sense of duty. He never turned a blind eye to undue scamperings or a deaf ear to shrill cries.

Watching the boys critically he noticed that only twelve of them left the song school. There had been fourteen at matins. Two of them had slipped back into the cathedral, and Dennis, with his quick, intuitive sympathy with the boyish mind, knew that they were up to mischief of some sort. Except for the purpose of doing something wrong no boy would remain in the cathedral longer than he was forced to. Dennis knew who these two boys were. One was Jimmy Bent, a naturally mischievous urchin of twelve years old. The other was Tom Hodson, the son of a re- tired London policeman of the C.I.D., who had done his share of tracking criminals and settled down in Carminster. Hodson, the father, was a Nonconformist, with a vigorous dislike to the cathedral, but Tom, the boy, had a voice so sweet and desirable that he was offered one of Lord Carminster's new scholarships. Hodson, the father, was the same detective officer who had tracked down the burglars who took Lady Carminster's emer- alds. When his pension became due he retired to Carminster, the original home of his wife. His Nonconformist principles did not oblige him to refuse the offer of a scholarship in the cathe- dral school for his son, but the fact that he accepted it increased his original bitterness. Tom became a choirboy not unwillingly. He knew that with a voice like his he must sing somewhere, and on the whole preferred anthems in the cathedral to very tuney hymns in the Methodist chapel. But the father's non- conforming instincts were strong in the boy. Rules were to him what rubrics were to his father, abhorrent. If there was anything wrong done, Tom Hodson was sure to be either the doer or the instigator of those who did.

Dennis, noticing that Tom Hodson and Jimmy Bent had not left the cathedral, felt certain that they were doing something wrong. He was quite right. The boys had conceived the idea of paying a visit to the organ loft. They knew the stories, whispered in the school, of whisky bottles found empty beside the organ, whisky bottles by no means empty brought in Mr. Cresswood's pocket, emptied during lessons, sermons and other interludes of organ playing. This seemed a golden opportunity of discovering the actual truth of such tales. Slipping out through a side door of the song school, the boys made their way into the Lady Chapel. Dodging behind pillars, passing swiftly over open spaces when the head of the verger on duty was turned the other way, they reached the screen and the winding steps which led to the organ loft. They climbed on tiptoe, very softly. A minute later, with white faces, they were racing down the steps again. They ran through the gates of the screen, past the verger who was closing them. They ran, almost breathless, into Dennis, who was looking for them.

'He's dead, sir! He's dead!' said Tom Hodson.

'His neck's broke!' said Jimmy Bent.

'His head's twisted something horrible.'

'His eyes is wide open.'

'His feet's up on the organ stool.'

'Stop shouting,' said Dennis, 'and tell me what's happened. Here, Tom, you're generally the more sensible of the two. What are you talking about?'

'It's Mr. Cresswood, sir,' said Tom. 'He's dead, sir.'

'In the organ loft,' said Jimmy.

'It's no wonder he didn't play this morning, sir. He couldn't, seeing as how he's dead. Could he, sir?'

Dennis took the boys by their arms and led them over to some chairs.

'Sit down there,' he said, 'and don't stir or speak till I come back to you.'

He ran up the stairs of the organ loft. He did not expect to find Cresswood dead. There seemed no reason why he should be dead, no way in which he was likely to have been killed. He did expect to find the unhappy man very drunk indeed – so drunk, even at that hour of the morning, that he was lying with his head on the ground and his feet on the organ stool.

He reached the organ loft and gasped. Cresswood was lying in a grotesque, it seemed an impossible, position. His head pushed forward horribly, rested on the edge of an oak chest, used for storing music, which stood behind the organ stool. His body, bent nearly double from the hips, was on the ground. His feet, as the boys said, were on the organ stool. Dennis stooped down and took one of the outstretched hands of the man. It was stone cold. There was very little doubt that Cresswood was dead and had been dead for some time.

Dennis left the organ loft and went back to his two boys.

'Tom,' he said, 'go off to Dr. Harrowby and tell him to come to the cathedral at once. Tell him that there's been a serious accident in the organ loft. Then run on to the police station and ask Inspector Smallways to come. Jimmy, you follow me to the Deanery.'

5

THE DEAN, LOOKING VERY old and frail, had sunk into a large chair near the window of his study. Sybil, cool and confident even in an emergency, but anxious about her father, stood beside him. The archdeacon, a frown of perplexity and annoyance on is face, paced up and down in front of the dean's chair.

Dennis had told his story. Jimmy Bent, thoroughly frightened, had given a stammering account of what he saw in the organ loft.

'It's my fault,' said the dean feebly, 'altogether my fault. I heard him fall. If I had gone to his help at once I might have saved him. But I didn't. I went away and left him.'

'You heard him fall?' said the archdeacon. 'How could you have heard him fall?'

Then, for the archdeacon was annoyed as well as perplexed, he turned to Jimmy Bent.

'Boy,' he said, 'leave the room at once.'

Jimmy Bent would have liked to hear a little more about the tragedy, but he was too wise to linger when the archdeacon gave an order. He slipped out of the room at once and consoled himself with the thought that though he had not heard all there was to hear he had a fine budget of thrilling news for the other boys.

'Now, dean,' said the archdeacon, 'tell us what you mean.'

'I was in the cathedral last night,' said the dean. 'I was listening to the organ. Cresswood was playing, and then suddenly he fell. I heard him fall. Oh, if I had only gone to his help! But I thought —'

'You thought he was drunk, I suppose,' said the archdeacon, 'and you were perfectly right not to go near him.'

'If I'd imagined for a moment that he'd really hurt himself — But such a thing never occurred to me. I was angry. I was disgusted. I went away. I did nothing. I just went away.'

The dean was babbling pitifully. The thought that he was responsible for Cresswood's death horrified him. Sybil, moved by a feeling of pity most unusual in her experience, took her father's hand and patted it gently. It was a futile and almost useless thing to do. But Sybil was not good at expressing sympathy.

'The dean ought to have a glass of wine,' said Dennis.

'The dean ought to be in bed,' said the archdeacon sternly. 'He has had a shock – a severe shock. We've all had a shock. I think he ought to be got into bed at once, Miss Grosvenor. I suppose' – he turned to Dennis – 'I suppose that the unfortunate man really is dead? You're quite sure about that?'

'Quite,' said Dennis. 'But I sent for Harrowby. He was the nearest doctor. He'll be here in a minute or two no doubt to give us his report. I sent for Smallways, the police inspector, too. But there's not the slightest doubt in my mind that Cresswood is dead, and has been dead for some hours.'

'And a certain priest,' murmured the dean, 'saw him and passed by on the other side. I ought to have helped him. I might have saved him.'

'Don't be morbid, dean,' said the archdeacon.

'And by chance a certain priest came down that way,' murmured the dean.

'Surely,' said the archdeacon, 'this is a most unsuitable time for quoting Scripture.'

'I feel like a murderer,' said the dean. 'In reality I am a murderer.'

'Miss Grosvenor,' said the archdeacon, this time very firmly, 'the dean ought to be in bed.'

'With a good stiff whisky and soda,' said Dennis.

Sybil disapproved strongly of whisky and soda. She also disapproved of people who went to bed in the daytime, unless they had some definite and recognisable disease to which doctors could give a name, preferably something which came out in spots. To go to bed out of mere feebleness seemed to her a moral fault. But it was plain that her father was not likely to be of any use while he sat in his chair muttering to himself, and she was accustomed to respect the judgment of the archdeacon in practical matters. She put her arm round her father's waist and led him away. She did not go so far as to provide the whisky and soda which Dennis prescribed, but she told Redington, an aged and reliable butler, to bring the dean a glass of port and to see him safely into bed.

'In my opinion,' said the archdeacon, 'it will not be necessary to say anything about this story of the dean's having been in the cathedral at the time of the accident. What happened is clear enough.'

'I suppose so,' said Dennis. 'Cresswood must have fallen backwards off the music stool and struck his head on the edge of the oak chest behind. That's what it looked like, but we'll know better when we hear what Harrowby has to say.'

'In any case,' said the archdeacon, 'whatever Harrowby says, there's no need to mention that the dean was there. This shock has been too much for him. He's a very old man, and just at present he's not himself. Besides, even if he were in the cathedral and heard the fall, there is nothing to be gained by publishing the fact. Cresswood's death is a scandal – a grave scandal – most injurious to the reputation of the cathedral. It would be worse, far worse, because the news would spread further and be given greater publicity if the dean's story is told.'

Dennis understood that. The death of a drunken organist while actually playing his instrument in the cathedral is bad enough. The newspapers, greedy of sensation, would publish that with appropriate headlines. But they would make much more of the news and go on publishing it for longer if they got hold of the picturesque story of the presence of the aged dean in the cathedral at the time of the tragedy.

'A fresh scandal in connection with this cathedral,' said the archdeacon, 'would be disastrous.'

He was thinking – could scarcely help thinking – of the earlier scandal occasioned by the arrest of one of the vergers for burglary.

Then Sybil came back into the study, having left her father to the care of Redington. The archdeacon felt sure of her support.

'I was just saying to Mr. Dennis,' he said, 'that we must do all in our power to minimise the scandal which will be occasioned by the death of this miserable man. It is unfortunately not the first time that this cathedral has suffered from unpleasant publicity. Mr. Dennis has not been here long enough to remember, but you and I, Miss Grosvenor, know how very disagreeable it was when — I am referring to the theft of the Carminster emeralds.'

Dennis, though he had only been a year at Carminster, had heard that story. In a small cathedral town sensational happenings are exceedingly rare. A first-rate burglary, arranged and carried out by a verger, is subject matter of gossip for years, and a stranger is welcomed, because he offers a chance of telling a good story again. Dennis had been told about the burglary twenty times at least before he had been three weeks in Carminster.

There was also, in addition to the burglary itself, the thrilling fact that the emeralds had never been found. There were at least a dozen theories to account for their disappearance. Cautious men shook their heads over every wild guess, and said that nothing ever would be heard of them. Hodson, when he settled in Carminster, declined to commit himself to any expression of opinion. It was generally believed that Hodson knew more than he would say, and a man of that temperament is never popular anywhere. Hodson, partly because of his dissenting hatred of the cathedral, and still more because he refused to gossip, was both disliked and distrusted in Carminster. The stories of the burglary which Dennis heard almost always ended with a hint that Hodson had discovered more than he told at the time of the trial.

The archdeacon and Sybil Grosvenor were probably the only two people in Carminster who never told the story of the burglary. To them the memory of the dreadful scandal which followed the arrest of the burglar was too bitter for words. And now – they looked at each other with despair in their faces – now there would be fresh scandal even more dreadful than the last.

'We know,' the archdeacon went on, 'how disastrous another scandal would be. It is absolutely necessary in the interests of the cathedral, of the Church in general, of religion itself – absolutely necessary to say nothing likely to give occasion for additional publicity.'

'All the same,' said Dennis, 'suppressing facts in a case like this is a serious thing.'

'Suppressing facts!' said the archdeacon. 'I beg of you, Mr. Dennis, not to suggest that I am doing anything of the sort, or advising such a course. If the presence of the dean in the cathedral were of any material value in the business of eliciting the facts – if there were anything to be gained by repeating what he has just told us – I should be the first to counsel complete frankness at whatever cost to our feelings and the reputation of the cathedral. I am sure, Miss Grosvenor, that you agree with me.'

Sybil did, completely and wholeheartedly. She saw nothing to be gained by publishing the story of her father's visit to the cathedral. She saw, too, that his conduct might be easily made to appear heartless. The world is far too fond of giving nicknames to deans. She did not want to see her father described in the newspapers as the 'Callous Dean'. And there was that verse which her father had quoted from St. Luke's Gospel about the priest who had passed by without succouring the wounded man. It would be most unpleasant if someone else hit on that verse – a newspaper man, perhaps.

'My father,' she said, 'is suffering from shock.'

'Severe shock,' said the archdeacon.

'I don't think,' said Sybil, 'that we can absolutely rely on the accuracy of what he says. When he has recovered —'

'Exactly,' said the archdeacon. 'In a week or two.'

By that time the newspapers would be thoroughly tired of the subject and it would not much matter what the dean said.

'In the meanwhile,' the archdeacon went on, 'we can decide nothing, and should certainly say nothing until we hear what Dr. Harrowby has to tell us.'

Dr. Harrowby's report, when he made it a few minutes later, was brief, and, from the archdeacon's point of view, as satisfactory as any report of such an event could be. The cause of death was a fracture of the base of the skull. About that Dr. Harrowby was perfectly certain. He was almost equally certain about the cause of the fracture. The unfortunate organist had fallen backwards off the high stool on which he sat while playing and had struck his head violently against the edge of an oak chest behind the stool.

Like everyone else in Carminster, Dr. Harrowby had regard for the welfare and reputation of the cathedral.

'The fall,' he said, 'might have been the result of a sudden fainting fit.'

'Ah,' said the archdeacon, 'quite so. A sudden fainting fit.'

This was better than anything he had dared to hope. If it could be represented that Cresswood had suddenly fainted, or even might have suddenly fainted, there need be no scandal at all. Anybody might faint, and no cathedral can be blamed because its organist has a weak heart. It was true, unfortunately, that everyone in Carminster knew all about Cresswood and his fondness for whisky, but the editor of Carminster's only newspaper could easily be persuaded to be discreet, and no editor outside Carminster – certainly no editor of a London paper – would have any reason to suppose that a cathedral organist was anything but a perfectly sober man. The archdeacon became almost cheerful.

'I take it, then, Dr. Harrowby,' he said, 'that in your opinion poor Cresswood fainted and then fell, a sudden giddiness perhaps, a failure of the heart's action. Poor fellow! Poor fellow!'

But Dr. Harrowby was a member of the most cautious profession in the world. Not even for the sake of saving the cathedral from scandal was he going to commit himself to a definite statement about Cresswood's heart.

'I mentioned a fainting fit as a possibility,' he said. 'There might have been some other cause of the fall.'

'Oh, quite so, quite so,' said the archdeacon. 'Still, he might have fainted.'

'There must be an inquest of course,' said Dr. Harrowby. 'I am sure you understand that.'

'I quite understand that. But in a case like this the cause of death is perfectly plain. You said a fracture of the skull, Dr. Harrowby.'

'There's no doubt about that – none at all.'

'Then,' said the archdeacon, 'the proceedings at the inquest will be more or less formal.'

'The coroner will want the fullest possible information,' said Dr. Harrowby.

'Yes, yes. Naturally. Quite rightly. Let me see now. Mr. Clayton is the coroner, isn't he? I am certain that Mr. Clayton will have no desire for any unnecessary exposé of unpleasant facts. Nor will Smallways, the police inspector. Smallways is a member of our voluntary Sunday evening choir. He won't want to stir up mud needlessly. So long as the nature of the accident is clear and the immediate cause of death undoubted there will be no need for going into remote speculations. Perhaps I might myself have an opportunity of giving a hint to Mr. Clayton. Perhaps if you happen to be talking to him, Dr. Harrowby?'

'I can't possibly do that,' said Dr. Harrowby; 'and, if I were you, archdeacon, I shouldn't try. The coroner has his duty to perform, and any attempt to induce him to burke the facts...'

'My dear Dr. Harrowby. Surely you don't suspect me of wishing to influence the coroner to suppress material facts! All I mean to suggest – all I ever intended to suggest – is that there are certain facts very injurious to poor Cresswood's reputation which perhaps – I only say perhaps – need not be brought out at the inquest. "De mortuis" – you remember, Dr. Harrowby. Cresswood fell off his organ stool and fractured his skull. That we know, and that is all we know. It can scarcely be necessary – I hope it won't be necessary – to inquire whether he was under the influence of drink at the time.'

'Well,' said Dr. Harrowby, 'Clayton may take that view of it, and the police aren't likely to press him to go further. I hope he does. I'm sure he doesn't want any scandal connected with the cathedral any more than the rest of us do. We all have the interests of the cathedral at heart, archdeacon. In the meanwhile

I'll tell the police that they may remove the body from your organ loft. It can be taken to the poor fellow's own house.'

6

IT IS OFTEN SAID and sometimes lamented that the Church no longer possesses the power which once enabled her to make the lives of her opponents very uncomfortable, or even to put an end to their lives altogether. It is, of course, perfectly true that no college of cardinals or bench of bishops can any longer put a Galileo into prison or burn a Latimer; but it is a mistake to suppose that the power of the Church has totally disappeared everywhere. In Carminster, for instance, men think twice and very carefully before they do anything likely to offend the dean and chapter. The little town exists mainly because of its cathedral. It would be much smaller than it is, certainly less prosperous – it might even cease to exist altogether – if the cathedral disappeared. The trade of the shopkeepers depends on their securing the patronage of those who are connected, directly or indirectly, with the cathedral. The patronage of local boards which distribute minor but much-coveted offices is influenced by the wishes of the cathedral authorities, whenever such wishes are expressed or even hinted. There is therefore, widespread among all classes, a sentiment of loyalty to the cathedral like that of the Ephesian silversmiths to the Temple of Diana. Everyone knows that the flourishing Mitre Inn would be emptied, the old furniture shops bereft of customers, the influx of charabancs in summer checked, if anything were to happen which seriously diminished the prestige and glory of the cathedral.

The inquest held on the body of the unfortunate Cresswood was a good example, if example were needed, of the influence of the Church in local affairs. Mr. Clayton, the coroner, a solicitor of good standing, was a man who would have done his duty without fear or favour in any matter which came under his jurisdiction. But Mr. Clayton was firmly convinced of the wisdom of the proverb which discourages the washing of dirty linen in public. The cause of Cresswood's death seemed perfectly plain, and would not be made any plainer by dwelling unnecessarily on the unfortunate fact that the dead man sometimes took too much whisky. '*De mortuis nil nisi bonum*,' the proverb quoted by the archdeacon, is respected by men of good feeling everywhere in England. Common decency forbade any emphasis on the poor fellow's failings, and the publication of the fact that the cathedral organist was a drunkard would annoy the dean and chapter and attract an unpleasant notoriety to the cathedral affairs. Mr. Clayton did not see that the interests of truth, justice, and law would be advanced by announcing that Cresswood was drunk when he fell off his organ stool.

The first witnesses called were the police. Superintendent Smallways, and then a constable, gave evidence about the removing of the body from the organ loft to the house. They described exactly the position in which the body lay – the feet on the organ stool, the head on the edge of the oak chest behind, the trunk on the ground between the stool and the chest, almost doubled up. Inspector Smallways gave it as his opinion that the body would be found in just such a position if the dead man had fallen backwards off the stool and been killed by the striking of his head against the oak chest. The coroner asked one or two unimportant questions and then dismissed the two policemen. The next witnesses called were the doctors.

Dr. Harrowby and the other two doctors who had joined him in making the post-mortem were very much of Mr. Clayton's way of thinking. Cresswood might or might not have been drunk. They preferred to keep to themselves any opinion they might have on that point. The blow on the back of the head which fractured the skull was undoubtedly the cause of death. About that they were quite definite. They gave their evidence clearly and unhesitatingly, and the coroner only asked them two questions:

'Was the fracture of the skull in your opinion such an injury as might have been occasioned by the fall backwards off the organ stool?'

The doctors were unanimous that it was, provided that behind the organ stool at a suitable distance there was an oak chest with a sharp-edged lid.

'And there was such a chest?'

'Yes.' It was Dr. Harrowby who answered this; 'and the head of the deceased rested on the lid of the chest.'

After that the coroner would have allowed the doctors to go; but there was a foreman of the jury who wanted more information. This was Hodson, the retired London detective. Hodson, as a sound dissenter, deeply disliked the power and influence of the dean and chapter in Carminster, and took every opportunity – the poor man got very few – of being unpleasant to the Church. The inquest, and the fact that he was foreman of the jury, gave him his chance, and the coroner was uncomfortably aware that he was likely to make the most of it.

'I should like to ask Dr. Harrowby,' he said, 'whether he has formed any idea of the cause of the fall – in other words, why did the deceased fall backwards off the stool on which he was sitting?'

Dr. Harrowby had a very clear idea of the cause of the fall. So had everybody else. But nobody wanted to talk about that.

The coroner would, if he could, have disallowed the question. But Hodson was not an easy man to snub, and his experience in the London police had given him a knowledge of law which the coroner respected. The question, once put, had to be answered. Dr. Harrowby fortunately was a man of resource.

'There are several ways in which such a fall might be accounted for: a sudden fainting fit, for instance, an attack of giddiness, a slight, possibly quite temporary, irregularity of cardiac action.'

The doctor rolled out his medical words with sonorous emphasis. A less vigorously independent man than Hodson would have subsided at once. Even Hodson did not care to start an argument with a doctor about cardiac functions. But he was not quite defeated.

He tried each of the other doctors in turn with his question about the cause of the fall. He took very little by his efforts. One doctor treated him to a short lecture on what he called aneurysm. The other became exasperatingly eloquent about valvular derangement and intermittent syncope. After learning that syncope was an ordinary consequence of cerebral anaemia, Hodson, wisely perhaps, gave the doctors up.

The next witness was Carson, the dean's verger.

He was, so it appeared, the last person who had seen Cresswood alive. His evidence was given with all the firm dignity natural to a man of his position.

'I happened to be in the Mitre on the night of the accident,' he said. 'I was there from nine o'clock till about nine thirty. I often go there of an evening for a glass of beer. There were several other people there that evening. Mr. Cresswood was there. He was talking to a gentleman whom I did not know. He and I left the Mitre at half past nine or thereabouts. We walked together as far as my house, where we said good night. Mr. Cresswood went on in the direction of the cathedral. That is the last time I saw him.'

'Did Mr. Cresswood seem in his usual health and spirits?' asked the coroner.

'He seemed to me perfectly well and quite cheerful.'

'How far is it from your house to the cathedral?'

'About five minutes' walk.'

'Is there any other house at which Mr. Cresswood might have called, after saying good night to you, on his way to the cathedral?'

He meant any other public house in which Cresswood could have got more to drink. Every one knew the purpose of the question and everyone who lived in Carminster knew what the answer must be.

'There is no other house between mine and the cathedral, except the residences of the canons in the close.'

That finished the coroner's examination. He had not asked whether Cresswood was sober or not, but he had succeeded in leaving the newspaper reporters with the impression that he was. Hodson, still desirous of throwing mud at the cathedral staff, demanded to be allowed to ask a few questions.

'What was the deceased drinking when you saw him at the Mitre?'

'Beer,' said Carson. 'He had two glasses of draught beer.'

It is not possible to suppose that even a young child would be intoxicated by two glasses of the beer ordinarily sold in England today. If Cresswood was sober when he entered the Mitre and drank no more than two glasses of beer while he was there he was certainly sober when he left.

'Was that all he had? No whisky?' asked Hodson.

'That was all.'

Hodson was a man of great pertinacity. His power of nagging was unsurpassed, even by that of the woman whom Solomon compared to the dropping of water on a very rainy day. This must have been most useful to him when dealing with witnesses brought to Scotland Yard for examination. But Carson possessed a shield – perhaps the only effectual shield – against the persistence of the nagger. His dignity was immense and unshakable. He had not, of course, been able to bring his silver mace into the court with him, but even without that weapon he was able to overcrow Hodson. His 'That was all' was final and unanswerable.

Hodson tried another line of attack.

'Can you give us any information about the deceased, his character or habits, which would throw light on his fall from the organ stool?'

If he expected to get a statement that Cresswood was a heavy drinker he was disappointed.

'Mr. Cresswood,' said Carson ponderously, 'was, so I am given to understand, a superior organist and very fond of music. He often went into the cathedral at night to play.'

That was, undeniably, a reply to Hodson's inquiry. In order to fall off a music stool a man must be on it. Carson had satisfactorily accounted for the fact that Cresswood was on his stool. As for what happened after he reached the stool – well, the doctors talked about aneurysms and functional derangements.

'Look here,' said Hodson, evidently annoyed, 'what I'm trying to get at is this: Was he drunk or sober?'

'Now, now,' said the coroner, 'that question—'

There was a general murmur through the court. It was felt that Hodson had gone too far, had shown a want of decent feeling in asking such a question about a man who was dead, who when alive had been a thoroughly good sort, even if inclined to drink too much. Only Carson appeared wholly unmoved. He answered the question without waiting for the coroner to finish his protest.

'Mr. Cresswood,' he said, 'was perfectly sober when he left me – as sober as I am now.'

There was a slight gasp of amazement. Carson was a credible witness. No one could suspect him of deliberate lying, even to save the honour of the cathedral. But if Cresswood were sober... Nobody had paid much attention to the doctors' talk, but perhaps after all the man's heart had failed for some unknown reason. Either that or... There was the choirboys' legend of empty whisky bottles in the organ loft. But even Hodson did not care to ask a question about that in open court.

The next witness was Powell, the proprietor of the Mitre Inn, a stout man with pleasant manners. He confirmed the evidence that Carson had given. Cresswood had two glasses of beer and no more. He was sober when he came into the inn. He left it, still perfectly sober, at nine-thirty in the company of Mr. Carson. While in the inn he had talked to a Mr. Bently, a stranger, who was spending a night in the Mitre.

'Who is Mr. Bently?' asked the coroner.

Powell knew nothing about him except that he had come to Carminster that day, had engaged a bedroom in the Mitre, had dined there, and after dinner had gone out. He had returned in Mr. Cresswood's company at about 9 p.m. He might have been a friend of Mr. Cresswood's. Powell knew nothing about that. Or he might have been one of the many casual tourists who came to Carminster to visit the cathedral.

Hodson wanted to know why this man Bently was not called as a witness. The coroner explained that Mr. Bently had left Carminster by an early train for London on the morning after the accident. The police had given this information. No one knew his address, and it did not seem worth while to make a search for him. He could add nothing to what Carson and Powell had told the court.

Hodson was not satisfied.

'Did he leave the Mitre that night in company with the deceased?' he asked.

'No, he didn't,' said Powell. 'He finished his beer, said good night to me, and went to bed.'

'Was he sober?'

'He was as sober as a Methodist minister at a temperance meeting,' said Powell.

The audience in the court tittered delightedly. Even the coroner smiled. Hodson was a Methodist, and given to taking the chair at temperance meetings, a most objectionable form of activity. It was generally felt that Powell had scored neatly and quite fairly. There were no other witnesses. Hodson was as dissatisfied with that as he had been with the evidence he heard.

'It seems to me,' he said, 'that we ought to hear what the dean has to say about the deceased.'

Here the coroner grasped his opportunity of finally snubbing Hodson.

'The dean,' he said, 'is no longer a young man. He has suffered a shock – a very severe shock – and is at present confined to bed. He has, I feel sure, the sympathy of everyone in the court, and we all hope that he will soon be restored to health.'

'May we have this inquiry adjourned,' said Hodson, 'until we hear what the dean can tell us about the deceased?'

The coroner was of opinion that nothing would be gained by adjourning the inquiry. He had heard of the dean's presence in the cathedral on the night of the accident. The archdeacon told him that, but he had not heard the dean's story of what happened. The archdeacon kept that to himself, believing, as Sybil Grosvenor believed, that the old man's mind had been so much affected by the tragedy that his statements were not to be relied on. The archdeacon was most unwilling to attract public attention to the dean's mental condition. He was very old. He had in his time been a great scholar. It would be unkind and in every way undesirable to expose the fact that his mental powers were failing. The coroner, though he did not know all that the archdeacon did, was quite sure that the dean ought not to be called on to appear in court.

'I do not propose to adjourn the inquiry,' he said firmly. 'I do not see that the dean can have anything useful to tell us.'

'It is desirable that we should have his evidence about the character of the deceased.'

That was Hodson again. He had been baffled by the doctors, by Carson, and by Powell. He thought that if he had the dean in the witness box he might get from him a public admission of Cresswood's drunkenness.

'We have heard,' said the coroner, 'that Mr. Cresswood was completely master of himself, in full control of his bodily and mental powers when he went into the cathedral. I do not see that further evidence about his character will aid us in determining the cause of death, which indeed seems to me perfectly plain.'

That finished Hodson. The other jurymen were as anxious as the coroner was to get the inquiry over without drawing public attention to Cresswood's failing.

They followed the advice of the coroner, very plainly given, and returned a verdict of 'Death by misadventure'.

7

DENNIS, WHO HAD BEEN present at the inquiry, left the court in the company of Powell, the plump and pleasant landlord of the Mitre. Powell, though usually a genial man, was in a very bad temper. He was pleased, as everyone else was, with the jury's verdict. He was very well satisfied with his own share in the snubbing of Hodson. But he was thoroughly disgusted with the persistent way in which the ex-policeman had tried to drag unpleasant facts to light.

'That fellow Hodson,' he said, 'ought to be kicked. And if I were younger I'd do the kicking with pleasure.'

He looked appealingly at Dennis, who was still a young man. But Dennis, though young, was a precentor, and a precentor cannot lightly undertake to assault a retired police sergeant.

'I quite agree with you,' said Dennis, 'but it wouldn't do for me to take on the job.'

'Why should he want to drag up things about poor Cress-wood?' said Powell. 'That's what he was at from start to finish – trying to make out that Cresswood was drunk.'

'I suppose he really was sober?' said Dennis. 'I know you said so, and Carson said so, and of course I believe you thought he was. All the same, it seems odd. Sober men don't crack their skulls by tumbling backwards.'

'He was sober when he came in,' said Powell, 'and all he had in my house was two glasses of beer. Mind you, I'm not saying that Cresswood didn't take a drop too much sometimes. He did. But that night he had what I said in court: two glasses of beer, and no more. I put it to you, Mr. Precentor, as a gentleman who knows the world, could a man get drunk on two glasses of beer?'

'He could not. Nobody could. Certainly Cresswood couldn't. He was accustomed to far more than that.'

'Well, that's all he had,' said Powell. 'He and that fellow Bently had two glasses each. Bently paid the first time and Cresswood the next.'

'That fellow Bently,' said Dennis, 'was he a friend of Cresswood's?'

'He may have been. All I know about him is that he went out after he had dinner, at about eight-thirty, and came back at nine with Cresswood. They seemed friendly enough. They were talking to each other while they were drinking their beer. But for all I know they might have met for the first time outside the door. Anyhow, friends or not friends, they were both sober.'

Powell and Dennis, walking briskly as they talked, entered High Street, a narrow, winding thoroughfare, at the end of which is the Mitre Inn. A few yards ahead of them was Carson, the dean's verger, walking more slowly, almost as slowly as he walked up the cathedral in front of the dean with his silver mace on his shoulder.

Powell caught sight of him.

'There's Carson,' he said. 'He'll back me up about Cresswood's being sober if you don't believe me.'

'Of course I believe you,' said Dennis.

But Powell was not satisfied. He hailed Carson, who stopped at once.

'Now, Mr. Carson,' he said, 'did poor Cresswood have more than two glasses of beer that night in the Mitre?'

'He had no more than two glasses,' said Carson. 'I was standing beside him all the time he was there, though I wasn't talking to him, not till we went out together. He was talking to a man I didn't know all the time he was in the Mitre.'

'Bently,' said Powell.

'Not that Mr. Cresswood was saying much,' said Carson. 'It was the other man who did most of the talking.'

'Did you happen to hear what they were talking about?' said Powell.

'I'm not in the habit of listening to other people's conversations,' said Carson with great dignity. 'That's a thing I wouldn't do even if I could have heard what was being said. And as it happened I couldn't have heard that night, for they weren't speaking loud. All I know is that Bently did most of the talking. And all Cresswood said was "No", or words to that effect, as if Bently was asking him for something and Cresswood did not want to give it.'

'Cresswood hadn't much to give to Bently or anybody else,' said Powell.

They reached the door of the Mitre and paused there before Powell went in.

'I dare say you know, Mr. Precentor,' he said, 'that poor Cresswood was up to his neck in debt. He owed me a tidy sum. I wouldn't say anything about it if it was only myself. But he owed money to pretty nearly everyone in the town. He owed a good lump' – here he sank his voice – 'to that fellow Hodson, though how he ever came to get money out of him beats me. I dare say that's what made Hodson so bitter against him after he was dead.'

'He owed me five pounds,' said Carson, 'which he borrowed from me six weeks ago.'

'You may reckon that lost money,' said Powell. 'And now, gentlemen, I'll have to say goodbye to you unless you'll come in and have a glass of beer.'

Neither Dennis nor Carson accepted the invitation. They went on together towards the Cathedral Close.

'Look here, Carson,' said Dennis. 'Where did Cresswood get the drink that night? You say he was sober when he left you.'

'I'm sure of that.'

'But he was drunk when he fell off the music stool. He must have been. He wouldn't have fallen off with a crash bad enough to crack his skull if he hadn't been very drunk indeed. What bothers me is how he managed it.'

'You heard what the doctors said.'

'I did, but I didn't believe a word of it. Nor did the doctors themselves. Cresswood hadn't a dicky heart. If he had the doctors would have found it out at their post-mortem, and if they'd found out anything of the sort they'd have said so. They'd have wanted to say so, if it was only for the sake of scoring off that beast Hodson. But all they said was that a fellow might have a syncopated aneurysm or some rot of that sort, a thing which a man like Cresswood would never dream of having. No. You know just as well as I do, Carson, that Cresswood must have been dead to the world when he toppled off that stool. Now, how did he do it?'

'There are stories,' said Carson – 'I don't say that I believe them, but—'

'Don't be so infernally cautious. I know all about those stories of empty whisky bottles in the organ loft. The choirboys are always telling them.'

'Those choirboys,' said Carson, 'would say anything. It was they who put it about that Cresswood had whisky in the organ loft.'

'I dare say he had, sometimes,' said Dennis. 'And supposing he had, supposing he had six dozen bottles there, that doesn't explain things in the least. You and he left the Mitre together at half past nine. You're sure of the time, aren't you?'

'It was nine-thirty when we left,' said Carson, 'for it's always nine-thirty when I leave the Mitre every night I go there; and Cresswood left with me.'

'I suppose it took you ten minutes to walk to your house?'

'It took me a quarter of an hour. I'm not a fast walker. I always take a quarter of an hour.'

'Good. That brings us to nine forty-five. Give Cresswood five minutes to get into the cathedral and up to the organ loft.'

'It would take more.'

'We'll say five minutes. The dean was in the cathedral – I suppose you know that, Carson?'

'I heard it,' said Carson cautiously.

'Well, it's true, The dean was in the cathedral listening to Cresswood playing. He says he listened for some time before he heard the fall. And the dean was back in the deanery, in Miss Grosvenor's room, by ten-fifteen. Miss Grosvenor told me that, and she's not the sort who makes mistakes about things of the kind. It took the dean ten minutes to get from the cathedral to the deanery. He couldn't have done it in less. That means that Cresswood fell at five minutes after ten or thereabouts. But he only got into the organ loft at ten minutes to ten at the soonest. And the dean listened to his playing for some time. Will you tell me when Cresswood managed to get drunk? Could he have done it in the time, as drunk as all that?'

'If he had a bottle of whisky in the organ loft,' said Carson, 'and if he took a good swig as soon as he got there, and if he happened to take it on an empty stomach, it mightn't affect him just at first, but—'

'That's a plausible theory,' said Dennis; 'but there's one objection to it. There was no whisky bottle, empty or full, in the organ loft next morning. I looked. I looked pretty carefully, for I'd heard the stories the choirboys tell. Mind you, Carson, I expected to find a whisky bottle there, and I didn't. There wasn't one, so unless Cresswood swallowed the bottle as well as the whisky it wasn't that way he got drunk.'

'If he didn't get drunk that way,' said Carson, 'he didn't get drunk at all. He was sober when he left me.'

But that was exactly what Dennis found it difficult to believe. It was not likely that Carson had lied when on oath in a coroner's court. It was still more unlikely that he and Powell had agreed together about the lie they meant to tell. Yet it was possible that they had. Moved by a desire to avoid a horrible scandal which would have gone sounding all over England, a titbit for sensation-loving newspapers, they might have actually perjured themselves. That was unlikely, very unlikely, but possible. It seemed to Dennis impossible that Cresswood, while sober, should have fallen backwards and broken his skull.

He felt perfectly sure that the doctors did not believe in their own aneurysms and synoopes, that is to say, believe that such things had suddenly seized Cresswood.

'I'd very much like,' said Dennis, as he said goodbye to Carson, 'to have a chat with that man Bently.'

'You're not likely to,' said Carson, 'for he left the town early that morning before anybody knew about the accident.'

But unlikely things – even very unlikely things – sometimes happen. Two days later Dennis had as much talk with Bently as he wanted.

8

THE SUDDEN DEATH OF a cathedral organist, while actually engaged in playing his instrument, is news. Even shorn of its more thrilling details, Cresswood's death was worth a short paragraph in the daily papers. Thanks to the discretion of the coroner and the doctors, no one outside of Carminster heard of the man's unfortunate fondness for whisky, and the newspapers gave no hint that he was drunk when he fell. Thanks to the prompt action of the archdeacon, supported by Sybil, no one except Dennis heard the dean say that he was in the cathedral when the accident happened. The archdeacon had got the old gentleman safely to bed, and Sybil kept him there. She was all the more anxious to do so because she suspected that her father's mind, the fine mind of a great scholar, was beginning to fail at last. The shock of the death in the cathedral had been too much for him. She was troubled about the way her father talked. He kept on saying that Cresswood had fallen forwards over the keyboard, whereas it was perfectly plain that he must have fallen backwards. Though the dean spoke feebly, there was no misunderstanding his meaning, and he insisted that he had heard Cresswood moving about in the organ loft after the fall, a thing that was plainly impossible. The man had fractured the base of his skull and lay exactly where he had fallen. Sybil, who had heard all about the coroner's inquest and the evidence given there, was driven to the conclusion that her father's mind had been seriously, though she trusted only temporarily, affected by the shock. She hoped that rest and complete quiet would restore him. Old Dr. Harrowby, though the dean did not talk much to him, agreed with Sybil that rest and quiet were the proper treatment.

Though the most interesting things about Cresswood's death – the drunkenness and the dean's delusions – never got into the papers, the news itself excited the attention of several people. Two days after the inquest a well-dressed and well-mannered gentleman called at the Deanery. He presented his card to Redington, the butler, and asked to see the dean. On the card, in neat copperplate, was his name, 'Mr. A. C. Bently'. and written underneath it, 'Representative (Special) of the Harpsichord Company'. It was impossible for him to see the dean, who was still in bed, but the butler was impressed by the clothes, the manner, and the card of the visitor. He told Mr. Bently that he might perhaps be allowed to see Miss Grosvenor. Sybil, like everyone else in England who was interested in Church music, had heard of the Harpsichord Publishing Company. It is, and has been for more than a century, one of the largest of our musical publishers, and for fifty years or so has specialized, not unprofitably, in Church music. Almost every popular *Te Deum*, in A, B, C, D, or any other key, flat, sharp, or natural, brought out of recent years has come from the Harpsichord Company. Its list of harvest anthems is so bewilderingly long that village organists study it with envious despair. Sybil, very anxious about her father, did not want visits from strangers, but the representative (special) of such a firm could scarcely be ignored.

'You will allow me, I hope,' said Mr. Bently, 'to express on behalf of our firm the feelings of deep regret with which we read in yesterday's paper of the death of Mr. Cresswood. In our opinion his decease is a loss not only to the cathedral at Carminster but to English music. We have too few first-rate men among our younger composers. Mr. Cresswood was one of the few. His loss will be felt – terribly felt.'

Sybil knew that Cresswood was a good organist. It was part of the loyalty to the cathedral which is strong in Carminster to believe that Cresswood was the best organist in England. Sybil also knew that before his death he had been composing tunes for her father's translations of his favourite medieval lyrics. These might be good or bad. Sybil knew nothing about that, for she had never heard one. But, whatever their merits, she regarded them as unsuitable work for a cathedral organist, just as the translation of the cheerier lyrics was unsuitable work for a dean. It surprised her to hear Mr. Bently speaking of Cresswood as a great composer. So far as she knew he had written nothing else except the two or three tunes for her father. But Mr. Bently, Representative (Special) of the Harpsichord Publishing Company, must know what he was talking about. Sybil, for the first time, began to feel a faint respect for Mr. Cresswood. His morals were deplorable; but good morals and good music do not necessarily go together.

'But my call on you this morning,' said Mr. Bently, 'was not made solely with the intention of expressing the feelings of our directors, and, if I may say so, my own feelings. We have been given to understand – in fact, there is no reason for concealing the fact – we were told by Mr. Cresswood himself that shortly before his death he had completed, or very soon would complete, a composition of some importance, nothing less than a *Te Deum*, intended for cathedral choirs on occasions of national rejoicing. Now our desire is —'

Mr. Bently's desire, which it took him some time to explain, was to get the manuscript of this composition before anyone else did. The Harpsichord Publishing Company wanted to have the honour, and perhaps the profit, of bringing out the work. Mr. Bently hinted that there might be considerable profits, thus showing himself to be a publisher of a most unusual kind. Few members of the publishing profession ever expect anything except losses, and musical publishers lose more steadily and more largely than their fellows who deal with books. The profits, admitted as possible by Mr. Bently, would be divided, so Mr. Bently said, in any way the dean thought proper.

They might go to the cathedral or to the representatives of Mr. Cresswood or – indeed to anyone except the Harpsichord Publishing Company. Sybil was greatly impressed. Mr. Bently's manner was impressive. The reputation of the Harpsichord Publishing Company was more impressive still. But, though impressed, she refused to consult her father about the matter. She explained that the condition of his health was such that he could not take any part in the arrangement of Mr. Cresswood's affairs. But Sybil wished to be helpful if she could.

'Perhaps,' she said, shedding one of her bright, efficient smiles on Mr. Bently, 'perhaps you could see the archdeacon about the matter.'

Mr. Bently was perfectly ready to see the archdeacon or anyone else who would give him leave to search among Mr. Cresswood's papers for the manuscript of the *Te Deum*. He bade a respectful and gratified goodbye to Miss Grosvenor and left the Deanery.

The archdeacon, like Sybil, was favourably impressed by Mr. Bently's card and by his manner. He was even more surprised and gratified than Sybil was when he heard how high an opinion the directors of the Harpsichord Company had of Mr. Cresswood's musical compositions. Surely there were no men in England, and therefore none in the world, who were better judges of music than the Harpsichord directors. He began to feel that Cresswood might after all turn out to be a credit instead of a disgrace to the cathedral. His drinking, if anyone outside Carminster knew anything about it, would very soon be forgotten. The fame of his festal *Te Deum* seemed likely to survive. But the archdeacon, though willing to help Mr. Bently in any way he could, was not quite sure of his position. The police had taken possession of Mr. Cresswood's house after they carried the body there. The house itself would no doubt be handed over to the cathedral authorities in due time, for it was their property, the official residence of the organist. In the meanwhile he supposed that Mr. Cresswood's furniture and effects, his music along with the rest, would be handed over to his relatives. So far as the archdeacon knew no relatives had appeared.

'But Mr. Dennis, our precentor, will know all about that. Perhaps you would be so good as to call upon Mr. Dennis. His residence, a small, red brick, Georgian house, not easily mistaken, is at the far side of the close.'

Mr. Bently, suave and courteous as he had been with Miss Grosvenor, thanked the archdeacon for his kindness and said that he would be delighted to call on the precentor.

He began his third interview as he had begun the other two by expressing his firm's sorrow at the untimely death of so eminent a musician as Mr. Cresswood. This time the opening failed of its effect. Dennis knew, as everybody else knew, that Cresswood could play the organ, but Dennis knew, as neither Sybil nor the archdeacon did, that Cresswood's compositions, the settings for the dean's translations, were very poor stuff.

'Come now, Mr. Bently,' he said, 'I've every respect for Cresswood's memory and all that sort of thing. I liked him and I admired his playing. But the things he wrote, any I've seen, were tripe – simply tripe. I never heard of his composing a *Te Deum*. But if he did it's probably tripier still.'

Here Mr. Bently showed himself to be a man of real ability, fit representative (special) even for so great a firm as the Harpsichord Publishing Company. Instead of attempting to maintain the opinion he had expressed of the value of Cresswood's music, he promptly accepted Dennis's judgment.

'Quite so,' he said. 'Quite so. But we musical publishers are business men. We know, and you probably know too, that there's money in tripe, a great deal more money than there is in decent music. The fact is, Mr. Precentor, speaking confidentially, the public wants tripe. That's where the money comes in.'

'I see that,' said Dennis; 'but who's going to get the money?

Again Bently showed himself a man of ability and understanding. Instead of suggesting as he did to Sybil that the cathedral might profit, or as he did to the archdeacon that a small fortune was waiting for Cresswood's heirs, he saw the wisdom of being cynically frank.

'We shall get most of it. We always do. But we are honest people. There is something for Cresswood's heirs if we publish the *Te Deum*.'

Dennis remembered what Powell, the landlord of the Mitre Inn, had told him about Cresswood's affairs. He had heard a good deal more since Powell spoke to him, and he knew that the unfortunate organist owed money to everyone in the town from whom it was possible to obtain either credit or a loan. Even if the *Te Deum*, supposing there was a *Te Deum*, turned out to be all that Bently hoped, and even if the Harpsichord Publishing Company gave enormous royalties, Cresswood's heirs were not likely to benefit. When the furniture of the house was sold, including the grand piano, the dead man's assets would be quite insufficient to pay his debts. And some of the creditors – Powell, for instance – were Dennis's friends. He felt sorry for them. If possible he would like to secure something from the sale of the manuscript music. He did not believe in the existence of the

Te Deum, but there might be something among Cresswood's papers which would turn out to be worth a few pounds.

But Dennis was a shrewd man, shrewder than either Sybil Grosvenor or the archdeacon. He was much less impressed than they were by Bently's excellent manners. Besides, as he remembered, he had heard Bently's name before. Powell had mentioned it. A Mr. Bently – possibly the representative of the Harpsichord Publishing Company, certainly some Mr. Bently – had been in Cresswood's company drinking with him on the evening of the accident in the Mitre Inn.

'By the way,' he said, 'had you approached Cresswood at all about the *Te Deum*? Had you any negotiations with him?'

'I thought I mentioned,' said Bently – 'I certainly did mention to the archdeacon – that it was from Cresswood himself that we first heard about the *Te Deum*.'

'Oh, you did mention that all right,' said Dennis. 'I was thinking more of actual negotiations. Had you made him any kind of offer? Talked to him about it at any time?'

Bently hesitated and glanced keenly at Dennis, but the glance was very rapid, and the hesitation only momentary. There was scarcely a perceptible pause before he replied.

'Yes. I saw Cresswood the night before he died and made him a definite offer for the *Te Deum*. I came down to Carminster on purpose to see him. I called for him after dinner at his house and we walked together to the Mitre, where I was staying. As I said, I made him an offer.'

'Which he accepted?'

'No. He refused.'

Dennis was satisfied. Bently's story fitted in exactly with what he had heard from Powell and Carson. The two men had been drinking together, as Powell said. Bently had wanted something from Cresswood, which Cresswood was unwilling to give. That was Carson's report. Now everything appeared plain. Bently wanted the *Te Deum*. Cresswood had held out for a bigger price. The only thing that still puzzled Dennis was that there should be a *Te Deum*. It seemed extremely unlikely that Cresswood had ever composed such a thing. But perhaps – men do the most surprising things sometimes.

'Very well,' he said. 'I'll get the key of the house from the police. They'll give it to me all right. Then I'll take you there and go over Cresswood's music with you. If you find the *Te Deum* you can take a look at it. Then, if you like it, you can make an offer for it, an advance on royalties calculated on a reasonable percentage. I shall submit it to the executors of Cresswood's estate, whoever they are.'

'I fear,' said Bently, 'that I shall not be in a position to do that without consulting my directors. If it is as good as I hope —'

'As tripey as you expect.'

'As good as I hope,' said Bently, 'from a business point of view, I shall take the manuscript to my directors. You will surely allow me to do that. The reputation of our firm is safeguard enough against any attempt at piracy.'

Dennis knew that the directors of the Harpsichord Company were not likely to commit an act of open robbery. They might, and probably would, make a very good bargain for themselves and a very bad one for Cresswood's executors, but they would certainly not steal a manuscript. If, on the other hand, he refused to let Bently have it, there would be no bargain at all, and the creditors, that decent fellow Powell among them, would be so much the poorer.

'Very well,' said Dennis. 'Come along and we'll see what we can find.'

Superintendent Smallways, the head of the local police force, made no difficulty about handing over the key of the organist's house to Dennis. One of the advantages of belonging to the cathedral staff in a town like Carminster is that there is no difficulty about obtaining the key of anything, except, perhaps, a bank safe. But even if Superintendent Smallways had been a man with a great respect for legal procedure he could scarcely have refused to give the precentor the key of a house which belonged to the dean and chapter.

The search was not a very troublesome business. Cresswood had quantities of music, stacked in piles, or strewed about the room in which he kept his piano. But it was all music which had already been printed and published. A mere glance through it was sufficient to convince Bently that the manuscript of the *Te Deum* was not there. Another room, used as a dining room, contained a rolltop desk. This was crammed with papers. Every pigeonhole and every drawer was full to overflowing. Here were sheets of ruled music paper, some of them with notes and phrases scribbled on them in pencil or ink. Bently seized these eagerly, but found nothing which could possibly be supposed to be even the roughest draft of a *Te Deum*. There was not a hint to show that the praises of the noble army of martyrs had ever engaged Cresswood's attention, or that he had the smallest wish to be numbered with the saints. The only composition which was nearly complete – nothing was quite complete – was an attempt to set a tune to the dean's translation of one of his drinking songs. Dennis, who had been shown the thing by the dean, recognised the words, and pointed out the music to Bently. He seemed totally uninterested in drinking songs. What he wanted was a *Te Deum*.

Besides the ruled music paper there were bills, apparently hundreds of bills, notices of meetings and musical festivals, some of these more than a year old, advertisements of gramophones, wireless sets, and published music, chiefly Church music. Everything was in wild confusion as if each paper had been shoved into a drawer or a pigeonhole or flung on to the writing slab of the desk without any regard to order or arrangement.

69

There was only one exception to the general confusion. In one drawer there was a small bundle of letters fastened together with an elastic band. Dennis picked up the bundle and laid it aside.

'You won't want to look through these,' he said.

'I should like to.'

'But your *Te Deum* can't be here. Nobody could write a *Te Deum* in four parts with an organ accompaniment on half a sheet of notepaper. Besides, I think I know what these letters are. Cresswood was engaged to be married. These look like letters from the girl. They're in a woman's handwriting. I don't think we ought to look at them.'

'I don't want to read them,' said Bently. 'I don't even want to touch them. I'll be quite satisfied if you'll turn them over one by one, just so that I can see that no music has slipped in among them.'

'There can't be any music among these letters,' said Dennis.

'There may be. Cresswood seems to have been extraordinarily careless with his papers, and the *Te Deum* must be somewhere. We know it's somewhere. My firm is anxious, really anxious, to secure it. A man who muddles up his papers as Cresswood did might very easily strap up a piece of music with his love letters.'

Dennis could scarcely deny that this was possible; and Bently seemed very eager.

'Very well,' he said. 'I'll slip off the elastic band and turn the letters over one by one, but I won't have them read. I'd rather not even see the signature.'

But it was not possible to avoid that. The lady wrote a large, sprawly hand, and on the back of every letter was an enormous Elsie, spread right across the page. Fortunately for Dennis's feelings of respect due to love letters and their writers, no surname appeared anywhere. There was no sign of the smallest scrap of music.

'If he wrote a *Te Deum* at all,' said Dennis, 'it must be up in the organ loft. Would you like to search there? It's certainly not anywhere in these rooms. Unless he kept it in his bedroom, it's not in the house.'

Bently, a most thorough man, tried the bedroom, but after the first glance without much hope. Cresswood's clothes were as untidy as his papers. But there was just this one sign of orderliness about the man. He did not mix up his music with his shirts. The bedroom had no papers of any kind in it.

'And now I'll have a look through the music in the organ loft, if I may,' said Bently.

'Oh, certainly. But I can't see why you're so keen on getting the thing. You admit yourself that Cresswood's stuff is tripe. There are hundreds of men who could turn out that sort of muck for you by the ream. I could do it myself for you if I tried, and I will if you offer me a decent price.'

'There's money in tripe,' said Bently; 'but only in some tripe, not in all. As it happens Cresswood's is the kind of tripe we can sell. And that sort of tripe, if you will use the word, is nearly as hard to get as good music.'

Carson was on duty in the cathedral when Dennis and Bently arrived there. He produced the key of the door at the bottom of the stairs which led to the organ loft. As dean's verger he carried the keys of all the doors and gates which were kept locked. Of this particular door he possessed at the moment two keys. That which Cresswood had used on the night of the accident had been found in his pocket and handed over to Carson by the police.

'You'd better take charge of this, Mr. Dennis,' he said. 'It ought to be kept along with the key of the door in the south transept, to be handed over to the new organist when he's appointed.'

'Very well,' said Dennis. 'Give them both to me.'

71

'I beg your pardon,' said Carson, 'but I haven't got the key of the transept door. It wasn't in Mr. Cresswood's pockets when the police examined his clothes.'

'He must have had it with him,' said Dennis. 'He couldn't have got into the cathedral at night without it.'

'It wasn't in his pockets,' said Carson; 'that's all I know.'

'He must have dropped it somewhere.'

That seemed likely enough. If a man is drunk enough to tumble backwards off an organ stool he might easily have scattered broadcast a whole bunch of keys.

'I'll take a look for it in the organ loft,' said Dennis, 'and if you come across it anywhere about the cathedral keep it and give it to me. Come along, Mr. Bently.'

The search in the organ loft was as vain as that in Cresswood's house. There was music in abundance – loose sheets, bound albums, even some scraps of manuscript, but nothing which could possibly be regarded as part of a *Te Deum*. Bently was plainly disappointed.

'It's not here,' he said at last, after turning over the piles of music.

'I don't think it's anywhere,' said Dennis. 'I don't think Cresswood ever composed a *Te Deum*. He may have meant to, but he evidently didn't do it. Did he – there's no harm in telling you that Cresswood was generally hard up; in fact he was up to his neck in debt to anyone in the place to whom he could possibly owe money – did he by any chance ask your firm for an advance payment on the promise that he would deliver the music?'

Bently hesitated for a moment.

'Yes,' he said at last, 'and, what's more, he got it. It wasn't a large advance, but it gives us a right to the manuscript if we can find it. I hadn't meant to say anything about the advance, but as you ask the question I don't mind answering it.'

The answer more or less explained Bently's extreme eagerness in his search for the music. It also – and this was satisfactory to Dennis – justified him in allowing the search and would justify him in handing over the manuscript if it ever was found.

Yet Dennis still felt puzzled and slightly uneasy. He knew enough about the publishing of music to be sure that advance payments for unfinished manuscripts are exceedingly rare in that business. He knew enough about the Harpsichord Company to feel sure that they would be the very last firm in England likely to make such an advance. He knew enough about Cresswood's music to be sure that nothing he wrote would be good enough or bad enough to make any publisher so eager to get his next work as to pay for it in advance before it was finished.

'Is there really nowhere else that the music could possibly be?' said Bently.

'Nowhere.'

'No office or anything of that sort?'

'There's the Song School,' said Dennis. 'There is a piano there, but I don't think Cresswood ever used it except for practising the boys. He did not keep any music of his own there; but you can look if you like.'

It was not much of a chance, but Bently was unwilling to let it slip.

Carson, producing his bunch of keys again, opened the door of the Song School.

9

'EXCUSE ME, MR. DENNIS,' said Carson. 'I'd be glad of a word with you if you can spare the time.'

A man must have a good deal of time to spare who consents to listen to a word from Carson. He is a man who talks at great length if he gets the chance of talking at all. But Dennis was not specially eager to watch Bently poking about among the boys' surplices and cassocks, a thing he felt sure Bently would do before giving up his search for the *Te Deum*.

'You go ahead, Mr. Bently,' he said. 'You don't want me to help you. As soon as you've finished you'll find me in the cloisters with Carson. Now then, Carson.'

'Perhaps I ought not to mention the matter,' said Carson, 'for it's not exactly my business, and I'm a man who doesn't care to push himself in where he has no concern. Still —'

'Still you are going to mention it. And quite right. If it was your business it would certainly be dull and uninteresting. As it isn't your business it may be quite interesting.'

'What I would like to speak about,' said Carson, 'is that gentleman along with you – the gentleman you took up into the organ loft. If you don't mind my asking the question, do you know who he is?'

'I don't in the least mind your asking. I don't even mind answering. I do know who he is. I'll go further – I'll tell you who he is. His name is Bently, and he's the representative, the special representative, of the Harpsichord Publishing Company.'

'That's all right. So long as you know who he is and so long as you're satisfied, I've nothing more to say.'

'You have something more that you'd like to say, though. Come now, Carson, out with it, whatever it is.'

'Perhaps you are aware, Mr. Dennis – no doubt the gentleman has told you himself – that he was with Mr. Cresswood on the evening of the accident, drinking beer with him in the Mitre Inn.'

'I know all about that,' said Dennis. 'Mr. Bently told me so himself.'

'That's all right then. I only just wanted to mention the matter in case you didn't know.'

'Now that you have mentioned it,' Said Dennis, 'you might perhaps mention a little more.'

'There's nothing more to mention. They were drinking beer. I said that at the inquest.'

'Just drinking? Silently swigging?'

'No, Mr. Dennis. Not silently. They were engaged in conversation.'

'What about? Now, don't tell me you didn't listen to what they said, Carson. You told me that before, but I know jolly well you couldn't help listening to anything you could hear.'

'You'll excuse me, Mr. Dennis,' said Carson, 'but that's not a thing that anybody ought to say to me. I have my own self-respect, Mr. Dennis, and to be called an eavesdropper or a Peeping Tom is what I won't put up with from you or anyone else.'

'Nobody's accusing you of eavesdropping. All I think is that you must have heard something and you could tell me if you chose.'

'I told you all I knew on the day of the inquest when you and I and Mr. Powell were walking together. The gentleman seemed to me to be asking Mr. Cresswood for something and Mr. Cresswood didn't want to part with it.'

'But what? Come now, Carson, you must have some idea what it was,'

'They were speaking very low – at least the gentleman was. Mr. Cresswood hardly spoke at all except to say "No".'

'But didn't you hear anything? Not a single word?'

'I heard the word "tune",' said Carson. 'I gathered that it was a tune the gentleman wanted, and Mr. Cresswood didn't mean to part with it.'

'You're sure he said "tune"?'

The word puzzled Dennis. Nobody would describe a *Te Deum*, however meretriciously tripey, as a tune.

'Tune was the word used,' said Carson, whose memory seemed to be improving. 'And the gentleman seemed very keen about getting it. "It'll be worth nothing to you," he said, "and I'll give you a good price for it".'

'Thank you, Carson.'

'You'll understand, Mr. Dennis, that I couldn't help hearing that. The words came to me though I wasn't wanting to listen, or trying to. But that's all I heard. The only time the gentleman raised his voice was when he said that.'

Carson's report of the conversation, since he professed to be able to repeat exact words, was likely to be accurate. There was no reason why he should have invented such a speech. Indeed, his unwillingness to repeat it went to show that he had really remembered it. But it seemed extraordinarily unlikely that any publisher trying to buy the rights in a *Te Deum* should talk in such a way. That he should call such a composition a tune was improbable enough; but it was quite incredible that he should offer a good price for it, saying at the time that it would be no use to the composer. The Harpsichord Publishing Company is no doubt the greatest firm of music publishers in England. But there are others. If the *Te Deum* was as valuable as Bently seemed to think, then it would be of some use to Cresswood. He would take it to some other publisher and get a price from him. Besides – Dennis was becoming more and more convinced of this – there was no *Te Deum*, and never had been. Bentley's search for it was simply inexplicable. Only one thing seemed clear. There was something of value among Cresswood's effects. Dennis very much wanted to know what it was.

Bently came out of the choir school. He was satisfied, it may be supposed, that no choirboy had purloined the manuscript of the *Te Deum* and hidden it in his cassock pocket. Dennis, standing with Carson in the cloisters, made up his mind to ask some questions about the *Te Deum* and to find out if he could what Bently really wanted. Unfortunately he got no chance of doing this. Before he said a word to Bently, one of the junior vergers came hurrying to him with a message. The archdeacon wanted to see Mr. Dennis as soon as possible and would be glad if Mr. Dennis would call on him at once.

Now, a rector may ignore a summons from his bishop, or a verger may postpone the doing of a duty laid upon him by a dean, but no minor canon in Carminster dare ignore or neglect a summons from the archdeacon. Dennis was as bold as most men, and had the true Irish dislike of all persons in authority, but even Dennis knew that when the archdeacon called him he must go at once.

'Sorry, Bently,' he said. 'Must trot off at once. But I'll see you again, won't I? Drop in for tea after evensong this evening and we'll talk about Cresswood's *Te Deum*.'

But Bently could not accept the invitation. He said that he was leaving Carminster by an early train that afternoon.

'But if you come across the *Te Deum*,' he said, 'or any other music of Cresswood's likely to interest me, you'll let me know at once, won't you?'

The archdeacon, when Dennis was shown into his study, was kindly, but stern. The sternness, quite apparent in the set of his jaw and the glitter of his eyes, showed that he was seriously annoyed with somebody about something. The kindliness, which appeared in the tone of his greeting, showed that Dennis was not the culprit. There was evidently no question of whistling while crossing the close in a surplice, or achieving punctuality by an undignified race.

'It has been brought to my notice,' said the archdeacon, 'that the unfortunate Cresswood was heavily in debt at the time of his death. Have you any reason to suppose that this is so?'

'Not much room for doubt about that,' said Dennis. 'Roughly speaking, I should say that he owed the whole of his salary for the next year. I can't think how he managed it. Nobody would trust me for a quarter as much.'

The archdeacon, who had never been in debt in his life, was not interested in the ways in which extensive credit was obtained.

'Miserable man!' he said.

No one knows whether debts incurred on earth weigh heavily on the spirits of those whom the archdeacon liked to call the departed But unless some great change had come over Cresswood he was not likely to be made miserable in the next world by the thought of his creditors' sufferings in this. While living, while still liable to be haled before a County Court, he had always been quite cheerful about his debts.

'His assets?' said the archdeacon. 'Have you any idea what his assets amount to?'

An answer to this question might be of considerable personal interest to the archdeacon. Cresswood's debts had to be paid.

For the sake of the honour and dignity of the cathedral every creditor must be satisfied. If Cresswood's assets were insufficient the money would have to be raised by Mr. Cresswood's friends to save the cathedral from disgrace. The dean, no doubt, would bear his share, but the dean was not a wealthy man. The other residentiary canons might give something; but the archdeacon, who was very well off, would have to give more than anyone else. He recognised this as inevitable, but he did not like the prospect. He wanted to know, or at least to form some idea, how much he would be called upon to pay, and since the sum was certain to be considerable he felt justified in speaking of Cresswood as a miserable man.

'So far as I know,' said Dennis, 'Cresswood had no money except three shillings and sixpence, which the police found in his pockets. But of course there's his piano, a Bechstein, and a pretty good one. I dare say it might fetch a hundred pounds with luck, if we can find a buyer. As for his furniture – well, I should say seventy-five pounds would be a liberal offer for every chair and bed in the house.'

'Is there nothing else?' said the archdeacon with a sigh. 'No life insurance or anything of that sort?'

He foresaw that he would have to give £200 or £250 towards the settling of Cresswood's debts, and that, without even the satisfaction of seeing his name highly placed in a list of sub-scribers. These things must be done privately, if done at all.

No one – not even a man who pays super-tax on the un-earned part of his income – likes parting with £200. But the archdeacon, being a Christian man, knew that there were some-things in life much more valuable than money. The honour and reputation of Carminster cathedral were, in his opinion, worth more than any money. He had once given £1,000 to support a tottering tower in which dangerous cracks had appeared. And a tower is part only of the outward fabric of the building. Its honour, threatened by Cresswood's debts, was much more precious than any stone and mortar. The archdeacon was prepared to write his cheque not cheerfully, but without groaning very loudly.

Dennis felt sorry for him. A poor man himself, with nothing but his salary to depend on, he could not be expected to enter fully into the feelings of a rich man who has to part with some money. But he was intelligent enough to realise, as few people do, that a man who has a great deal finds it hard to part with what he has. He was so sorry for the archdeacon that he felt justified in holding out a hope that Cresswood's estate might be more valuable than it appeared.

'A representative of the Harpsichord Publishing Company called on me today,' said Dennis.

'Ah,' said the archdeacon, brightening a little. 'He called on me too. Indeed, it was I who sent him on to you. He said something about a *Te Deum* which Cresswood had composed, but I don't suppose it's worth anything.'

'It would be worth something,' said Dennis, 'at least I think it might, if we could find it. I gathered from Mr. Bently that the Harpsichord Company would pay something, perhaps something considerable, if we could hand over the manuscript.'

'But surely,' said the archdeacon, 'if he wrote a *Te Deum* it must be somewhere.'

'It isn't. Bently and I have searched everywhere and there isn't a sign of it.'

'How very odd!' said the archdeacon. 'A *Te Deum* in manuscript! I don't know that I ever saw a *Te Deum* in manuscript, but it must occupy a good deal of paper. It wouldn't be very easy for such a thing to disappear completely.'

'It has though,' said Dennis. 'Bently and I have ransacked Cresswood's house. We have searched the organ loft and the Song School. The thing simply isn't there.'

'It may turn up.'

'If it exists it certainly will. But I'm very much afraid that Cresswood never wrote it.'

'Perhaps,' said the archdeacon, 'there may be some other music of his which will fetch something. I happen to know that he was engaged in composing tunes for some of the dean's translations of medieval hymns. The dean is a little reticent about his work and seldom talks to me about it. But I understand from Miss Grosvenor that many of his translations are complete and that Cresswood was composing tunes for them.'

'I came across a few notes of something of the sort among his papers.'

'Perhaps the Harpsichord Company might buy them,' said the archdeacon.

'Bently didn't seem to want them. I showed them to him, but he scarcely glanced at them. At the same time —'

He hesitated. Bently certainly wanted something. If it was neither a *Te Deum* nor a tune for a medieval lyric, what was it? According to Carson he had offered a big price for the something, whatever it was.

Dennis did not feel inclined to repeat to the archdeacon all that Carson had told him, but he felt that he might safely say that the Harpsichord Company wanted something of Cresswood's and was prepared to pay for it.

'I think,' said the archdeacon, that I had better write direct to the Harpsichord Company myself. If their representative, this Mr. Bently, is mistaken about the *Te Deum* they will tell me what it is that they want. In the meanwhile will you be so good as to look over Cresswood's music again and bring me any manuscript compositions which you may find.'

The archdeacon had never approved of the dean's fondness for Latin lyrics. He agreed with Sybil that drinking songs and love songs which the dean preferred to the hymns were bad

Latin, shockingly bad Latin. The archdeacon was more inclined to dwell on the fact that the translation of such things was bad form, in a dean. Highly placed ecclesiastics ought to be occupied with quite different things, an edition, for instance, of the Cur Deus Homo. If the dean must read medieval Latin, Anselm's theology would be a more reputable work for his study. And yet, the dean was a scholar with a reputation. A volume of songs from his pen, set to music by a cathedral organist – there would be a novelty about the thing. The archdeacon was a shrewd man. There might be money in a series of drinking songs by a dean, set to rollicking tunes, which had been composed on a cathedral organ.

'Yes,' he said firmly, 'I'll write myself to the Harpsichord Company, mentioning the visit of their representative today. Then if you do find the *Te Deum* you can send it to them.'

'What astonishes me,' said Dennis, 'is that a firm like the Harpsichord Company should be prepared to make an advance payment on a *Te Deum* by Cresswood, even supposing he wrote such a thing, which seems to me unlikely.'

'It is surprising. But their representative expressly said so, didn't he?'

'Yes, he did.'

'Then,' said the archdeacon, 'they will surely pay something for the other music which we are prepared to offer them – music, I regret to say, much more likely to make a popular appeal than a *Te Deum*.'

'I suppose,' said Dennis, 'that the dean won't have any objection to our selling the tunes? I mean to say, we should have to sell his words along with them if the tunes are to be of any value.'

'I don't see why the dean should object. He must have been contemplating publication when he asked Cresswood to write the tunes. I imagine he would be pleased if we arrange the whole thing for him.'

The dean's words, so the archdeacon reflected, must be worth something too, perhaps as much as Cresswood's music, perhaps more. If a substantial sum could be secured from the Harpsichord Company, the dean's share of it, as well as Cresswood's, might very well go to the paying of the debts. The archdeacon had no doubt that the dean would agree to that, for he was the least worldly of men and would certainly contribute to the utmost of his ability to a fund which was to save the honour of the cathedral.

'I shall see Miss Grosvenor about it,' said the archdeacon. 'What we propose is plainly the right thing to do. I feel certain that Miss Grosvenor will agree with us about it.'

His confidence was founded on long experience. Sybil almost always agreed with the archdeacon.

10

FOR SIX DAYS AFTER Cresswood's death the dean stayed in bed, unwillingly, kept there by the firm care of his daughter. On the seventh day Sybil went to luncheon with Lady Carminster, and the dean got up. He dressed himself in his ordinary clothes, instead of the dressing gown which the butler recommended, and crept down to his study.

He looked shattered and was very pale. The shock of the organist's death and his own failure to go to the poor man's help had affected him. Sybil's rigid nursing had done even more than the shock to reduce his vitality. But what did him most harm was the feeling that he was regarded as a dotard, a doddering old man with a feeble mind. The dean was quite convinced that he was nothing of the sort. His recollection of what happened in the cathedral was perfectly clear. Cresswood had fallen forward on the keyboard of the organ. He had pulled himself together sufficiently to shut off the electric current and silence the instrument. He had walked about the organ loft afterwards, stumblingly, the dean thought, and with some difficulty. But he had certainly walked. He might have sat down on the organ stool again afterwards. He might have had a fainting fit and then fallen backwards and struck his head on the oak chest. All that was possible. If that was what had happened then the dean was to blame for not going to the man's help at once. The dean was a sensitive man. He felt that, if not actually a murderer, he was certainly responsible to God and man for Cresswood's death.

But Sybil would not let him tell his story. Every time he began she said, 'Now, father, don't think such things. They're not true, and it is very bad for you to think them.'

Dr. Harrowby took almost exactly the same line.

'You must keep quiet,' he said. 'The essential thing in your case is complete rest and the avoidance of mental effort. Don't let your thoughts dwell on what happened that night.'

They were both perfectly polite – Sybil a little less so than the doctor – and extremely kind. But the dean knew exactly what they were thinking and no doubt saying about him. He did not like it at all.

When he got to his study, leaning rather heavily on Redington's arm, he went straight to his writing table and opened the book of medieval lyrics. He set to work again on the '*potatores exquisiti*' drinking song. That required mental effort. The dean was determined to convince himself, and in the end other people, that his mind was alert and vigorous. If he could find a translation for *exquisiti* he would prove to Sybil and the doctor and everybody else that his mind was as sound as ever. No man with a failing intellect could possibly translate *potatores exquisiti*.

The dean had been no more than ten minutes at work when Redington came into the room again.

'A young person has called, sir,' he said, 'who wishes to speak to you.'

The word 'person' when used by servants is invariably feminine. It is also a term of contempt. The dean did not particularly want to see or be seen by a despicable girl. He was quite sure that Sybil, if at home, would keep such a creature far away from him. But he was in a defiantly independent mood. The proper translation of *exquisiti* still eluded him. But there were other ways of proving mental competence. He would see this young person, hear what her business was, and deal with it, quickly, decisively, competently.

'Show her in here at once,' he said.

'In here, sir?' said Redington doubtfully, for the dean's study was a sacred place. Even the archdeacon only dared to enter it after making an appointment.

'I said "here".'

The dean spoke firmly, almost fiercely, and was greatly pleased with himself. Feeble-witted old men hesitate and are doubtful.

After that the butler had no choice. He showed in the young person.

Her appearance did more than justify Redington's description of her. She wore – the dean began his survey at the top – a kind of skull cap, bright blue in colour, fitting very closely to the head, which it completely covered, like one of the rubber helmets worn by bathers who mean to dive or play water polo. It gave the impression at the first glance that she was completely bald, and, owing to some unusual disease, had a bright blue skull. Her lips, which were enormous and of singular shape, were puce-coloured. Her face, except for two red spots on the cheeks, was of a greyish mauve colour. Her eyelashes and eyebrows were thick and very black. Her eyes were large and appealing. The dean gathered the impression that she either had been crying or intended to cry very soon. He hoped that she had got the business over and would not shed tears in his study.

Her clothes were silky and fitted her from her collarbone to her knees like a tight sheath. It was difficult to suppose that she had on any garments beneath those which were visible. Her stockings – a slight wrinkling at the knees proved to the dean that they were stockings and not skin – were exactly the colour of her legs, or the colour which she wished it to be thought that her legs were. Her shoes were a pale fawn colour, made of a kind of rough leather, which might perhaps once have been the skin of a crocodile.

'Young person' was a mild and charitable description of her. If Sybil had seen the girl she would certainly have enrolled her among the 'cases' to be considered by the Committee for Social Purity. She would very likely have given her without further inquiry an order for admission to the Diocesan Rescue Home, an institution which the Committee for Social Purity kept going. She would have given the order tactfully, kindly, but with a firm intention of having it used. Such a gift would have been, in her opinion, by far the most appropriate way of dealing with this 'young person'.

The dean, though he too might have given an order for admission to the institution, did not think of doing such a thing. His mind was entirely occupied with the hope that the young person was not going to cry, a hope rapidly turning into a fear that she was.

'I came to speak to you about poor Ben,' she said.

Then she cried. Or the dean thought she did. She certainly dabbed her eyes with a small blue pocket handkerchief.

'Poor Ben?' said the dean vaguely.

'Yes. Poor dear, darling Ben. I was his fiancée. Elsie, you know, his fiancée.'

The dean did not know. He felt that he was getting confused. Perhaps, after all, Sybil was right in her fears. Perhaps Dr. Harrowby was right. His mind must be beginning to give way.

The young person dabbed her eyes again, and this time the blue pocket handkerchief seemed quite damp.

'I'm Elsie Hill,' she said. 'Surely you know that Ben and I were engaged to be married?'

'No,' said the dean, 'I didn't know. Or perhaps I did. I may have known. The truth is I don't know who Ben is. I don't think I know anyone called Ben.'

The large, appealing eyes opened very wide indeed.

'But Ben was your organist,' she said.

'Oh, yes. Of course. How stupid of me! Cresswood of course? But I thought his initial was R. Reuben. Surely his name was Reuben?'

'It was,' said Elsie. 'But I always called him "Ben". I couldn't call him Reu, could I? It would have sounded just like Prue, and that's a girl's name. I couldn't call him that, so I decided on Ben, and he rather liked it.'

'I am very glad he did,' said the dean.

'But now he's dead. Poor darling Ben! He wasn't always what you'd call a good boy. Not in every way; but in other ways he was such a dear. And now he's dead. I'll never see him again.'

This time she really did cry. A tear escaping from the blue pocket handkerchief trickled halfway down her cheek, and was then absorbed, like water running over dry sand, by the mauve-grey powder.

The dean felt that he ought to speak words of sympathy. But he had never in his life come in contact with a young person like Elsie Hill, and he did not know what kind of sympathy was most suitable.

'We shall all miss him,' he said, feeling that he had hit on a safe beginning. 'He was a musician of quite unusual talent. His organ recitals in the cathedral —'

'Topping, I expect,' said Elsie, who had stopped crying abruptly.

It was almost as if the dean's words of sympathy had dried up her tears, an unusual effect of words of that kind, though occasionally produced if the listener has a strong sense of humour.

'Quite topping,' said Elsie. 'He always used to say they weren't. That was modesty, I expect. Ben was very modest, though he may not have looked it. Especially if he'd been — You know what I mean. "Drink's a curse. Down with it." That's what Ben used to say – and do. The down with it part, I mean.'

Again the horrible suspicion seized the dean that his mind was giving way. He found himself quite unable to follow what Elsie was saying.

'Is there anything,' he said rather feebly, 'that I can do for you?'

'Yes, there is,' said Elsie, 'and if you're half such an old pet lamb as you look you won't say "No" when I tell you what it is.'

She crossed the room as she spoke, came quite close to the dean, and laid her hand on his shoulder in a manner which he felt to be caressing. He was acutely embarrassed. A young woman who was capable of calling him an 'old pet lamb', who laid her hand caressingly on his shoulder, might put her arm round his neck, might even kiss him. The dean shrank from the thought of being kissed by a strange young woman with enormous carmine lips.

'I want you to get me back all my letters,' she said; 'the letters I wrote to him – love letters. You know what love letters are like, don't you?'

The dean had, very long ago, written love letters to Sybil's mother before he married her. She had, he supposed, written letters to him, and they must have been love letters. But what they were like — Elsie confidently assumed that he knew what they were like. But he did not. It was all very long ago and the dean had forgotten. Elsie kindly explained.

'Not the sort of letters you want strangers to read. I wrote him hundreds, sheafs, and I expect he kept them. That's the sort of boy he was. So sweet, though he had his failings. We all have. I expect you have a few yourself, dean, though I must say you don't look it. I'm sure whatever you do wrong, it isn't gin and ginger like poor Ben, though I must say you look as if one would do you good – a double gin, with half a small ginger. Now what about the letters? You'll give them to me, won't you?'

The dean saw no reason why Elsie should not get her own letters back. Indeed, he would at the moment have been willing to give her any letters she wanted whether they were her own or not. The hand which had been laid on his shoulder was slipping round his neck, and he could not help feeling that at any moment he might feel the carmine lips on his cheek. He felt exceedingly glad that Lady Carminster's luncheon parties always lasted a long time. Sybil would not be home for an hour or two. By that time Elsie would be safely out of the Deanery.

'If you wait a minute,' he said, 'I'll give you a letter to Mr. Dennis. I think he's in charge of Mr. Cresswood's papers and things.'

'Mr. Dennis? Who's he?'

'Our precentor,' said the dean.

'My hat!' said Elsie. 'A precentor! I suppose he's even a bigger pot than a dean? Is he – is he as old as you?'

'Not nearly,' said the dean. 'In fact he's quite young. So you needn't —'

'I won't,' said Elsie. 'I promise I won't. I'm far too sorry for poor Ben to take up with any other young man for months and months.'

'What I intended to say,' said the dean, 'is that you needn't be frightened. I wasn't thinking of your – er – taking up with him.'

'Frightened! Good gracious me! I never was frightened of a man in my life.'

The dean realised that this was probably true. She was certainly not in the least frightened of him. As if to show her complete fearlessness she slipped the hand on his shoulder right round his neck and gave a little squeeze. He wrote his note to

Dennis, suggesting that if possible and convenient – the dean was always considerate – he should give Miss Elsie Hill any letters she wanted at once. He even managed to add a P.S., though he feared that Elsie was reading it over his shoulder: 'Please see her safely into the train as soon as you have given her the letters.'

11

DENNIS ᴛᴏᴏᴋ ᴀ ɢᴏᴏᴅ look at Miss Elsie Hill before he opened the dean's letter. Though a precentor he was a young man of broad and liberal views without any taint of puritanism in him. He had no prejudice against girls with carmine lips and mauve faces. He quite understood, when he grasped who she was, how it was that she had attracted Cresswood. There was no sign of moral severity about her, and Cresswood would certainly choose a girl who would not condemn life's simpler and more obvious pleasures. He also understood, when he read it, the postscript of the dean's letter. Elsie Hill might have, and no doubt had, many lovable qualities, but she was not the sort of girl who would get on well with Sybil Grosvenor. If she stayed in Carminster and paid visits to the dean she would certainly meet Sybil sooner or later. Dennis understood that when that happened there would be trouble.

While Dennis was reading the dean's letter, Elsie was taking a good look at him. She found that he was young, pleasing in appearance, and that he had eyes capable of merry twinkling. He was a clergyman, and a clergyman of a very clerical sort, a precentor. But he was also a man, and Elsie's experience of men led her to believe that her own eyes were useful in dealing with them. As soon as Dennis looked up from the letter she 'cast on him' – the phrase is Shakespeare's – 'most speaking œillads'. The effect surprised her. An innocent and modest young man, the sort of man a clergyman ought to be, would have blushed and looked away. An experienced man with natural instincts would have cast back at her other œillads more speaking still. A Puritan – Elsie believed that there were such people – would have frowned and scowled. Elsie would have been prepared to deal with any of these ways of receiving her glances. What Dennis did and said startled her.

'Look here,' he said. 'Before we start looking for the letters you want, get this clearly into your head. You're not to make eyes at me. I haven't the slightest objection to girls making eyes at me at proper times and in proper places. In fact I don't mind admitting that I rather like it. But this is Carminster, and I'm the precentor of the cathedral. If you'd ever seen the dean's daughter or his verger, you'd know that the sort of thing you're doing isn't tolerated here.'

'Crikey!' said Elsie, brightly. 'Should I have had to be as good as all that if I had married poor Ben and come to live here?'

'You would,' said Dennis.

'Every day and all day?'

'Every weekday, and even better on Sundays.'

'Well,' said Elsie, 'I'm heartbroken about poor Ben, and when I think of him I cry whole bucketfuls of tears, but I dare say it's really just as well that things have turned out so that I can't marry him. I couldn't have kept it up, not being as good as that, for very long.'

Dennis was much of the same opinion. Elsie would have been a strange and disturbing creature in the Cathedral Close.

'Now that we've got that settled,' said Dennis, 'and you quite understand – you do, don't you?'

'Rather. The modest village maiden stunt for yours truly.'

She pressed the palms of her hands together, like the child Samuel saying his prayers, touched her chin with the tips of her forefingers, let her head droop slightly to one side, and almost shut her eyes.

'Good!' said Dennis. 'Now we'll go along to the police station.'

Elsie dropped her impersonation of the village maiden with a start.

'Goodness gracious me!' she said. 'But I've done nothing. You can't have a girl arrested for looking at a man. You couldn't have had me arrested even if I'd kissed you, and I didn't do that.'

'Don't be silly,' said Dennis. 'Nobody wants to arrest you.'

'Oh, of course, if you're only pulling my leg it's all right. But I wish you wouldn't do it that way. I don't like police stations. They make me jumpy.'

'We've got to go to one whether you like it or not,' said Dennis, 'for Inspector Smallways still has the key of Cresswood's house.'

Elsie was reassured, but certainly not happy. She was quiet and subdued as she walked through the streets to the police station. Dennis decided that she must have more than the usual instinctive dread of the police. The fact did not altogether surprise him.

Inspector Smallways produced the key of the house again, with a suggestion that this time Dennis might as well keep it. The police, having done their duty by Cresswood's body, had no wish to be mixed up with his affairs. Dennis pocketed the key and took Miss Elsie to the house.

When she got there she repeated the performances she had gone through with her pocket handkerchief at the Deanery. Dennis was entirely unembarrassed. If Miss Hill chose to weep, she could do so without any interference from him. It was, Dennis recognised, quite natural and right that she should cry when she entered the house of her dead lover – if she was one kind of girl, the simple and innocent kind. If, as he suspected, she was quite a different kind of girl, it was equally natural and right that she should pretend to cry.

'Poor darling Ben,' she snivelled. 'I can't help thinking of him when I come into the room where he lived, with his writing table in it and all. I just seem to see him, sitting here composing hymns and practising scales and thinking of me.'

The picture was a touching one, but Dennis remained unimpressed. He went straight to the writing table, opened a drawer, and took out the packet of letters.

'Here are your letters,' he said.

He handed her the packet still held together by its elastic band. She stopped snivelling at once. She slipped off the band and turned over the letters one by one, glancing at each. When she had finished she went through the whole set again, slowly and more carefully. There was a look of puzzled anxiety on her face when she had finished her second scrutiny.

'They're not all here,' she said. 'There's one missing.'

'I'm sorry,' said Dennis, 'but that's all there are. If there ever were any more he must have torn them up or burned them.'

'Ben never burned that letter,' said Elsie. 'Give it to me, at once. Do you hear, give it to me!'

The girl was unmistakably angry. This was a new side of her character, and Dennis felt more embarrassed than he had been by the minx, the demure maiden, or the mourning virgin, widowed before she was wedded.

'My dear Miss Hill,' he said, 'I've given you all the letters I have. If you can find another anywhere you're welcome to it.'

'Likely I'll find it!' she said, her anger growing. 'You've taken jolly good care I shan't find it. Oh, I know your sort, as pi as a saint in a window, turning up your eyes and calling everybody a miserable sinner if a girl so much as looks at you. But you're ready enough to steal a letter when it suits you. Call yourself a precentor, indeed. A nice kind of precentor! You're a low, sneaking, nasty beast of a cat, stealing a poor girl's letter.'

It is to Dennis's credit that he kept his temper even under this shower of abuse.

'My dear girl,' he said soothingly, 'do try to be reasonable. Why on earth should I steal your letter? What use would it be to me if I had it? I assure you I don't want to read it.'

Elsie was not in the least mollified by this appeal to her reason.

'If you want to read my letters you can,' she said. 'I don't care who reads them. I don't care what you do with them. There they are for you.'

She gathered the letters on her lap into a bundle, snapped their elastic band round them, and flung them at Dennis. He caught the packet before it struck him, and, holding it in his hand, stared in bewilderment at Elsie.

'I don't know what you want,' he said. 'I've given you all your letters – all I have; and just because you think there's one missing, you shy the whole lot at me.'

'The one that's missing,' said Elsie, 'is the only one I really want. Look here' – her anger appeared to be cooling a little – 'I'll give you five pounds for it if you'll let me have it. It's no use to you, not the least, so you may just as well give it back.'

'I'd give it back with pleasure if I had it,' said Dennis. 'What I'm trying to get you to believe is that I've never seen it, much less stolen it. I quite understand' – he had been thinking rapidly and felt that he really did understand – 'I quite understand that there may be things in that letter which you wouldn't like any-one to see. You may have gone a bit too far in your expressions of affection, or there may have been allusions to things which happened. You and poor Cresswood may —'

Girls have from time to time written things in love letters which were not meant for the eyes of anyone but the lover, things which, if read by others, might lead to unpleasant reflections about the writer's character. Dennis thought it likely that he was concerned with a letter of that sort. He quickly saw his mistake. Elsie suddenly laughed aloud.

'Great suffering Jupiter!' she said. 'Do you think I'd write that kind of thing to Ben, even if I'd done it, which I didn't! And do you really think I'd mind your reading it if I had! I'm not the kind of girl who gets ratty over a trifle like that.'

'If it wasn't – wasn't a' – Dennis hesitated. He was, after all, a clergyman and a precentor. Such men have to pick their words – 'if it wasn't a very intimate love letter, why are you so anxious to get it back?'

'It wasn't a love letter at all,' said Elsie, 'at least the love letter part doesn't matter in the least. What I want to get back is a tune.'

Dennis saw a glimmer of light. Could this be the piece of music which Bently had been so anxious to get? Cresswood, supposing he had really composed the festal *Te Deum*, might have sent it to the girl he was going to marry, for criticism if she was musical, for admiration if she were not. It was odd that both Bently and Elsie should call such a composition a tune. But the girl at all events might know no better. The word 'piece' is used by child students of the piano in the same indiscriminate way.

'Was it,' he said, 'a setting of the *Te Deum*?'

'The *Te Deum*,' said Elsie, thoughtfully. 'Would that be a great big thing?'

'Huge,' said Dennis. 'A *Te Deum* in four parts, possibly eight parts, with an organ accompaniment, would cover sheets and sheets of music paper – great big sheets. If the orchestration was done it would be larger still.'

'Then it's not a *Te Deum*,' said Elsie. 'The tune I'm looking for is — Will you absolutely swear a solemn, Bible dying oath that you haven't got it?'

'I'll do nothing of the sort. I don't approve of miscellaneous swearing about trifles, and, anyhow, I can't swear a dying oath when I'm alive and well. But I haven't got your tune. I'll give you my word for that.'

'All right,' said Elsie, 'I'll believe you, and I'll tell you what it was so that you'll be able to help me to get it back. It was a tune, written on half a sheet of notepaper, not just ordinary notepaper, but paper with blue lines on it.'

'I know Cresswood wrote tunes,' said Dennis, 'and I think I can lay my hands on one or two of them if you'd like to see them.'

'Cresswood! Ben! Who's talking about him?'

'I thought we both were. Surely it's one of his tunes you want?'

'No, it isn't. Ben didn't write it. I sent it to him.'

'Oh! A composition of your own. I see.'

'Good gracious me!' said Elsie. 'What do you take me for? First you think I'm the kind of girl who'd blush because Ben or somebody kissed me, and now you think I've nothing better to do than to write hymns! Why, if I'd written it myself I'd write it again, or write another. Anyhow, I wouldn't care a hang whether I got it back or not. As a matter of fact – I'm trusting you a lot when I tell you this; but if a girl can't trust a clergyman who can she trust? Not that I'm much of a one for curates. Still I will say that I'd as soon trust a curate as anyone else. And of course you're a precentor.'

'If there's any secret about the tune, perhaps I'd better not hear it.'

'Oh, I don't know that it need be a secret,' said Elsie. 'If you swear not to tell anyone. But of course you won't swear. You told me that before. Though I can't think how you manage to get on without a good damn now and then. But if you won't you won't, and I shan't ask you to. Nobody will ever be able to say it of me that I taught a precentor to swear. But if you promise – just promise without any swear about it – not to tell anyone else what I tell you, I will tell you.'

'I'm not sure about promising,' said Dennis. 'I like to know what I'm going to promise before I do it. What are you going to tell me?'

'Who wrote the tune.'

Dennis saw no possible harm in promising not to reveal that, though he could not guess at any reason why he should be asked to promise it.

'Very well,' he said. 'I promise.'

'Faithful and true?'

'No. Just promise.'

'All right. I'll trust you. My poor dear Dad wrote it when he was dying. I sent it to Ben so that he should play it in the cathedral.'

'I see,' said Dennis, thankful that he did see at last.

There was, apparently, no connection between Bently and Elsie. The fact that they were both seeking for a piece of music among Cresswood's papers was a mere coincidence, though an odd one. Bently wanted a *Te Deum* composed by Cresswood; Elsie wanted a hymn tune composed by her father, who was dead.

'Poor Dad,' she said. 'I sob and sob when I think of him composing that tune when he was dying. Just like – I forget his name, but I know he was a clergyman, who walked about the sea-shore writing "Abide with Me". I rather love "Abide with Me", don't you? I always feel inclined to cry when I hear it, which isn't very often, for I'm not a whale on going to church. Perhaps if I heard it oftener I wouldn't want to cry so much.'

Dennis, who had a tender heart, was touched by this story. Elsie, with her painted lips, heavily-powdered face, and her strange oaths, weeping over "Abide with Me" on the few occasions on which she heard it, was touching enough. Elsie, a dutiful daughter, receiving a hymn tune from the hands of a dying father, was more touching still.

'Let's go right through Cresswood's papers,' said Dennis, and find it. 'It must be here somewhere.'

Once more the search was in vain. Various tunes were found, more or less complete and a rough jotting of the notes for the *potatores exquisiti*; but these were all on large sheets of music paper, and Elsie threw them aside at once.

'Dad's tune,' she said, 'was on a half sheet of notepaper – thickish paper, but nasty. I do think a man might be given a decent sheet of paper when he's dying, don't you?'

Dennis reflected that the inferior quality of the paper must have been Elsie's own fault. It must have been she who gave it to her father.

'If it turns up anywhere,' he said at last, 'I will send it to you.'

'It won't turn up,' said Elsie. 'And I'll tell you why it won't turn up. It's been stolen. At first I thought you'd stolen it, but I don't believe now that you did.'

'Thank you,' said Dennis, 'but I don't see why anyone should have stolen it.'

'Lots of people would. If they knew about it. And some people did. Binder knew, for he came to see me, and tried to get it from me. I say, has Binder been down here?'

'Not that I know of. He's certainly not been near me.'

'And that policeman might,' said Elsie. 'I forget his name. But he might hear about it. The police tell each other everything. Has there been a policeman snooping about among Ben's things?'

Dennis remembered that Inspector Smallways had carried Cresswood's body home from the cathedral, and emptied his pockets. Afterwards he had charge of the key of the house. But it really was impossible to suppose that Smallways, rather fat, obviously upright and beyond suspicion, could have stolen a hymn tune from a dead man.

'And that nasty old devil who walks about your cathedral with a silver club,' said Elsie. 'He always hated poor Dad. He'd steal it like a shot, just out of spite if he knew about it.'

'Carson?'

'That's him, stinking, jealous old skunk. He'd steal it if he got the chance.'

These suggestions were becoming more and more absurd. Of all men living Carson was the least likely to steal a hymn tune. Apart from his position and character, which set him far above suspicion, his whole life was spent among hymn books, each crammed with tunes. He could have as many as he liked all day, and if he chose to take a few home with him at night no one would object to his doing so. It was ridiculous to think of Carson stealing anything, but actually grotesque to suspect him of stealing a manuscript hymn tune.

'Well,' said Dennis, 'I'll do all I can to help you, and if I come across the tune anywhere I'll send it to you. Will you give me your address?'

'My address is here,' said Elsie firmly. 'The Mitre Inn, and I don't intend to budge out of this till I get Dad's tune.'

It seemed likely, if she stuck to her resolution, that she would spend the rest of her life in Carminster. Dennis was a little troubled at the thought that it was impossible for him to obey the instructions given him in the dean's postscript.

12

THE ARCHDEACON RECEIVED A prompt and most disturbing reply to the letter he wrote to the secretary of the Harpsichord Publishing Company.

> 'DEAR SIR' (he read), 'In reply to your valued inquiry re Mr. Bently, we greatly fear that there must have been some mistake in re —'

When the archdeacon got as far as 'in re' he clicked his tongue against his palate. 'Re' was bad enough, a vile Latinism, but 'in re' following hard in the same sentence was too much. If he had been a layman he would have sworn. The archdeacon was not a scholar, as the word might be used of the dean, but he was an educated man, and 're' affected him as a split infinitive affects some stylists. He had once given up dealing with a tailor for no reason except that the unfortunate man wrote 'in re' as an introduction to some statement which he wanted to make about gaiters.

> ' – in re the visit to you of a gentleman purporting to be a representative of our firm, I am directed

> to inform you that we have no one connected
> with the firm, as representative, or in any other
> capacity, bearing the name of Bently. I am further
> directed to inform you that we are unable to trace
> any correspondence with the organist or other
> member of the Carminster Cathedral staff re —'

'Good heavens!' said the archdeacon, driven to a mild kind of oath either by the repetition of the word 're' or by the startling news which the letter contained.

> ' – re a Festal *Te Deum* or similar musical com-
> position submitted to us by your organist. No
> representative of our firm has visited Carminster
> during the months inst. or ult.'

'Inst.' And 'ult.' are, in the archdeacon's opinion, as bad or worse than 're' and 'in re'. But he did not pause to make clicking noises over them. The news which the disgusting words contained was too serious for that. Nor did the rest of the letter, though very civil and even flattering, soothe him in the least.

> 'May we add that if now or at any future time
> you should desire to submit to us for publica-
> tion a setting of the *Te Deum*, or other sacred
> musical composition, the work will receive the
> most careful and favourable consideration of our
> directors.'

The archdeacon was seriously annoyed. It seemed plain that someone had been playing a practical joke. No one, except the perpetrator, ever enjoys a practical joke, and those who occupy positions of dignity – archdeacons, for instance – detest this kind of wit even more than common men do. But the archdeacon of Carminster, though dignified, was not personally a vain man. He was certainly no vainer than every man is who has achieved a moderate success in life and reached the age of sixty. What vexed him, indeed made him actually angry, was not that he had been the victim of a joke, but that anyone had played off a joke on the dean and chapter. That struck him as atrocious, an offence against good taste so grievous as to be actually sinful,

He could think of only one person in the world who would have dared to do such a thing. Dennis, the precentor, was young, was Irish, was singularly lacking in good taste, had little or no sense of decency or reverence. A man who whistled in the cloisters on the way to matins and ran across the close with his surplice over his arm, might make a practical joke with the dean and chapter of Carminster as victims.

The archdeacon rang his bell. A messenger was sent to find Dennis.

'He may be in the cathedral,' said the archdeacon, 'or in the Song School, or in his own house, or somewhere else in the precincts. Wherever he is, please find him and ask him to call here at once.'

If he had said, 'Fetch him, alive or dead,' his order would have been scarcely more impressive.

Dennis was found almost immediately. He was bowling to Sam Hodson at the nets in the boys' playing field. Sam Hodson was a promising bat, and Dennis found it hot work bowling to him. He hastily put on his waistcoat, coat, and collar, which lay on the ground at the end of the pitch, wiped the sweat from his face, and hurried to the archdeacon's house.

'Read that,' said the archdeacon, handing him the letter from the Harpsichord Company.

Dennis read it.

'Great Scot!' he said.

'What?' said the archdeacon.

'A bit thick,' said Dennis, by way of making clearer what he meant by 'Great Scot'.

'It seems to me,' said the archdeacon, 'that someone has been playing a practical joke on the dean and chapter. I can only say that if the perpetrator is a member of the cathedral staff his performance strikes me as not merely wicked but actually vulgar.'

The archdeacon, in calmer moments, might have inverted the terms of his climax, but just then he was so profoundly shocked that he spoke exactly as he felt.

He looked at Dennis so fiercely that it was impossible to miss his meaning.

'I assure you,' said Dennis, that I had nothing whatever to do with it. I was just as much taken in as you were. I should never have thought of such an original spoof.'

'I see nothing in the least original about it,' said the archdeacon.

'Come now, Mr. Archdeacon,' said Dennis. 'Hang it all, be fair. To set the dean and chapter and the precentor and the minor canons and Carson, especially Carson, scraping the cathedral with fine combs to find a *Te Deum* which never existed – I almost wish I had thought of it myself. That fellow Bently, whoever he is, must have a brilliantly inventive mind.'

'I'm afraid,' said the archdeacon, 'that I cannot share your admiration for this kind of originality. It strikes me, to be perfectly candid, as simply lamentable. I am, however, sincerely glad, more glad than I can easily say, that you had nothing to do with it.'

'Nothing whatever,' said Dennis. 'Absolutely nothing.'

'I'm all the more glad,' said the archdeacon, 'because I feel it my duty to place the matter in the hands of the police at once, a thing I should be sorry to do if any member of the cathedral staff were involved.'

'Do you think,' said Dennis, 'that that's the best thing to do? I mean to say, isn't there a risk? If the thing was simply a joke won't we look rather silly when we tell the story against ourselves?'

'This is far beyond a joke. The man Bently ought to be arrested for – for misrepresentation.'

'We might have had him run in,' said Dennis, 'for obtaining money under false pretences, if he had obtained money. But he didn't. He didn't even try to. He never so much as attempted to borrow the price of his railway ticket home.'

'He endeavoured by means of gross and abominable misrepresentation to obtain something of value.'

'The *Te Deum*? But he didn't get it. And besides, he kept on offering to pay for it.'

But the archdeacon had made up his mind. He had, as he put it to himself, 'decided on his course of action'. He lifted the telephone receiver from his writing table and asked to be put through to the police station.

'I shall be glad, Mr. Dennis,' he said, 'if you will accompany me. You saw more of the man Bently than I did, and what you can tell Inspector Smallways may be of great assistance to him in bringing this – this malefactor to justice.'

Dennis, for one reason or another, had seen a good deal of the police since Cresswood's death. He had always been on friendly terms with Inspector Smallways, and was by this time quite intimate with him. He liked him, having come to regard him as a good-humoured and obliging man with a great deal more sense and intelligence than he appeared to have. He did not altogether enjoy the prospect of telling the story of Bently's practical joke to a man who would certainly chuckle over it afterwards, even if he preserved his official gravity in the presence of the archdeacon. He would have been glad to avoid this visit to the inspector, but the archdeacon was a masterful man, and when he said that a thing was to be done it generally was done – in Carminster.

Inspector Smallways listened to all that the archdeacon had to say. He listened to Dennis's much longer story. He made some notes when he was given a description of Bentley's appearance. Dennis, expecting to see a twinkle of amusement in the inspector's eyes, was surprised to find that he took the whole story seriously. He certainly seemed to regard it as something more than a practical joke.

'We heard at the inquest,' said Smallways at last, 'that a man calling himself Bently stayed in the Mitre Inn on the night of Cresswood's death. He was seen in Cresswood's company, talking to him and drinking with him that evening. Have you any reason to suppose that he and the man who called on you and the archdeacon were the same?'

Dennis remembered what Carson had told him.

'Yes,' he said, 'it's the same man. Carson saw him in the inn and saw him afterwards in the cathedral with me.'

Then he remembered something more – Carson's account of the conversation in the inn.

'Bently,' he said, 'was trying to get something from Cresswood. That looks as if he really was after the *Te Deum*, and I'm bound to say that when he was with me he seemed pretty keen. I mean to say I got the impression that he was trying very hard to find it.'

Influenced by Smallways' manner and by his own recollection of his interview with Bently, Dennis was inclined to abandon the idea of an elaborate and ingenious hoax. He began to think that he had come on something much more interesting than that.

'Does the name Bently suggest anything to you, Mr. Archdeacon?' said Smallways.

The archdeacon shook his head.

'Or to you?' said Smallways to Dennis.

'Only a kind of motor,' said Dennis, 'the kind I'd have if I could afford it.'

'We may take it, then,' said Smallways, 'that Bently was an assumed name, intended to mislead us, like his alleged connection with the Harpsichord Publishing Company.'

Smallways reached his conclusions slowly, but they were thoroughly sound when he got to them. There seemed little doubt that the name of the man who wanted Cresswood's *Te Deum* was something else, not Bently.

'Is there anything more that you'd like to say to me?' said Smallways.

'Only that I should be glad to see the man arrested at once,' said the archdeacon.

'Quite so,' said Smallways, 'and I can assure you, Mr. Archdeacon, that the man, once we get in touch with him, will be kept under observation, even if it is not possible to arrest him.'

'So far as I can see,' said Dennis, 'there's precious little chance of your getting in touch with him. He left Carminster as soon as he made sure that he couldn't find the *Te Deum*. He said he was going to London, but he may have gone anywhere. If his name isn't Bently, you have nothing whatever to go on except a rather vague description of his appearance. You're not likely to find him.'

'I think,' said the archdeacon, 'that we may safely leave that to Inspector Smallways. The police have their own methods of obtaining information about the movements of the criminal classes.'

He shook hands courteously with the inspector and left the office. Dennis went with him. But ten minutes later Dennis was back at the police station. He went straight to the inspector's room.

'Look here, Smallways,' he said. 'Now that the archdeacon's gone – I never can stand the archdeacon, can you? Pompous old ass!'

Smallways smiled slowly.

'The archdeacon,' he said, 'occupies a very important position in Carminster.'

It was his smile, not his words, which encouraged Dennis to go on.

'Anyhow he's gone,' said Dennis, 'so perhaps you won't mind telling me what you really think about this Bently business? Is it simply a practical joke played off by some silly blighter, or is it — What on earth else can it be?'

'I think,' said Smallways, 'that it's curious, very curious.'

'That means, I suppose, that you're taking it seriously?'

'I shall have inquiries made about Bently,' said Smallways, 'and find out what I can about the man.'

'"The police",' said Dennis in a very fair imitation of the archdeacon's voice, '"have their own methods of obtaining information about the criminal classes".'

Smallways smiled.

'You called the archdeacon a pompous ass,' he said, 'but he has very proper ideas about the police.'

'You may be omniscient,' said Dennis, 'but I suppose you're not above taking a hint.'

'We are omniscient,' said Smallways, 'just because we never neglect hints.'

'Very well,' said Dennis. 'I don't see any connection myself between Bently and what I'm going to tell you. I dare say there isn't any. But Bently isn't the only man who wants Cresswood's music. Did you ever hear of anyone called Binder?'

Inspector Smallways was a heavily built and very impassive man. He gave many people the impression that he was dull. He certainly never displayed undue excitement or gave any sign of being surprised.

'Yes,' he said, 'I know something of a man called Binder.'

'Is he,' said Dennis, 'the kind of man who'd steal a hymn tune?'

'I don't think he'd steal a hymn tune, but I'm quite willing to believe that he'd steal pretty nearly anything else. It was before your time here, but you may have heard of the robbery of Lady Carminster's jewels.'

'I've heard of precious little else since I've been here.'

'Well, Binder was the name of one of the men convicted for that burglary. He wasn't the ringleader, but he got five years for it.'

Dennis thought rapidly and did a small sum in his head.

'So Binder is just about due to be out again,' he said. 'That burglary was five years ago.'

'He is out again,' said Smallways. 'I make it my business to know things like that. And now will you tell me why you ask me about Binder? You'd never heard of him in connection with the burglary, had you?'

'No,' said Dennis. 'I'm tired listening to the story of that burglary, and, anyhow, I don't believe I heard the names of the convicted men. If I did I've forgotten them.'

'Then what put his name into your head? And why did you ask me whether he was likely to steal hymn books?'

'I didn't say hymn books. I said a hymn tune. I'm afraid I can't tell you that, Smallways. I've gone as far as I can in giving you the name. It would be – I'll not talk about the seal of the confessional and that sort of stuff – but it would be a gross breach of confidence if I told you any more. I'm not sure that I haven't told you too much already.'

'Perhaps you will feel inclined to tell me a little more,' said Smallways, 'if I tell you something. I had a visit from Carson yesterday...'

'The dean's verger?'

'Yes.'

'I suppose he didn't come to confess that he'd stolen a hymn tune?'

'No. He didn't. He came to tell me that you brought Bently with you to the cathedral, into the organ loft, and afterwards into the Song School.'

'I told you that myself,' said Dennis. 'What's the use of repeating back to me things I've said to you?'

'Carson told me a little more,' said Smallways. 'He told me that he had seen Bently with Cresswood in the Mitre Inn, and then again with you.'

'I told you that too. How extraordinarily slowly your mind works! It seems to take you half an hour to grasp the simplest thing. We've got it all settled and fixed about the two Bentlys being one and the same Bently. Don't go harking back in that way.'

'Carson told me one thing more,' said Smallways. 'He had a feeling that he knew the man's face when he saw him in the Mitre, and he felt sure of it when he saw him again with you in the cathedral. But he couldn't put a name to him or remember where he had seen him before. Well, you know how these things come and go in the memory. Two days afterwards Carson remembered where he had seen the man and who he was. Bently was one of the prisoners tried for the robbery of the Carminster jewels, tried and convicted. Carson couldn't remember which he was, but he was in court every day during the trial, and he was sure that Bently was one of the gang. Well, that interested me, as you may imagine. I thought I'd like to be sure of it, so I asked Hodson if he could identify the man.'

'Hodson? That's the fellow who made the fuss at the coroner's inquest, trying to publish the fact that Cresswood was drunk?'

'Yes,' said Smallways, 'but Hodson was also the Scotland Yard detective in charge of the Carminster jewels case. He would remember the prisoners and be able to identify them. Unfortunately he did not see Bently, either during his first visit here, on the night of Cresswood's death, or afterwards when he went about with you: So he was no use to me, and I was left guessing whether Carson was mistaken or not. Then you come here and ask me if I know anything about a man called Binder. You won't give me your reasons for asking the question and you won't tell me what put the name into your head. You simply spring Binder on me when we were talking about Bently. Now will you tell me a little more?'

'Sorry,' said Dennis, 'but I can't.'

'Mr. Precentor,' said Smallways very gravely.

'Oh, drop that,' said Dennis. 'I call you Smallways. Why can't you be friendly and call me Dennis?'

'I'll call you anything you like, but I want to warn you that if this business turns out to be as serious as it very well may you will have to tell me all you know. You won't be given any choice.'

'Don't you talk that way to me, Smallways. That might-of-the-law business doesn't impress me one bit. I'll tell you all I know if this turns out to be a really serious business. But so far I've no evidence to show that it's anything of the sort. It may be just a mixture of a practical joke and some silly stunt about a hymn tune. There hasn't been another burglary, has there?'

'Not yet.'

THE HYMN TUNE MYSTERY

'And I don't see any likelihood of another. So far as I can see nobody wants to steal anything except a *Te Deum* or a hymn tune.'

'Very well,' said Smallways. 'I think you ought to tell me what that girl, whoever she is, said to you about Binder. But if you won't, you won't.'

'I'll tell you what I'll do, if you like,' said Dennis. 'I'll ask her if I may tell you all she told me. She may give me leave, though I don't expect she will. The fact is she seems a little bit afraid of the police.'

'Some people are.'

'It doesn't in the least follow that she's a burglar. Lots of quite innocent people hate being mixed up with the police. You're all far too fond of your official manner, if you don't mind my saying so. You're just like the archdeacon in that. Look at the way you tried to talk to me just now – "Mr. Precentor", and so forth. It doesn't worry me in the least, but you can't expect a girl to like it. It frightens her. However, I'll ask her and see what comes of it.'

'Thank you,' said Smallways. 'In the meanwhile we seem to have got this far: a man who calls himself Bently comes here looking for a *Te Deum* to be published by the Harpsichord Company. It turns out that his name isn't Bently, and the Harpsichord Company knows nothing about him. That's right so far, isn't it?'

'Quite right,' said Dennis, 'and you may add, if you like, that there's no *Te Deum*, and never was.'

'Carson,' Smallways went on, 'thinks that Bently is really Binder, a burglar just out of prison. Then you meet a girl who suspects that Binder is trying to steal a hymn tune. That's what you said, isn't it?'

'Not quite. I asked you whether you thought Binder would steal a hymn tune. I didn't say the girl accused him of trying.

113

And, look here, Smallways, I don't like the way you are talking about that girl. It sounds to me as if you thought I'd been picking up stray girls all over the place and was worming secrets out of them. As a matter of fact, it was the dean who sent that girl to me with a letter of introduction. If he hadn't I don't suppose I'd ever have spoken to her. There is such a thing as defamation of character, Smallways, and I can't have you taking it for granted that I'm a man who runs about with dozens and dozens of strange girls, particularly that sort of girl.'

'Oh, she's that sort of girl, is she?'

'I don't say she is,' said Dennis, 'but I don't mind telling you she rather looks it. Nothing extreme. I'm not suggesting that. Just skittish. If she'd been anything worse the dean would never have handed her over to me.'

'By the way,' said Smallways, 'how is the dean? I heard —'

'If you heard that he's gone dotty in the head you heard what isn't true. I know that's the sort of thing they're saying, and old Harrowby shakes his head and bleats about "shock", which simply makes the talk worse. As a matter of fact, the dean is as sane as you or I. I don't say he's a good judge of a girl. He's not. But then he never was. He's no worse in that way now than he was twenty years ago. At the same time he wouldn't pass on a regular bad one to me. I'm a young man and innocent. The dean knows that, though apparently you don't.'

'Leaving the girl's character out of it for the present,' said Smallways, 'she did mention Binder's name to you?'

'Yes, she did. I told you that. I'm sorry now that I did tell you, but I won't go back on it.'

'And you gathered from what she said that Binder would steal a hymn tune if he could.'

'Confound you, Smallways, don't practise that sort of cross-examination on me. I won't say another word, good or bad, unless I get her permission.'

114

13

DENNIS LEFT THE POLICE station and walked quickly towards the Mitre Inn. He wanted to see Elsie Hill at once. In all probability she would refuse to allow him to speak to Smallways about her father's hymn tune. He remembered her unwillingness to go to the police station when he wanted to get the key of Cresswood's house. It was most unlikely that she would agree to telling the police what she regarded as an important secret. But Dennis hoped to learn something from her, even if he could not get absolution from his promise. He was becoming interested in what at first seemed a meaningless business. If he questioned her tactfully Elsie might tell him why she thought Binder, a burglar who had once had his hands on £30,000 worth of jewels, should want to steal a hymn tune. Or why she suspected Carson of such a thing. Or who the policeman was – she had spoken of a policeman – who was likely to turn thief for the sake of such unlikely booty as a tune.

But Dennis, though he hurried along the street, did not reach the Mitre Inn for nearly half an hour. He was stopped on his way by the one man in Carminster whom he would have particularly wished to avoid. It was Carson – stalking from the Mitre in the direction of the cathedral – who stopped him; and when Carson caught a victim he kept him.

'I beg your pardon, Mr. Dennis,' he said, 'but there's a little matter I'd like to speak to you about.'

'Certainly,' said Dennis. 'Tomorrow morning after matins.'

'If it's all the same to you,' said Carson, 'and if it's not inconvenient, I'd rather say what I have to say at once, before more mischief is done.'

'Say it quick then. I'm in a hurry.'

'I'll say it as quick as I can. But there's somethings that must be said properly if they're said at all. For if they're not said properly they shouldn't be said any other way. Of course it's not my business, strictly speaking.'

'If it's not,' said Dennis, 'I wish you'd leave it to whoever's business it is.'

'At the same time,' said Carson, 'I feel it my duty to acquaint you with the facts, for if I don't somebody else may be telling you what isn't facts.'

'Go ahead, then. What's it all about?'

'It's about what most trouble and vexation is about,' said Carson. 'Them choirboys.'

The iniquities of choirboys are numerous. A whole hour might be spent in merely naming the wicked things which choirboys do. Carson, who lived at open feud with all the boys, would want to do a great deal more than mention their sins. Dennis groaned.

'Anything fresh?' he said. 'Don't tell me that story of Hodson's cricket ball and your scullery window. I've heard it before, and to be quite frank with you I don't believe it. I expect your cat broke that window, or that your wife threw a shoe through it to stop you talking.'

'Is it in accordance with the wishes of the dean and chapter that the boys should be playing on the piano in the Song School whenever the fancy takes them?'

'No, it's not. You know that as well as I do.'

'So I've always been given to understand,' said Carson. 'It's no business of mine, of course, but I've always been told that the piano in the Song School is a valuable instrument, purchased by the dean and chapter for the use of the organist in teaching the boys to sing.'

'You've got it exactly right, Carson, and the boys have a piano of their own that they can play on whenever they like.'

'So I've always understood. And what I want to bring to your notice is that this morning I caught one of them at it.'

'At what?'

'Playing on the piano in the Song School.'

'Well, he'd no right to, and you ought to have stopped him. What did you do?'

'What I would have done was box his ears for him, and well he knew it. For the moment I opened the door – I was going along the cloisters at the time and it was that door I opened, hearing the piano being played and thinking I ought to know who it was – well, as I was saying, before I had the door properly open, he was off through the other door, into the cathedral, and away before I could lay hands on him.'

'Just you tell me who he was,' said Dennis, 'and I'll deal with him.'

'That's what I can't do,' said Carson. 'I got no more than a glimpse of his back. And, anyway, one of those boys is much the same to me as another. They're all young devils.'

Dennis was very much of the same opinion, but this particular evildoing rather puzzled him. A cathedral choirboy gets music enough imposed on him by authority. The very last thing he is likely to want to do is to make more music, voluntary and unnecessary music. Should such an unnatural desire possess the mind of one of the Carminster boys he can gratify it without the risk of blame. There is in the big schoolroom of the choir school an aged and disreputable piano given over to such use as

117

the boys choose to put it to. It is difficult to imagine why any boy should enter the Song School when he need not and play a forbidden piano. He can get little pleasure out of such evildoing and the punishment, if he is caught, is likely to be severe.

'Oh, all right,' said Dennis. 'I have to take the practice this afternoon, and when I get them all there I'll try and make the culprit confess.'

'Thank you, Mr. Dennis; and there's another little matter —'

'No, there isn't. At all events not now.'

'If you'll excuse me,' said Carson, 'it's rather an important matter.'

'You said "little" a moment ago. And, anyway, your idea of importance is not mine. You think that the world is likely to stop going round the sun just because some wretched choirboy plays the piano when he ought to be playing cricket. That's what you call an important thing, Carson. And the next thing you want to say is probably just as trivial. Goodbye.'

It is very difficult to shake off Carson when he is determined to talk; but Dennis is a vigorous man. He pushed Carson gently through the door of an antique dealer's shop and left him there. Antique dealers lead leisurely lives and always seem to have time to spare. Carson could, if he liked, repeat the whole story of the choirboy and the piano. Afterwards he could go on to his other important matter. Dennis hurried on to the Mitre Inn.

He found Miss Elsie Hill in the smoking room. She was lying back in the deepest of the leather chairs with which Powell had furnished this room – chairs which justified him in advertising the Mitre as 'replete with every comfort'.

Her feet were on another chair. She had a cocktail on the table beside her and a cigarette drooping from the corner of her mouth. When she caught sight of Dennis she jumped up and welcomed him warmly.

'Got it?' she said. 'Good man! I knew you would.'

'No, I haven't. And I don't think I'm likely to. Unless you'll allow me —'

'I'll allow you to do anything you like,' said Elsie, 'except go to the police about it.'

'But that's exactly what I want to do.'

'You're not to. And just remember this, that you've sworn a most frightful oath that you won't tell anyone a word about poor Dad and that tune.'

'I didn't swear,' said Dennis, 'but I quite admit that I promised.'

'Same thing with a parson, specially a precentor. I'd say myself that a nod from a precentor is as good as a terrific curse from a bookmaker or anybody else. It ought to be, anyhow. I don't think much of parsons in most ways, not even precentors and deans, but I expect them to keep their promises.'

'I'll certainly keep mine,' said Dennis.

'You darling! I'd like to kiss you.'

'If you make the slightest attempt to do anything of the sort,' said Dennis, 'or if you call me darling again, I'll go straight to the police and take you with me.'

'My hat!' said Elsie. 'I didn't think anybody could be as pi as all that. Fancy making such a fuss about a kiss! I should have thought that even a precentor — But if you'd really rather I didn't, I won't. At least not until you've found Dad's tune for me. After that I must, whether you like it or not. And I expect you will like it really, in your heart, though you may go on pretending not to.'

Dennis felt that he might safely ignore this threat. The discovery of the tune seemed a long way off, and without Smallways' help scarcely possible.

'It's about that tune I came to speak to you,' he said. 'I haven't found it and I'm not likely to, unless —'

'Don't start talking about the police again. I won't have them.'

'I won't mention the police again if you'd rather I didn't. But I'd like to find out from you why you think anyone wants to steal that tune. You suggested, for instance, that I'd stolen it. Why should I?'

'I took that back,' said Elsie, 'and I apologised all I could. I'll apologise again if you want me to.'

She dropped suddenly on her knees and held up her clasped hands as if in supplication.

'Please, Mr. Precentor,' she began, 'forgive me for saying that you stole the tune. I didn't mean it, and I won't ever say it again. Amen.'

'Get up,' said Dennis, 'and don't play the fool. If you really think that tune has been stolen try and explain why anyone should want to steal it.'

'Lots of people would want it. Almost anybody would, if he knew that poor darling Dad wrote it. Carson would. He looks like an owl, but you can't go by looks. Carson may be all there when it's a question of L S D.'

'But that's exactly what it isn't. Your father's tune may be a very good one, but you may take my word for it that no hymn tune ever written would fetch a ten-pound note. Tunes of that sort are a drug in the market. And besides, everybody thinks that being meant for hymns they ought to be a free issue.'

'Dad's tune would fetch a lot,' said Elsie. 'And you may bet your hat that Carson knows it. He knows a lot, that old boy. Binder knows it too. He started off by offering me fifty pounds for it. Then he rose to one hundred pounds. Then when I told him to go and boil his silly head, he suggested fifty-fifty on whatever we got out of it. I might have let it go at that, for to tell you the truth I couldn't quite get the hang of the tune myself, but by that time I had sent it to poor Ben. Dad said I was to, on account of his being musical, you know. He had to be more or less musical, being an organist. I thought he'd play it. That's why Dad said he was to have it, so that he could play it on the cathedral organ.'

'About that man Binder,' said Dennis. 'Do you think he's the kind of man who would come here calling himself Bently and saying that he represented a firm of musical publishers?'

'Binder,' said Elsie, 'would call himself Alexander the Great and say he represented the patriarch Obadiah if he thought he'd make five pounds out of it. If Binder was down here mouching about, it was Dad's tune he was after, and he'd steal it if he couldn't get it any other way.'

'As a matter of fact he didn't get it.'

'Don't you be too sure of that. Binder is a very wary bird. He wouldn't tell you if he had stolen it.'

He might not. Dennis saw that it was most unlikely that he would confess such a thing to one of the cathedral clergy. But he could hardly credit him with being wary enough to pretend great eagerness in a search for something which he had safely in his pocket. And Bently had been eager enough, unmistakably eager.

'But if Binder didn't get it,' said Elsie, 'then Carson did. Or if it wasn't Carson it must have been that policeman.'

'Surely you don't suspect Inspector Smallways?'

'Smallways,' said Elsie, 'is a pussy cat, quite harmless. I know all about him. The man I have in mind is a Scotland Yard fellow, detective and all that, called Hodson. If he's been down here —'

'He lives here,' said Dennis. 'He's a leading light in Dissenting circles, preaches in chapels on Sundays, though one of his boys sings in our choir.'

'Oh, he preaches, does he?' said Elsie. 'Well, he might. In fact, I shouldn't wonder if he preached better sermons than you do. A man must be a hypocrite to preach a really good sermon, the sort that makes you feel all quaky in the tummy on account of hell. You know that kind of sermon. So if that's what Hodson does I expect he's the man who's stolen Dad's tune. Only I don't quite see how he got to know about it. For the matter of that, I don't see how Carson could have known about it either, unless Ben told him. But I don't think it can have been Carson, though I suspected him just at first, until I knew that Hodson was down here. I don't suppose that Ben would tell Hodson, but the police are all in league together. Whatever one knows all the rest know. I expect some other policeman told Hodson.'

To Dennis it appeared that Elsie suspected Smallways of goading Hodson on to steal a piece of music from Cresswood. This was obviously absurd, and the more he tried to think it out the more absurd it seemed. He began to think that Elsie must be suffering from some form of mental aberration. Dislike of the police, like St. Paul's learning, had made her mad. It would be a mere waste of time and energy to argue with her.

'It seems to me,' he said, 'that if anybody has stolen that tune or anything else, the simple thing is to tell the police about it. It's their job to catch thieves. I do wish you'd let me tell Smallways about it. I really think he'd be able to help.'

'I won't let you do any such thing,' said Elsie. 'You've given your promise, and I hold you to it. I won't have the police mixed up with my business at all.'

'Very well,' said Dennis. 'I expected you to say that, and I'll keep my promise.'

14

INSPECTOR SMALLWAYS IS A man of simple and straight-forward mind. If he wants information he goes to someone who knows the facts and asks a few questions. This is not a method of inquiry favoured by people with subtle intellects. They prefer to get at anything they want to know by tortuous ways. But Smallways' way of working is sound and effective. It generally produces excellent results. The great drawback to it is that it brings little or no glory to the man who adopts it. It is so simple that everybody feels he could have done the thing quite as well as the professional investigator. That is why Smallways has never made a reputation as a great detective. There is no subtlety about his methods and therefore they remain quite unimpressive.

This time he wanted to know who the woman was who had been talking to Dennis about a stolen hymn tune. Instead of noticing a long yellow hair on Dennis's coat sleeve – a hair which was not there – and deducing from it that the lady belonged to the London demi-monde, as he might have deduced if the hair had been obviously a dyed one – he made up his mind to go to the Mitre and ask Powell what guests he had staying there. It was plain to him that the woman must be a stranger, for Dennis had incautiously admitted that she was 'that kind of girl', though not excessively so. And Carminster, a cathedral city, only produces girls of the other kind. If she was a stranger she would be almost certain to be staying in the Mitre. Powell would know at least her name, probably a good deal more about her.

Smallways wrote a letter to an inspector in Scotland Yard asking for information about Binder. When he had finished that he walked down to the Mitre Inn and found Powell.

'I want you to tell me,' he said, 'whether you have a young woman staying with you, a girl of sorts, who's been running about the town with the precentor.'

'I don't know about running about with the precentor,' said Powell, 'but there is a girl here. She's in the smoking room, if you want to see her, and – mind you, I'm not saying there's anything in it; very likely there isn't – the precentor's with her.'

'I thought he might be,' said Smallways. 'Who is she?'

'Her name,' said Powell, 'is Hill – Elsie Hill.'

'That doesn't tell us much about her, does it? Hill is a common enough name.'

'The country is full of Hills,' said Powell. 'I know half a dozen at least.'

'And there are plenty of Elsies knocking about.'

'Dozens.'

'That man Hill,' said Smallways, 'the verger in the cathedral, who got run in for the Carminster jewels robbery had a daughter, hadn't he? I seem to remember that there was one.'

'Get on with it, inspector,' said Powell. 'What the use of beating about the bush? You know just as well as I do that Hill had a daughter called Elsie. She was about seventeen the time her father was convicted. I suppose you want to know whether this is the same girl?'

'Is she?'

'I can't swear to it,' said Powell. 'A girl changes a lot between seventeen and twenty-two, and I never knew her well. But I'm inclined to think it is the same girl.'

'What's she doing here?'

'There you have me,' said Powell. 'She came yesterday and went straight off to call on the dean, and now the precentor has called on her. That's all I know about her.'

'I suppose you don't know what she wanted to see the dean about?'

'No, I don't.'

'Or what she and the precentor are talking about now?'

'If you want to know that,' said Powell, 'why not ask them? They're in the smoking room.'

'I don't think they'd tell me if I did ask them.'

'No,' said Powell, 'I don't suppose they would. And quite right too. Look here, inspector, you and I have always been pretty good friends. You won't mind my giving you a bit of advice. Don't go starting a scandal about the precentor and this girl. You'll only burn your fingers if you do. The dean and chapter won't like it, and it'll turn out afterwards that you're wrong. The precentor's not that kind of man, and even if he was it's no business of yours. There's no harm in a man calling on a girl, even if she is a convict's daughter.'

'I'm not accusing the precentor of anything,' said Smallways.

'I'm glad to hear it, and if I were you I shouldn't accuse the girl of anything either. I don't say she's a member of the Young Women's Christian Association, she's not that type – not to look at anyway. But so far as I know she hasn't done anything that the police need interfere with.'

'I suppose you don't happen to know,' said Smallways, 'whether she was mixed up with Cresswood in any way?'

'I don't know anything about that. Cresswood was engaged to be married to some girl or other. He used to talk to me about it, but I never heard her name. It might have been Elsie Hill, but it's far more likely to have been somebody else. I never saw her down here before, and, as I say, I never heard Cresswood's girl's name.'

'There's another matter I'd like to speak to you about,' said Smallways, 'and I may as well take the chance now that I'm here. You know old Redington, I suppose?'

'The dean's butler? Of course I do. Everybody in Carminster knows Redington.'

'And you know everybody in Carminster?'

'I know everybody who likes a glass of beer. And old Redington comes in for his pretty regularly between tea and dinner at the Deanery.'

'And talks, I suppose?'

'Everybody talks, mostly about the weather.'

'Come now, Mr. Powell,' said Smallways, 'trying to get anything out of you is like pulling a tooth out of a dead elephant. Why won't you open your mouth?'

'What is it you want to know? If it's gossip about the servants in the Deanery, who's the housemaid's young man and that sort of thing, I don't know any to tell you.'

'What I want you to tell me —' said Smallways. But he got no further than that at the moment.

Dennis had finished his talk with Elsie Hill and was leaving the inn. Smallways caught sight of him as he went out of the smoking room across the courtyard. He stepped out of Powell's room and stopped the precentor.

'Well,' he said, 'seen the lady?'

'Yes,' said Dennis, 'and it's no good. She won't let me talk to you.'

'And you won't do it without her leave?'

'No, I won't. No boy on a burning deck could be firmer than I am. "Would not go without his father's word", and so forth. Most heroic. Just my line.'

'Perhaps you'll change your mind if I tell you who the lady is,' said Smallways. 'She's the daughter of Hill, the convict, the man who was verger here and got seven years for burglary.'

Dennis whistled softly. He remembered that Elsie's 'darling Dad' was the composer of the lost or stolen hymn tune. The affair, always interesting, was becoming actually thrilling.

'And the father died in the prison hospital about a fortnight ago or thereabouts,' said Smallways.

Dennis remembered that the hymn tune had been composed by the 'darling Dad' on his deathbed. Elsie, in the character of a dutiful and affectionate daughter, had made great play with the pathos of the situation.

'Feel any more inclined to talk now,' said Smallways, 'or do you still think you are bound to respect the young lady's confidence?'

'I say,' said Dennis, 'this is getting a bit thick, isn't it? First of all, a fellow who calls himself Bently comes here searching for a *Te Deum*. He turns out to be a convict, just out of quod. Then a young woman who turns out to be the daughter of another convict — You're sure about that, Smallways?'

'Fairly sure.'

'Very well. The daughter of another convict, who is dead, turns up and starts a search for a hymn tune. Now, I don't say a hymn tune is a *Te Deum* but they're both more or less music, or are supposed to be. It looks rather as if Bently and the girl were after the same thing.'

'That's what I'm inclined to think,' said Smallways. 'But I'd be in a better position to know what is going on if you'd tell me what that young woman said to you.'

'At the present moment I can't tell you anything,' said Dennis, 'for I ought to be at the cathedral, taking the boys' practice in the Song School. In fact, I ought to have been there ten minutes ago, and I hate being late. I say, Smallways, I suppose your mind is so much occupied with this intriguing conspiracy about a hymn tune that you'd scarcely notice a petty theft even if you saw one committed?'

'If that young lady of yours, Miss Elsie Hill —'

'Oh, she's not the criminal this time,' said Dennis. 'Do you see that bicycle?' – he pointed to a dilapidated machine which was leaning against the wall outside the Mitre – 'well, that bike isn't mine,' said Dennis, 'but I'm going to jump on to it and ride as hard as I can to the cathedral. If the owner turns up you can tell him that he'll find it outside the Song School at the cathedral. If he asks you why you didn't stop me when you saw me stealing it, all you have to say is that you were meditating on the mystery of the stolen hymn tune.'

'Take the bike if you want it,' said Smallways. 'It belongs to Powell's messenger boy, and he won't mind. But I hope you'll come back and talk to me when you've finished with your boys.'

Dennis did not promise that. It is doubtful whether he heard what Smallways said. He had rushed from the hotel and bounded on to the bicycle as soon as he stopped speaking himself.

Smallways went back to Powell, who was waiting for him.

'Now, Mr. Powell,' he said, 'what I want you to tell me is this: there's a lot of talk going round about the dean and Cresswood's death, and it all goes back to Redington. I mean to say that Redington was the man who started it. Can you tell me exactly what he's been saying. So far I've only got it at third or fourth hand, and you know how these things get exaggerated.'

Why don't you ask Redington himself?'

'Because I don't know whether there's anything to ask him about. If it's all pure gossip, the invention of some fool with a lively imagination, I should look rather an ass going up to the Deanery and cross-questioning Redington. I don't think the dean would like it, and I'm sure Miss Grosvenor would kick up the hell of a row. Of course if Redington has been saying things I'll have to get at him in the end – at him, and the dean too if necessary. But I'd rather know first whether there's anything to make a fuss about.'

'Well,' said Powell, 'Redington says the dean was in the cathedral when Cresswood fell off the stool and killed himself.'

'I know that. It didn't come out at the inquest because the dean was too ill to be there, and the cause of Cresswood's death seemed plain enough without further evidence. But I knew it. So did the coroner. Is that all Redington's saying?'

'No, it's not all. He says the dean heard Cresswood crash and afterwards heard him walking about.'

'Ah,' said Smallways, 'the dean says that, does he?'

'Yes. He's said it to Redington, and Redington believes he's said it to Miss Grosvenor and the doctor. What's more, he says that according to the dean Cresswood fell forwards and not backwards, sprawled over the keyboards so that every note in the blessed old organ shrieked at once. That's Redington's story. He's told it here half a dozen times. It's all over the town now and everybody's talking about it.'

'And do you believe it?'

'I believe Redington heard the dean tell the story. Is that what you mean? Redington's rather an old fool, but he wouldn't invent a story like that and say the dean told it.'

'What I mean is this: do you believe the dean's story of what happened that night?'

'Of course I don't. Everybody knows Cresswood fell backwards. He couldn't have cracked his skull if he'd fallen forwards over the keyboards, and of course I don't believe that he walked about after he was dead.'

'Then you think that the dean's mind — Eh?'

'I think that Miss Grosvenor and the doctor are perfectly right to say as little as possible about that story, and I think Redington ought to have kept his mouth shut. Everybody knows that the dean is an old man, but nobody wants to think that his mind's going. I dare say it isn't. I dare say this is only a passing delusion and he'll get over it. Hang it all, Smallways, it's not to be wondered that he was a bit upset. I shouldn't have liked it if I'd been in the cathedral and heard Cresswood fall. You wouldn't have liked it yourself. It's no wonder the dean's gone a bit queer.'

'The precentor says,' said Smallways, 'that the dean's as sane as you or I.'

'I dare say he is,' said Powell, 'in most ways. But lots of fellows who are quite sane in other ways have a delusion or two.'

'I'd better see Redington anyhow.'

'You can if you like; but if you take my advice you won't. What is the good of advertising the fact that the dean's gone dotty in the head? That's all you'll do, you know, even if Redington repeats the whole story, which he probably won't.'

15

DENNIS REACHED THE SONG School and found thirty boys waiting for him outside the door. They were waiting hopefully and in good temper. Dennis was more than ten minutes late. It was possible – as the minutes passed it became actually probable – that he had forgotten about the practice and would not be there at all. There were boats on the river which might be borrowed, and there was, less than a mile away, a bathing pool. Boating and bathing were pleasanter occupations than singing anthems on warm summer afternoons. Perhaps the precentor had forgotten the practice.

Dennis's arrival was a disappointment, but the boys concealed their feelings very well. They welcomed Dennis with smiles, which shows that they were at heart good boys, for they knew very well that they were in for at least an hour's hard singing.

Dennis, though excited by the news which Smallways had given him, did not allow his private interests to interfere with his duty. He remembered Carson's complaint of the use which had been made of the Song School piano.

'Boys,' he said, 'before we begin our practice I want to know which of you was in here this morning playing the piano. You know jolly well that you've no right to do that. You've got a piano of your own, and if you want to thump you can thump it. I want to know who the culprit is. If he owns up I won't be too hard on him. If he doesn't own up I will drop on him heavily.'

The welcoming smile disappeared from the boys' lips. They stood in silence staring at Dennis. They were honourable boys, nurtured in the traditions of English school life. Every one of them knew who the culprit was, but not one of them so much as glanced in his direction to see whether he was going to confess or not. The idea of telling Dennis who he was never entered their minds. 'Sneaking' was unthinkable.

The culprit remained as silent as the rest. He was certain that none of his fellows would betray him, and he argued that Dennis's threat was mere bluff. How could Dennis drop on him heavily if he did not know who he was? And how could he find out except through a confession? So he reasoned, but he had not taken proper account of Dennis's intelligence and resource.

After a couple of minutes of complete and embarrassing silence it became clear that there was not going to be a voluntary confession.

'Very well,' said Dennis. 'Saturdays, as you know, are half-holidays, and half-holidays at this time of year are very pleasant things. We all enjoy them, don't we?'

The boys murmured 'Yes'. They were not quite sure what was coming next, but they were afraid that it would be something very unpleasant indeed.

'Next Saturday,' said Dennis, smiling cheerfully, 'will not be a half-holiday. The afternoon will be spent by every single boy in the school doing long division sums, the very longest I can think of. That is how next Saturday afternoon will be spent, unless I know on Saturday morning at the latest who meddled with the Song School piano. Don't get it into your heads that it will be as unpleasant for me as it will be for you. It won't. I shall rather like it. I shall have a hammock chair, a nice book, a jar of home-made lemonade, and a dish of strawberries and cream, which I shall consume in a leisurely way while you are doing long division sums. And don't take me up wrongly. I don't want anyone to sneak. In fact, I shall be seriously angry if anyone does, and I don't want to get an anonymous letter giving me the name of the criminal. We can't have that sort of spirit in the school. What I suggest to you is this: you have this evening — Let's see, it's Wednesday, isn't it?'

'Yes, sir,' said the boys, glad to be able to say something that did not commit them in any way.

'Very well. You have before you this evening, the whole of Thursday, and the whole of Friday. You have not, at this time of year, got any football boots, but you have got cricket stumps, and they can be applied forcibly to that part of the body which is usually kicked of the boy who thumped the Song School piano. If applied with vigour at all convenient times between this and Saturday morning that boy will probably come to me and voluntarily confess his crime. In that case there will be no long division sums. Otherwise there will. Got that? Sure you understand? Very well. We shall now go into the Song School and do our practising. The anthem for next Sunday afternoon' – he drew a paper from his pocket – 'ah, how appropriate! "How good and joyful a thing it is, brethren, to dwell together in unity" by Royds. You'll like singing that, I'm sure. The boy who thumped the piano will particularly enjoy it. He will be looking forward to a practical demonstration between this and Saturday of how good and joyful a thing it is when the rest of you are really united.'

He opened the door of the Song School as he spoke. The boys followed him in with rueful smiles on their faces. They recognised the astuteness and the fundamental justness of Dennis's plan; but they were evidently not sure whether, even with

133

the aid of cricket stumps, they would be able to secure their Saturday half-holiday.

There was a distribution of music, and the boys stood ready to shout the praises of brotherly unity. Dennis opened the piano and struck a chord. From the music stand in front of him a sheet of paper slipped down and lay on the keyboard.

It was rather an unusual sheet of paper, measuring nine inches by seven, neither foolscap nor quarto nor ordinary notepaper size. It was fairly thick, of moderate quality. It was ruled from top to bottom with blue lines, set close together. One side of it was blank; on the other side was some music, rather untidily scrawled, the ruled blue lines being used for the lines of the treble and bass clefs. Dennis glanced at it, but had no time to study it carefully. In response to the chord he struck the boys were off at full cry: 'Behold how good and joyful a thing —' Dennis stuffed the paper into his pocket, seized the baton which lay on top of the piano, and rapped sharply.

The composer of the anthem, in order to bring home to a congregation the meaning of the Psalmist's words, had ordained that 'joyful a thing' should be sung fifteen times over in quick succession. At the fourteenth repetition the boys missed a beat. That was why Dennis rapped with his baton and made them begin again. This time they triumphed over the whole fifteen 'joyful things', but came to grief at 'unity' when they reached that word for the first time. Dennis was a conscientious choirmaster. He pulled them up again. He pointed out that though unity is a thing which it is delightful to linger over they must cut it a little short for the sake of an important tenor lead which was to follow.

So for more than a quarter of an hour they struggled with the permutations and commutations of the words devised by the ingenious Dr. Royds. After that they spent another half hour over an entirely new Magnificat by a composer who thought that the idea of putting down the mighty from their seat could best be expressed by giving the words to bass voices and making them go lower and lower, until the final 'seat' came on F below the lowest line of the bass clef. The same line of thought had led him to write the passage for the boys descriptive of the exaltation of the humble and meek, an exaltation that went as far as A above the line, and on that note every single boy went dismally flat. They were getting tired, and Dennis, a humane man though a strict choirmaster, recognised that there was little hope that afternoon of getting the humble and meek up to the place prepared for them. He dismissed the boys.

Instead of darting straight out of the Song School in their usual way they lingered, whispering together. At last an unwilling spokesman was pushed to the front. This was Sam Hodson, the holder of Lord Carminster's latest and most valuable scholarship. He was obviously unwilling to come forward, but the others pushed and goaded him.

'Please, sir,' said Sam, and then stopped.

'Please, Hodson,' said Dennis.

'Please, sir,' said Hodson again. 'About that Saturday half-holiday?'

'Likely to be spent, I fear, in doing long division sums, while I shall be eating strawberries and cream.'

'Please, sir,' said Hodson, 'if the boys were to turn to and beat him with cricket stumps, wouldn't that be enough, sir? I mean to say, sir, please, sir – if the boys were to give him a good beating, we wouldn't have to stay in on Saturday afternoon, would we, sir?'

'If I were satisfied,' said Dennis, 'that the punishment was thorough I should not want to do anything more to him, and the whole school could play cricket as usual. But there must be no sham about it. A couple of taps with a stump will not be sufficient.'

'No, sir,' said the boys in chorus, joyfully. 'You trust us, sir. We'll give it to him proper. He'll get it in the neck.'

'Not in the neck,' said Dennis. 'In quite a different part of the body. A series of heavy blows on the neck with a cricket stump might injure the spinal cord, which would be an excessive punishment. No harm will be done by forty or fifty strokes on a part of the body which I propose to indicate.'

He fumbled in his pocket and drew out a piece of paper, the very sheet which slipped off the music stand. This time he looked at it, and for a minute studied the scribbled notes. It seemed likely that the culprit who had played the piano had left the paper behind him when he fled into the cathedral, terrified by the sudden appearance of Carson.

'Ah,' said Dennis, 'I see that our pianist is also a composer and was playing a tune of his own. That makes his fault worse. The punishment must therefore be more severe.'

'Yes, sir,' said the boys. 'We'll give it him, sir, hot and strong.'

'On the portion of his body,' said Dennis, 'which I shall now suggest.'

Dennis turned over the paper which he held. On the back of it he wrote a well-known and often quoted tag from Horace:

'*Post equitem sedet atra cura.*'

'Now, Hodson,' he said, 'can you translate that classical gem?'

Hodson took the paper and looked at it. His study of Latin literature had taken him as far as the third book of the Odes of Horace.

'Yes, sir,' he said. 'I think so, sir.'

'Very well, then,' said Dennis, 'translate aloud so that everyone can hear you.'

'"*Post equitem*",' said Hodson, '"behind the horsemen; "*sedet*", sits; "*atra cura*", black care.'

'That,' said Dennis, 'is the commonly accepted but quite erroneous translation of the line. The correct rendering is this: "*Post equitem*", after horseback riding; "*atra*" (feminine, you observe), the dark lady; "*sedet*", sits down; "*cura*" (ablative), with care.'

The boys giggled. One or two of them had actually ridden horses. All of them knew, by experience of one kind or another, what it was to sit down with care.

'Very well,' said Dennis, 'if the boy who played the Song School piano finds himself forced to sit with extreme care next Friday evening, the school will have its usual half-holiday on Saturday and nothing more will be said about the piano playing.'

This time the boys accepted their dismissal and tramped joyfully out of the Song School. The practice, owing to their failure to exalt the meek to the proper note, had been a little shorter than usual. They had a clear half hour before evensong.

Dennis sat down to the piano and propped up the sheet of paper with the notes on it in front of him. It is not every day that one comes across an original composition by a choirboy. He thought he would like to see what the thing was like. He struck a few notes and then paused, staring hard at the paper.

The time signature was plainly a mistake. Dennis ignored it and played the first four bars in their natural rhythm. He recognised at once that they were part of a tune which he knew, quite a familiar tune. He could not at the moment say what tune it was, but he felt fairly sure that it belonged to a hymn. The choirboy, whoever he was, was a shameless plagiarist. He had copied his first four bars – even the harmonies seemed familiar – straight from Hymns Ancient and Modern, the English Hymnal, or some other collection in ordinary use. The only touch of originality was the time signature, and that was so obviously wrong that no one with any knowledge of music could possibly have set it down. There was, indeed, no need to put a time signature at all. The rhythm was quite obvious, that march of a man with a game leg, so commonly used in English hymns.

Dennis played it over again as far as the double bar. He knew it – knew it perfectly well – but he could not fix the hymn it belonged to or decide which hymnal it came from. He left it for the moment and went on to the notes which followed the double bar. Here he found himself completely bewildered. There was neither time, tune, nor harmony. The thing was not music at all. It was a jumble of entirely meaningless notes. If one of the choirboys had written such stuff and, having written it, had gone into the Song School in order to play it, that boy deserved the worst beating any boy ever had. His musical education, toiled at by Dennis and the deceased Cresswood, had been entirely wasted.

Then suddenly he thought of something else that this odd jumble of notes might be. Was it possible that this was the composition which Bently had sought for so eagerly, which Elsie Hill wanted desperately? It was certainly not a *Te Deum*, or the beginning, or the roughest jottings of a beginning, of a *Te Deum*. The first few bars were part of a hymn tune, but most assuredly that hymn tune had not been composed by Elsie's father upon his deathbed. It was a common tune, copied out accurately enough, so far as Dennis could see, from some hymn book or other. What possible value could such a manuscript have unless the value lay in that jumble of notes after the double bar, notes which had no connection with the tune or with any other tune?

Dennis sat touching the notes of the piano lightly, humming the tune as he played it. In a minute or two he found himself able to complete the tune and hum the remaining bars. Then the words came to him:

Jerusalem, my happy home,
When shall I come to thee?
When shall my sorrows have an end?
Thy joys when shall I see?

Well, if Elsie's father copied out that tune on his deathbed the sentiment of the words which belonged to it was suitable enough. The aspiration of a dying saint! The man was apparently not a saint, or had not been a saint all his life. If Smallways was right he had been a burglar. But even a burglar, though not actually a saint, might have pious aspirations on his deathbed. Dennis was quite ready to believe in a tardy repentance; but, then, why had the man written those notes – a sort of musical printer's pie – after the first four bars of his tune? What on earth did they mean? And what about the perfectly unnecessary time signature? Any one could see how the time went, and no one could possibly suppose that it went in sevens and eights.

Dennis picked up a hymn book, an Ancient and Modern, to make sure that he was right in his recollection of the words. The hymn was there, but with a different tune. He tried the English Hymnal and was rewarded at once. There were the words, and there was the tune of which he had the first four bars in his manuscript. The words he had been humming were the first verse of an immensely long hymn, with no less than twenty-six verses, noted by the compilers of the book as suitable for singing in procession on saints' days. On account of its extreme length it was given three tunes, and the first of them was the tune which the choirboy, or Elsie's father, had copied out.

It was called 'A traditional English Melody'. Choirs were directed to sing it in moderate time, a minim being reckoned equal to 144 metronome beats. But none of this information was of the slightest use to Dennis. The hymn book suggested no explanation of the mad notes which followed the double bar, or of the ridiculous time signature. They certainly suggested no reason why Bently, or Binder, or whatever the man's name was, should want the thing so badly that he was prepared to pay for it. He could have got the tune, the whole of it, by buying or borrowing a copy of the English Church Hymnal. Indeed, if he disliked buying or borrowing, there would have been no great difficulty in stealing a copy of the book.

As to the other notes – those which followed the double bar – no one could possibly want them. Unless the choirboy, if it was a choirboy, had gone suddenly mad, or Elsie's father had become wildly delirious it was impossible to account for these other notes, and they could have no value or interest.

There was no way of explaining Binder's desire for the thing, and it was not easy to hit on a plausible explanation of Elsie's eagerness. A very sentimental girl, deeply attached to her father, might value his last attempt to express a spiritual and beautiful aspiration. But it was not easy to imagine Elsie swayed by such feelings. He found it difficult to believe that she cared much whether her father yearned for Jerusalem or not. It seemed unlikely that he had, but perhaps a man who stole emeralds while on earth might regard a very golden Jerusalem as his spiritual home.

It seemed on the whole more likely that the manuscript before him was the work of one of his choirboys; but Dennis was unwilling to believe this. It would be a dull explanation of what otherwise might be a really fascinating mystery. And there were good reasons for refusing to be driven back on to the choirboy. It was most unlikely that a choirboy would copy a tune out of hymn book. What pleasure or what prospect of gain was there in such a performance? And there was the paper to be considered. Where could a choirboy get such a piece of paper? Nothing like it in size, texture, or the way in which the lines were ruled was used in the school. Dennis had never seen paper exactly like it anywhere. He held it up to the light to discover a watermark. There was none discernible. The most careful scrutiny of it told him nothing except that it had been torn, probably along a fold, from another sheet of the same size. It would not have been easy for a choirboy to have obtained a double, folded, sheet of such paper.

Dennis was still speculating when the striking of the cathedral clock warned him that he had only a quarter of an hour left before evensong. He folded the paper and put it away in his pocket. If he were lucky he might get a cup of tea before evensong, though if he did he would certainly have to risk a rebuke from the archdeacon by running across the close afterwards.

16

A WEEKDAY EVENSONG IN Carminster Cathedral affords to the thoughtful man certain opportunities for quiet meditation, especially when the archdeacon is reading the lessons. He is the possessor of a soothing voice, and he has cultivated to the highest degree that emotionless kind of reading which is characteristic of Anglican dignitaries, especially those who come from Oxford. The archdeacon can reduce even the most exciting Old Testament stories to a gentle monotony not unpleasant to listen to, something like the distant cawing of rooks on a summer evening. On the evening of Dennis's threat to the choirboys he had to read a chapter from the first Book of Samuel, to which it would have been difficult to listen even if it had been declaimed by an old-fashioned Shakespearean actor. The prophet's objection to the establishment of a monarchy, read by the archdeacon, in no way disturbed the thought of anyone who wished to think.

Dennis had a good deal to think about, and welcomed the chance which the lesson gave him.

He wanted to make up his mind about the tune which he had found. Ought he to take it to Elsie Hill and ask her if it were what she wanted? Ought he to take it straight to Inspector

Smallways? Or should he assume that it meant nothing at all, tear it up, and forget all about it?

The archdeacon had reached the prophet's anticipation that the new king would require both confectioners and cooks, when Dennis decided that he was in honour bound to show the tune to Elsie. She might be the daughter of a convict, but that was no proof that she herself was a criminal. In any case her father's lapse from honesty did not absolve him from his promise to help her to find her tune. If it turned out that the tune was hers, composed or copied out by her father, he would ask her if she knew what it meant, why her father had chosen that particular hymn, and what the notes after the double bar were. If she gave him any satisfactory explanation he would hand over the tune to her and say nothing about it to Smallways or anybody else. If she could not or would not explain, then – Dennis was not sure what he would do then. He hoped that the occasion for dealing with that difficult question would not arise.

It did not. Indeed the necessity for asking Elsie for an explanation did not arise either. But Dennis did not find this out at once. As soon as evensong was over the archdeacon demanded his attention.

'You have, I understand, been looking into Cresswood's affairs?'

'Yes,' said Dennis; 'almost without a pause since he died.'

'Then no doubt you have found his keys. I think' – there was a mild reproach in the archdeacon's voice – 'I think I mentioned the matter to you before. I refer to the keys which he, as organist, had of the doors of the south transept and the Song School.'

'I haven't come across them,' said Dennis, 'but I told Carson to have a good look for them. I expect Cresswood dropped them somewhere in the cathedral.'

'I attach some importance to the recovery of those keys,' said the archdeacon, still reproachfully.

No doubt the keys were important, and the archdeacon was quite right to think so. Any good archdeacon would think so. Indeed, a man is not likely to become an archdeacon unless he has the kind of mind which realises the importance of lost keys. Dennis, who often loses his own keys, and regards lostness as the normal condition of all keys, may become a bishop (though this is unlikely) or a dean (which is scarcely more probable), but he will certainly never be an archdeacon, any more than a man with an unconquerable aversion to entrails could become a surgeon.

'I'll tell Carson to search again,' said Dennis. 'They must be in the cathedral. They weren't in his pockets or anywhere in his house.'

'When they are found,' said the archdeacon, 'they should be handed over to me at once.'

After this Dennis managed to disengage himself from the archdeacon and hurried off to the Mitre Inn to find Elsie.

He was met at the door by Powell, who told him that Miss Hill had left Carminster. She had just managed, after a hurried scramble, to catch the 3.45 train for London.

'Gone?' said Dennis, to whom this news was very surprising. 'Why?'

'She didn't tell me why.'

'She may not have told you,' said Dennis, 'but I expect you know without being told.'

'Girls,' said Powell sententiously, 'take sudden notions into their heads.'

'Every one knows that,' said Dennis. 'What I'm trying to get out of you is why this particular girl took this particular notion into hers.'

'There's no use trying to keep anything from you, Mr. Dennis, but I haven't much to tell. She came out of the smoking room ten minutes after you left and she saw Inspector Smallways standing there talking to me. It was about her he was talking, and she might have guessed that by the look of him, though she couldn't have heard what he was saying. Whether she did or not I don't know. Anyhow, as soon as she saw him she went straight up to her bedroom and packed her suitcase. Then she rang the bell and asked for her bill. She paid it too. Smallways may say what he likes about her being the daughter of a burglar, but she was honest enough so far as I had any dealings with her. She ordered a taxi to take her to the station. I thought myself that she'd miss the train, but she must have caught it, for she didn't come back here.'

'And you think it was the sight of Smallways drove her away.'

'I didn't say that,' said Powell.

'I know you didn't say it. If you had said it I'd take for granted that you thought it. It's just because you didn't say it that I'm asking you whether you thought it.'

'If it wasn't the sight of the inspector that sent her off I don't know what it was.'

Elsie Hill had shown a strong dislike of the police more than once since Dennis first met her. He began to suspect that she must have some good reason for her feeling. Only those afflicted with guilty consciences bolt at the sight of a policeman. Elsie must have thought that Smallways was making inquiries about her. Perhaps she had heard him say something which frightened her – her own name or her father's. At all events her flight seemed to absolve Dennis from his promise of secrecy. If she were planning any kind of evil-doing it was plainly his duty to tell Smallways all he knew about her.

He left the inn and went to the police station.

'Smallways,' he said, 'that girl we were talking about, Elsie Hill, has left Carminster.'

'I knew that,' said Smallways. 'I knew it before she got into the train. But don't let that worry you. I'll put my hands on her any time I want her. I sent a wire to Scotland Yard asking them to keep an eye on her.'

'Well,' said Dennis, 'I've changed my mind about telling you what she said to me.'

'I thought you would.'

'If you go in for being so infernally superior,' said Dennis, 'I'll change my mind again and not tell you a single word. Now don't shoot off any silly talk about compounding a felony and being liable to severe penalties. I'm not being frightened into telling you. And I'm not telling you because it's the duty of a good citizen to aid the law. I'm an Irishman and that sort of talk strikes me as piffle. Considering the ridiculous laws we have now, and the enormous number of them – fresh ones every day – I should be inclined to say that it is the duty of every good citizen to hinder the enforcement of law in every way he can, and to put as many obstacles as possible in the way of the police.'

Inspector Smallways chuckled fatly.

'So long as you tell me what you know,' he said, 'I don't care why you do it. But I'll be surprised if you've anything to tell me that I don't know already.'

That was perhaps the wisest thing he could have said. No one likes to be told that his cherished secret is valueless, and most people will blurt out anything in order to prove that what they know is important.

'I'm going to tell you,' said Dennis, 'out of simple curiosity. Not your curiosity, Smallways. My own. I wouldn't care if yours was never satisfied. But I do want to know what all this fuss is about. You understand that. Very well then. That young woman, Elsie Hill, came to Carminster to find a tune which she thought was among Cresswood's papers.'

'You told me that much before.'

'But it wasn't the tune which Cresswood had composed. I thought it must be when I first heard of it, but it wasn't. It was a tune she sent to Cresswood, hoping that he would play it on the cathedral organ. It was composed, or at all events copied out, by her father while he was dying.'

'I thought it might be.'

'You couldn't possibly have thought anything of the sort,' said Dennis. 'Nobody could have thought that. I couldn't have thought it myself unless I'd been told it by Elsie.'

He was a good deal irritated by this continued assumption of superior knowledge. He knew that Smallways' mind worked slowly, though methodically and correctly. He knew that he was far more likely than the inspector to make swift guesses. It was incredible to him that Smallways could have deduced the odd fact that Elsie's father wrote a hymn tune on his deathbed. For a moment he felt inclined to say nothing more, and to allow Smallways to guess if he could where the tune was. But the temptation to spring a surprise on the impassive inspector was too strong for him.

'I've got the tune in my pocket,' he said.

This time he succeeded in producing the effect he wished. Smallways did not actually express surprise or delight – that would have been too much to expect – but he was plainly eager to see the tune.

'I hope you mean to show it to me,' he said.

Dennis took it from his pocket and laid it on the table.

'Now what do you make of that?' he said.

Smallways looked at it carefully. He even whistled a few notes. 'I seem to know that tune,' he said.

As a member of the voluntary choir which sang in the nave service on Sunday evenings he knew a good many hymn tunes.

'Of course you do,' said Dennis. 'You've sung it scores of times, and so have I. "Jerusalem, My Happy Home", out of the English Hymnal.'

'Jerusalem!' said Smallways, lingering over each syllable. He was using the name of the Judean capital as an exclamation of surprise, not merely repeating the first word of the hymn.

'Now,' said Dennis, 'you go in for knowing everything before you are told. You've adopted an attitude of what I can only call offensive superiority ever since I came into this room. Each time I've said anything you've sneered and said that you were aware of that, although you weren't and couldn't have been. I'm not complaining of that. It's the natural and inevitable result of being in an official position of any kind. You all do it and I suppose you can't help it, but I think you ought to justify the attitude occasionally by showing that you really do know something which other people don't know. What do you make of that tune?'

'What are the chords after the double bar? They're not part of the tune.'

'To quote your own words,' said Dennis, 'I know that. I knew it before you told me. In fact I know more. Not only are those chords no part of the tune, they're not even proper chords. They're just notes set down higgledy-piggledy, as if someone had a large pepper box full of minims and crochets and shook it over a piece of paper.'

'And what about the time signature?' said Smallways. 'There's no such thing as 7/8 time, is there?'

'As a matter of fact there is,' said Dennis. 'It's very modern and hardly ever used, but it exists. As well as I can recollect, Tchaikovsky invented it. One thing you may be sure of is that nobody ever wrote a hymn tune in 7/8 time, or if anyone did it wasn't that tune.'

'Then why is that time signature there?'

'That,' said Dennis, 'is what I expect you to tell me. So far, Smallways, you haven't contributed a single point to the elucidation of this mystery. It's quite time you did.'

'Then I will,' said Smallways. 'The paper that tune is written on is the paper served out to prisoners in jail when they are allowed to write letters. It's uncommon paper. In fact, I don't think I've ever seen it in ordinary use anywhere. It's given out in double sheets, folded. If the other half of this sheet hadn't been torn off you'd find the official regulations governing prisoners' correspondence printed on the first page of the four.'

Dennis whistled.

'Then it did come from Elsie's father,' he said.

'We're not sure of that, even now,' said Smallways. 'All we know for certain is that the paper came out of a prison, from a prisoner. Whether it was Hill or not we can't be sure yet.'

'For goodness' sake, Smallways, don't be so slow and sure. The thing is as plain as anything could possibly be. There's not the slightest doubt that Elsie's father wrote down that tune. What I don't see is why he wrote out a hymn tune at all, and why he sent it to Elsie and told her to pass it on to Cresswood.'

'I can make a guess at that,' said Smallways.

'Well, do. Anything like a guess from you will be a startling novelty.'

'If I tell you all I guess and all I know about this damned affair will you help me to find out a little more?'

'Of course I will,' said Dennis. '"Damned affair"! I like that, Smallways. It's your first lapse from the correct official attitude. You're treating me now like a man and a brother and I'll do anything you like for you. "Damned affair"! Go on, Smallways.'

'I'll have to go back,' said Smallways. 'Before I go on I must go back five years to the Carminster jewel robbery.'

'Oh, that! Cut it as short as you can. I know it all already.'

'You know that Hill was convicted and four more men as well?'

'Yes.'

'And you know that the jewels were never found? They weren't sold. We know that, for not a single one of them ever came on the market anywhere. As you can guess, a pretty sharp watch was kept on all emeralds which were sold after that robbery. The presumption is that they were hidden somewhere.'

'I know all that. I'm rather enjoying this, Smallways. It's nice to be able to say "Buzz, buzz" which is Shakespearean for stale news, whenever you tell me anything.'

'Well, here's something that's perhaps new to you. Hill knew where the jewels were hidden. He was the leader and the brains of the whole party, but none of the others knew. The four who got five years each didn't know what Hill had done with the jewels. We're pretty sure of that. There was a good deal of pressure put on them to induce them to tell. The insurance company had to pay up to Lord Carminster, and naturally wanted to find the jewels so as to be able to get its money back. In fact – I'm telling you this unofficially, for I've no right to tell it at all – if one of those men would have told where the jewels were he could have got off altogether. The case against Binder or any of the others would have been dropped if he'd told. The men, Binder and the rest, were questioned and cross-questioned, threatened and offered bribes. The conclusion we came to was that none of them knew – except Hill. Binder, for instance, would have told like a shot if he'd known. He's the kind of man who'd blab out anything to save himself. And there was more in it than merely getting off. I happen to know that the insurance company offered him a thousand pounds and the police offered to withdraw the case against him if he told. He didn't, because he couldn't.'

'I see,' said Dennis. 'Hill, I suppose, meant to collar the whole swag for himself when he got out of quod. A pretty sickening sort of swine he must have been.'

'We are not sure of that,' said Smallways. 'Hill may have meant to play fair with the others, but he wasn't going to trust them. He knew he would get the longest sentence, and if they knew where to look for the jewels when they got out there mightn't have been much left for him when he did.'

'Yes. I see that. But Hill never got out. He died. Binder got out; but Hill died.'

'In the prison hospital, of pneumonia.'

'And the secret with him?'

'That's exactly what we aren't sure of. Hill might have passed the secret on. I'm telling you official secrets now, and if you go gossiping about them you'll get me into serious trouble. Hill was given every chance of passing on the secret if he chose. Binder was put into the hospital too – put beside Hill, into the next bed – and Binder was due for a release in a week or two. He was the first of the lot to get out, for he earned all his good-conduct marks and shortened his sentence. The idea was that when Hill knew he was dying he'd tell Binder where the jewels were. It seemed likely enough, didn't it? The secret would be no good to him when he was dead, and he couldn't tell it to anyone else.'

'Quite a sound scheme,' said Dennis. 'I'd no idea the police were so crafty.'

'As a matter of fact,' said Smallways, 'the idea came from the insurance company, and they had the devil of a job to persuade the prison authorities to adopt it. Contrary to regulations and that sort of thing, you know. In fact, only that Lord Carminster interested himself and put a squeeze on the Home Secretary it never would have been done. Lord Carminster is a pretty big bug and can get things done, even if they're not the sort of things that people talk about afterwards. Anyhow it was done, and friend Hill had every opportunity of telling Binder if he choose.'

'The next thing, I suppose, was to keep an eye on Binder when he got out. He was pretty sure to make a grab for the jewels, and by following him you would have collared the swag, which is what the insurance company wanted.'

'Exactly. The insurance company and Scotland Yard both meant to keep their eye on Binder, and they did – up to a point. They saw him off at Paddington with a ticket for Carminster in his pocket. That seemed all right – very much what they expected. The jewels were pretty sure to be somewhere in this neighbourhood. The obvious thing to do was to wire to me to keep an eye on the man when he arrived here, to follow him round, and so on. That was the simple, plain thing to do, but they didn't do it.'

'Why on earth not?'

'Oh, the usual reason,' said Smallways, a little bitterly. 'The country police aren't supposed to have any brains. Everybody thinks we're as stupid as owls, capable perhaps of arresting a small boy with a catapult, but nothing more difficult than that.'

'It's your figure does the mischief, Smallways,' said Dennis. 'I know you've got brains all right. Look at the way you spotted that hymn tune the moment you saw it; but you must admit that your figure is against you. Very few men have both brains and tummies. It's generally a choice of one or the other. You happen to have both; but you ought to thin down a bit – golf, or exercise after your bath before an open window – something.'

'What they did,' said Smallways, 'was to telegraph to Hodson. Of course he was a Scotland Yard man originally, before he retired, and he had been in charge of the case. He knew Binder far better than I did. There's that much excuse for them.'

Smallways, though he had his official position to consider and his own dignity, was a fair-minded man. He was ready to make excuses for the action of the Scotland Yard authorities and the insurance company, even though he felt that he had been unduly snubbed.

'I dare say he was really a better man for the job than I was. If I'd set one of my fellows tramping round the town after Binder he'd have tumbled to the fact that he was being watched and wouldn't have gone near the jewels.'

'And what did Hodson find out?'

'That's just the point,' said Smallways, and there was a note of satisfaction in his voice. 'Hodson found out nothing at all. He bungled the thing somehow, and never set eyes on Binder from the time he arrived till he left next morning. That was Binder's first visit here, on the day of Cresswood's death.'

'So that all we know about Binder's movements,' said Dennis, 'supposing the fellow who called himself Bently really was Binder, is what Carson and Powell told us. That's precious little.'

'He stayed at the Mitre,' said Smallways. 'He spent the evening with Cresswood, and that's all we know.'

'Except that he was trying to beg, borrow, or buy something from Cresswood. Carson seems fairly sure about that.'

'Yes,' said Smallways. 'But what?'

'This tune, of course,' said Dennis. 'What else could it have been? I say, we're getting at things a bit.'

'What do you think we're getting at?' said Smallways. 'I'd like you to tell me, because I'm getting at things too, or I think I am. And if we're getting at the same things there may be something in it.'

'What I've got at so far is this,' said Dennis. 'The insurance company's neat little scheme didn't come off. Hill wasn't such a fool as to tell Binder where the jewels were. That's obvious, for Binder never attempted to look for them. On the other hand, he felt sure that Hill had somehow sent the secret out of the prison to his daughter Elsie. We know that, for the first thing Binder did was to go to Elsie Hill and try to buy this tune from her. He went so far as to offer to share anything they got out of it on a fifty-fifty basis. Elsie would have taken that offer, but she'd already sent the tune to Cresswood, as her father told her to. Binder came straight down here and tried to buy it from Cresswood, who wouldn't sell. As soon as he heard of Cresswood's death he came rushing down here again with his story of a lost anthem, and on the strength of that was allowed to go right through Cresswood's papers. He didn't find the tune. Then Elsie came and had a try. But she didn't find it either. I picked it up in the Song School, and now you have it. That's what I make out of things so far. And now I'd like to know what you think. It seems to me that we're up against a most interesting little puzzle, with thirty thousand pounds' worth of emeralds as a prize if we solve it.'

17

'IF WHAT YOU THINK and what I think is right,' said Small-ways, 'we're up against something a good deal more serious than an intriguing mystery. But before we go further I'd like you to have a clear idea of what my position is. It's peculiar and it's difficult. I'll have to be uncommonly careful if I don't want to put my foot into a wasps' nest of trouble. There's nothing I'd like better than to work this thing out on my own. It would be a fine feather in my cap and a score off the insurance company who wouldn't trust me, the Scotland Yard people who think I'm a fool, and that fellow Hodson who's a swine. But I've got to go cautiously, for if I'm wrong in my guess —'

'If you've come to the same conclusion that I have,' said Dennis, 'you're not wrong. I'm never wrong in anything that requires intelligence.'

'If you're right —'

'We,' said Dennis. 'You say that you agree with me.'

'Very well then. If we're right so far, we've got to go a good deal farther. But I don't want to say anything about that till you see what my position is. At the time of Cresswood's death I didn't know that Hill had died in prison. I didn't know that Binder had come down here calling himself Bently. I didn't know that there was any fresh move on about the jewels. They didn't tell me these things. I suppose they thought I was too stupid to make anything out of them. Cresswood's death was reported to me, and I thought, what everybody else thought, that it was the result of an accident, due to the fact that Cresswood was helplessly drunk in the organ loft. I'd been told that the dean was in the cathedral at the time, but I didn't see any good in making that public. I hadn't heard the account the dean gave of what happened.'

'That story of Cresswood's walking about after he had fallen?'

'Exactly. I hadn't heard that; but I'm not sure that I'd have paid any attention to it if I had. I'd have thought the poor old gentleman's mind was wandering. That's what his daughter thought and what Harrowby thought.'

'The dean's mind isn't wandering in the least.'

'That brings me to the first thing I want you to do for me,' said Smallways. 'You can see the dean if you like, I suppose?'

'Oh, I can do that all right,' said Dennis. 'The dean rather likes me, though the archdeacon doesn't. He'll see me if I call, unless Miss Grosvenor catches me on the doorstep and shoos me away. Even if she does I can wait a while and then go again. She can't spend her whole time, day and night, on the doorstep. When she's not there I'll drop in on the dean.'

'Try and get him to tell you his story of what happened that night. You see the way I'm fixed. I can't do anything myself. If I attempt to question the dean I'll have Miss Grosvenor on my back.'

'And the archdeacon.'

'Exactly. And the archdeacon; which will be most unpleasant. If I persevere in spite of them they'll put the old gentleman to bed again, and Harrowby will back them up. Of course I can insist on seeing the dean and questioning him; but then if it turns out that the old man's mind really is wandering, and that he's imagining things, I shall have made myself unpleasant in a nasty, officious way, and I shall suffer for it afterwards. Don't think that I am funking things. I'm not. All I want is to be fairly sure of my ground before I start a fight with the archdeacon and Miss Grosvenor. At present I've nothing to go on but secondhand gossip. The dean may never have said half what Redington reports. What I want is an accurate and reliable version of the dean's story before I go any farther.'

'I'll get that for you,' said Dennis; 'but I hate going blindfold, and I don't want to be guessing ghastly things. I wish you'd tell me what the dean's story has got to do with Hill and the Carminster jewels.'

'I'll come to that in a minute,' said Smallways. 'Let me get at it my own way. The next thing that happened after the inquest was Binder's second visit to Carminster. You and the archdeacon reported that to me. I'd been thinking a bit before you came to me, and I'd made a couple of inquiries quietly. When you and the archdeacon brought me your story about Binder or Bently and the anthem, I began to think hard, and I made a few more inquiries. Now we know exactly what Binder did in Carminster that time.'

'He visited Miss Grosvenor and told her a cock-and-bull story about a *Te Deum* which Cresswood had composed. He visited the archdeacon with the same tale. He came to me and we went through Cresswood's papers together, looking for the *Te Deum*.'

'But you didn't find it.'

'No, we didn't. Because there wasn't such a thing.'

'But Binder was looking for something and if it wasn't a *Te Deum*, what was it?'

'It could hardly have been the jewels,' said Dennis. 'They wouldn't have been in Cresswood's house.'

'No. I don't think it was the jewels. But whatever it was he didn't find it. Then Miss Elsie Hill turns up, and she starts looking for something too – something which Cresswood had. She tells a story about a hymn tune, composed by her father on his deathbed. When she can't find it she accuses Binder of having stolen it.'

'She accused me too,' said Dennis. 'And Carson. And you. Don't forget that she accused you too, Smallways.'

'Anyhow,' said Smallways, 'she was pretty sure that there was a tune to steal.'

'Oh, she was quite sure about that. She had sent it to Cresswood herself. It was a most moving story. Dying father's last wish to have his tune played in the cathedral. Elsie engaged to the organist. Cresswood to work the thing into a voluntary. Affectionate daughter weeps behind a pillar. Spirit of the deceased father immensely gratified. R.I.P., and everybody satisfied. But then I find the tune. And it turns out that Elsie's dear Dad didn't compose it at all, simply copied it out of the hymn book.'

'Wait a minute,' said Smallways. 'You're still jumping at conclusions. You found a tune; but we don't know that it was Elsie's tune. Did she search the Song School when you and she were looking for that tune?'

'No, she didn't. But Bently, or Binder, or whatever the blighter's name is, did. He went over that Song School carefully, turned the boys' cassock pockets inside out, and flattened the ruffs they wear round their necks. It certainly wasn't there when he searched.'

'That tune of yours may have been,' said Smallways. 'But that may not have been what he wanted. It might have been some scrap of wastepaper which Cresswood dropped.'

'Do you mean to suggest that old Cresswood wrote that tune I found? He didn't. He couldn't have. Cresswood may have been drunk occasionally, but he never was drunk enough to write 7/8 as the time signature of that tune. And even if he had been in delirium tremens he couldn't have written those notes after the double bar. Cresswood was a silly ass about whisky, but, after all, he was a musician. If you think he wrote that thing in front of you you're wrong, totally and hopelessly wrong.'

'I don't think Cresswood wrote it. As a matter of fact, I think Hill wrote it, in the hospital before he died. But I want to make quite sure of that. There are odd points about the story of that tune – very odd indeed. Elsie Hill says it came to her in a letter from her father. She kept the letter and sent the tune to Cresswood. That sounds true. And the paper' – he took up the paper and handed it to Dennis as he spoke – 'the condition of the paper bears that out. It's been torn in two, along the fold. We've got half, but not the other half. Just what might be expected if Elsie's story is true. But how did that tune get past the prison censor – the man who reads all the convicts' letters? The letter was all right apparently, just a dying man's farewell to his daughter. But you'd think any censor would have been a little suspicious about the tune. Remember they were watching Hill, hoping to get the secret of the hiding place of the jewels out of him. Don't you think that anyone who read his correspondence would have been suspicious of that tune?'

'Great Scot!' said Dennis. 'I see what you're at! The tune is a – what do you call the thing? – a cryptogram, with the hiding place of the jewels wrapped up in it.'

'I'm not sure of that,' said Smallways. 'I'm going no further than saying it's odd that the tune should have passed out without being noticed. No notice was taken of it. The Scotland Yard people know nothing about it. Nor, apparently, does the insurance company. If they had known they'd have been after it before now. Either the censor who passed that letter with the tune in it was a very stupid man, even stupider than I'm supposed to be, or the tune didn't come from Hill.'

'It did. It must have.'

'There's one other possibility. But it's most unpleasant. Can you guess what it is?'

'The prison official,' said Dennis, guessed what the tune was, but let it go, hoping to make something out of it himself? Is that what you mean?'

Smallways nodded.

'Well,' said Dennis, 'he might. Thirty thousand pounds is a pretty big prize. He might have given the tip to some friend of his that such a tune had been sent to Elsie Hill. All that ever could be proved against him was carelessness. It would be up to his friend to get the tune, work out the secret, and collar the jewels.'

'Exactly. But you see where I shall be if I make a suggestion like that and it turns out to be totally unfounded. It would be bad enough to make Carminster too hot to hold me by enraging the archdeacon and Miss Grosvenor; but if I start a suggestion of scandalous corruption against the prison officials and it turns out to have nothing in it, it won't only be Carminster, it'll be England which will be too hot to hold me.'

'Yes,' said Dennis, 'I see that; but you've got to go ahead just the same.'

'I'm going to,' said Smallways. 'But before I do I want to be sure – absolutely dead sure – that Hill wrote out that tune and that it came out of the prison to his daughter. That brings me to the second thing I want you to do for me. Do you think you could see the chaplain of that prison and find out from him whether Hill sent the tune or not? He must have been with Hill pretty often in hospital. He ought to know something about him, especially as it was most likely from him that Hill got the hymn book. It sounds a roundabout way of getting what we want, but if I go to the governor or the head warder it becomes a matter of official action at once, and then if I'm wrong the fat's

160

in the fire, and me along with it. The chaplain is the least official person there is in the prison, but if I go to him he's bound to refer me to the governor, and I'm in the same trouble again. But if you go to him —'

'I see,' said Dennis. 'Brother parson interested in sorrowing daughter. Consolation for her in the story of her father's last hours, and so forth and so on. Yes, I think I can do that. In fact, I will. Any other little job for me?'

'Plenty. When you've done those two. I shall want to find out how that tune got into your Song School. Who put it there? And I shall want to find out what the damned thing means. You can help me in both inquiries if you will. But there's no use starting on them till we're tolerably sure that the tune matters. If it's just a scrap of wastepaper scribbled over by somebody with nothing better to do, there's no use our breaking our hearts trying to understand it. But if it's Hill's, that is to say, if Elsie's story is true, then it must mean something.'

'Very well,' said Dennis. 'I'll tackle the dean first. I'll see him tomorrow morning after matins. As a matter of fact, that will be quite easy. It's my job to make out a list of music for the week, anthems, services, and so on. I have to submit it to the dean for approval – a matter of form, for he never changes anything. In fact, very often I don't show it to him at all. I simply go ahead on my own. But this time I shall show it to him. I'll make it out tonight and take it to him tomorrow. Then with the utmost tact – tact is one of my strongest points – I'll steer a pleasant chat round to Cresswood's death, and the dean will tell me his story. That will be that. Your prison chaplain won't be quite so easy. What prison is it, anyway?'

'Bassmore,' said Smallways.

'Bassmore. That's about eighty miles from here. I can manage to run over there all right.'

'I'll pay for the car of course,' said Smallways.

'No, you won't. I'd rather take my own. A small Morris two-seater inspires confidence in a brother parson. These things must be done carefully and the proper atmosphere produced at the start. If I were going to call on some big financial bug to raise money for a gold mine in Cochin China I should hire a Rolls Royce and a dignified chauffeur as much like Carson as possible. The idea would be to suggest solid, old-established opulence and a general feeling of vintage port. If I were approaching the owner of a theatre with a view to getting him to produce a play of mine I should dash up in an eight-cylinder supercharged Bently, driving myself, and, if possible, running over a child just outside his door. Financially successful artistic temperament would be the idea there. If I wanted to rent a furnished house in a select neighbourhood without paying a half-year's rent in advance I should have a fairly new Humber saloon, about twenty horsepower, with an elderly chauffeur, rather untidy about the neck, old family servant style. That would be solid respectability, moderate private fortune, and no unnecessary swank. But I'm going to visit a brother parson to talk about the broken heart of the deceased convict's daughter, so the thing to go in is a shabby little Morris-Cowley.'

'Yours is shabby enough anyhow,' said Smallways. 'If shabbiness is a guarantee of piety...'

'Mere shabbiness isn't a guarantee of anything,' said Dennis. 'But an elderly Morris two-seater with a gentle and timid-looking parson driving it suggests simplicity of mind, total ignorance of the ways of the wicked world, and great tenderness of heart – in fact, makes the exact impression which in this particular case we want to make.'

'Do you think you'll be able to live up to all that? Simplicity now and tender-heartedness?'

'Not for long perhaps,' said Dennis; 'but then I don't mean to spend the whole day with that chaplain. An hour ought to be quite enough, and I can keep up anything for an hour. But, I say, what on earth do you mean by talking of my keeping it up? Do you mean to suggest that I haven't got a tender heart? I have. Just look at the way I love those choirboys. If my heart wasn't like a spring chicken I'd have murdered most of them long ago.'

'Oh, I expect your heart is all right,' said Smallways. 'All I meant was that I never saw much childlike simplicity about you.'

'I adapt myself to the company I'm in,' said Dennis. 'When I'm with you I try to be a hardened cynic, a very difficult thing for me to do. When I'm with the dean I let him feel that I read medieval Latin for pleasure every evening before I go to bed. That's tact, which is another name for sympathy, which is one of the most desirable of the minor virtues. Precisely what line I shall take with that chaplain I shan't know till I see him. It may be golf. It may be incense. But whatever it is the small Morris-Cowley is the note to start on. That's why I'm refusing your offer of a Buick saloon. But I haven't the slightest objection to your paying for the petrol. I get about twenty-five to the gallon out of my car. That'll be about seven gallons for the journey there and back. Work that out some time when you've nothing better to do. Then double the figure to cover oil and the wear and tear of tyres. I don't want to make money out of the trip, but if the county is paying I may as well get what I can.'

18

THE TACT WHICH DENNIS boasted of was not put to any very severe strain when dealing with the dean. The old gentleman was glad to have the chance of telling his story to someone who believed it, or at all events made a good outward show of believing it. He had not entirely got over his first feeling of intense self-reproach; but he was beginning to wonder how what he heard in the cathedral fitted in with the received account of Cresswood's death.

'He certainly fell forward,' said the dean, 'and he fell quite suddenly. He was playing, and there was no sign of fumbling at the notes, no uncertainty. I can't believe that he was so intoxicated as to fall off the stool.'

'That was Cresswood's peculiarity,' said Dennis. 'I hate to say it, especially now that he's dead, but the drunker he was the better he played.'

'But surely if he was very drunk, drunk enough to be unconscious, he couldn't play at all. If he tried he would have fumbled before he fell. And he didn't. Besides, he fell forwards and not back. He couldn't have fractured his skull by falling forward over the keyboards.'

'What makes you so sure that he fell forward?'

'The way the notes all sounded at once,' said the dean. 'That couldn't have happened unless he had sprawled over the keyboards. There's no other way of explaining the noise there was, the noise I certainly heard. Very soon it stopped. He must have switched off the electricity from the blowing apparatus. If only I'd gone up to the organ loft then! I ought to have gone up. If I had poor Cresswood would be alive now, for I could have helped him. But I shrank from it. I'm afraid I was very angry, and I felt disgusted.'

'Naturally,' said Dennis. 'I don't see how you could feel anything else. But he can't have been so very drunk when he switched off the electricity. And that wasn't all he did. He pushed in the stops. That's how they were when I went up in the morning. All pushed in.'

'And he walked about,' said the dean. 'I assure you that I couldn't have been mistaken about that. I know that everybody thinks I imagined all this, but I didn't.'

'I don't think so.'

'I'm so glad you don't,' said the dean. 'It's been very painful for me. My daughter, you know. She's so kind and does everything for me, and I don't know how I should get on without her; but she thinks I'm becoming fanciful. So does Dr. Harrowby. He's a first-rate doctor. I know that. So kind and sympathetic, but I'm dreadfully afraid that he — And I'm sure the archdeacon agrees with him. Tell me, Dennis, and like a dear fellow don't hide the truth from me, have you heard the archdeacon say that I ought to see a mental specialist?'

'I never heard him say that,' said Dennis. 'But he very well might. The archdeacon is capable of saying anything.'

'Please don't speak that way about the archdeacon,' said the dean. 'He's such an excellent man, so good at everything. I've the greatest respect for the archdeacon. If he'd been in the cathedral that night instead of me everything would be different now.

He'd have saved Cresswood. I'm sure he would. The archdeacon is so very efficient.'

'That,' said Dennis, 'is exactly what makes him so objectionable. Now listen to me, Mr. Dean, and take my advice. I know it's rather a cheek of me to give you advice, but I do thoroughly understand the archdeacon. If he says anything to you about a mental specialist, just you tell him to go out as a missionary to some country where the savages will appreciate him – boiled with parsley sauce. That will show him that your mind is vigorous.'

The dean smiled faintly. He was a very good and gentle man, but even to him there was something attractive in the thought of the archdeacon dropped, like a lobster, into a pot of boiling water while hungry cannibals kept the fire going and their chief whetted the tribal carving knife. But his smile quickly faded away.

'Most likely they won't say anything to me about it,' he said. 'They'll just bring some man here, to lunch, without telling me who he is. That's the way these interviews with mental specialists are managed. I'm getting quite nervous, Dennis. Every time I see a stranger I wonder whether he's an alienist. Fortunately I see very few.'

'Look here, Mr. Dean,' said Dennis, 'if they do try anything of the sort – I can't believe they will, though the archdeacon is capable of most things —'

'They'd mean it kindly,' said the dean. 'They'd think it was for my good. I know that.'

'Most of the mischief in the world is done by people who mean well,' said Dennis. 'And more harm is done by doing good to other people than in any other way. Look at the men, or rather the women, who insist on trying to revive things – village dramas, folk songs, silly old dances, and so on – making life a burden to sensible men. However, we needn't discuss that. If they do bring a mad doctor to see you, or anyone who looks as if he might be a mad doctor, don't say a word about Cresswood's death. Keep that story to yourself. And don't repeat it to anyone except me or Inspector Smallways, if he happens to ask you about it.'

'Thank you, my dear Dennis,' said the dean. 'I'm sure that's good advice and I'll act on it. I'm very glad we've had this little talk. I'm feeling all the better for it. I was – I really think I was sinking into a condition of great nervousness. You've cheered me up.'

Dennis left the Deanery and at once made his report to Inspector Smallways.

'I'm inclined to believe the dean's story,' he said. 'I don't know how you feel about it, Smallways, but if the story is true, then it looks to me as if Cresswood's death wasn't quite such a simple thing as it appeared at the inquest. I don't believe that he climbed up on to the organ stool again after doing all that the dean heard him do, and then fell off and cracked his skull. But if that wasn't what happened —'

Smallways held up a warning finger.

'Don't go too fast,' he said. 'When we've found out a little more about that tune we'll be in a better position to form an opinion about what happened in the organ loft.'

'Very well,' said Dennis. 'You're running this show and I won't try to hustle you faster than you want to go. I'll dart off now and get my little car. If I've any luck I'll be back this evening with a full account of what I get out of the chaplain.'

The Morris-Cowley behaved as if it had been a Rolls Royce, bounding along the roads at a speed which its makers may have advertised as possible, but which they can scarcely have believed in. Dennis reached Bassmore early in the afternoon and had no difficulty in finding the chaplain's lodgings.

The Reverend Theophilus Hartshorn was a middle-aged man, and, perhaps as a result of his peculiar calling, inclined to be reticent and suspicious. Every one who occupies an official position of any kind must be reticent. It is said that the Roman augurs smiled when they met each other. They were so far honest men that they did not pretend to each other to believe in their own business. If our official people smile at all it is in the strictest privacy.

Mr. Hartshorn held an official position and believed in official reticence, thinking, as all officials do, that it is very bad for the general public to be told anything about its own business, and that any member of the public who asks questions deserves to be snubbed. But Mr. Hartshorn was more than ordinarily reticent. He spent his days in ministering to criminals, and had been deceived so often in early life that now, in middle age, he regarded everyone he met as an insidious liar. This made him cautious in dealing with strangers.

It was in this spirit that he received Dennis, and the task of persuading him to talk was no easy one. Very few men could have got any information from him, but Dennis was no ordinary man.

'I have no doubt,' said Dennis, 'that you remember the death of one of your prisoners in hospital about a fortnight ago. Pneumonia, I think.'

Hartshorn nodded. He saw no harm in admitting that a man had died in the prison hospital.

'A man called Hill,' said Dennis.

'Number twenty-seven eighty-four,' said Hartshorn.

This is the strictly correct way for a prison official to refer to a convict, whether dead or alive, but it is a little discouraging for an outsider who hopes to establish some point of human contact with the criminal.

'I happen to know his daughter,' said Dennis. 'Elsie Hill. She appears to have been greatly attached to her father.'

It was possible that a prisoner's daughter might be attached to her father. It was even possible that the father might have some affection for her. But Hartshorn was not inclined to believe in anything of the sort without very good evidence.

'Poor girl,' said Dennis, 'she was engaged to be married to our organist – Carminster cathedral, you know. Did I tell you that I am precentor in Carminster? It isn't for me to swagger about our singing, but there's no harm in saying that it's by far the best in England. I hope you'll run over some Sunday afternoon and hear it. It's a pity you won't hear Cresswood playing. You'd have enjoyed that. But he's dead. A very sad business. Dropped dead quite suddenly. Very soon after your man Hill died. A double blow to poor Elsie. I dare say you heard about poor Cresswood's death? It was in all the papers. Inquest and so forth.'

'No,' said Hartshorn

He was not to be lured beyond a discouraging monosyllable, even by an invitation to Carminster Cathedral. He may have been one of those people who are bored by anthems.

'A very sad affair,' said Dennis. 'Terribly sudden. A severe shock to the poor girl. First her father, then the man she meant to marry.'

'Quite so. Yes.'

This was slightly better. Three monosyllables instead of one. Dennis felt that he was beginning to make headway.

'There was a letter,' said Dennis, 'written by the father before he died —'

'"All letters",' said Hartshorn, '"are read by the prison authorities".'

This was quite a long sentence – the longest he had spoken so far. Dennis might have been further encouraged if he had not suspected that the words were a quotation, as in fact they were, from the printed rules by which the correspondence of prisoners is regulated. The very respectful tone in which Hartshorn spoke suggested that he was quoting from some venerable document. Since the words are neither in the Bible nor the Prayer Book, Dennis, quite rightly, supposed that they came from the prison code.

'"Prisoners",' Hartshorn continued to quote, '"are permitted to write a letter at intervals, which depend on the rules of the stage they attain by industry and good conduct."'

'Hill,' said Dennis, 'had attained the stage of dying of pneumonia, but of course I don't know whether he got there by industry and good conduct.'

Hartshorn looked at him suspiciously. It was impossible to suppose that anyone would dare to poke fun at prison regulations, but Dennis's words sounded like an attempt at some sort of joke. Hartshorn deeply distrusted humour, as indeed all wise officials do. In a world held together by pompous officialdom humour is the deadliest of all microbes.

'I suppose,' said Dennis, 'that it would be quite contrary to regulations, the regulations you've just been quoting, for you to give me any information about that letter of Hill's?'

'Quite.'

That at all events was something. Dennis now knew for certain that Hill had written a letter and that it had been sent to his daughter.

'I suppose,' said Dennis cheerfully, 'that if a letter were handed to you by a prisoner in hospital it would be your duty to pass it on to the prison authorities, who would deal with it according to regulations?'

'"If there is anything in any letter of an objectionable tendency",' said Hartshorn, '"it would be suppressed".'

Dennis recognised another quotation from the same code of laws. It gave him a little more information. Hill had handed his letter to the chaplain, who had passed it on to the proper authority to be tested for 'objectionable tendencies'.

'Objectionable tendencies!' said Dennis. 'That gives the proper authority a pretty wide discretion doesn't it?'

'It's meant to,' said Hartshorn grimly.

'Still,' said Dennis, 'there must be some things – not many perhaps, but still some – which your proper authority would not regard as tainted with objectionable tendencies.'

'Of course.'

'For instance,' said Dennis, 'if a prisoner were to copy out a verse or two of a hymn – say Rock of Ages or some other well-known hymn – that wouldn't be regarded as having a tendency to the objectionable, would it?'

Hartshorn, so far, had been sitting with his eyes half closed and a look of boredom on his face. When Dennis spoke of a hymn his eyes suddenly opened and there was in them for a moment a look of interest. Almost as quickly as the look appeared it vanished again, but he had been stirred to the point of making a reply of some length.

'No,' he said. 'I shouldn't think a verse of Rock of Ages would be regarded as objectionable.'

'I suppose,' said Dennis, 'a prisoner could borrow a hymn book if he wanted to, especially if he were in hospital and dying?'

'If he asked for one he could have it.'

'Supposing he asked for a copy with the music in it,' said Dennis. 'I mean he might want to copy out the tune as well as the words, or even the tune without the words. That paper which you give prisoners to write on, all ruled over with blue lines, would almost suggest the idea of writing music on it. Did you ever come across a prisoner who wanted to copy out a hymn tune?'

This time Hartshorn gave up all appearance of being uninterested. He sat up and his eyes were wide open when he answered.

'I don't know what you're trying to get at,' he said, 'but if you want information about letters written by Hill, or any other prisoner, you'll have to go and ask the governor for it. You must know that I can't talk about things of that kind to outsiders.'

'Oh, don't think I want to get you into a row,' said Dennis. 'I hate all rules myself and make a point of breaking them as often as I can; but I quite realise you may feel differently.'

'I wish you'd go to the governor,' said Hartshorn, 'and ask him your questions.'

'I would,' said Dennis. 'I'd go like a shot if I thought there was the faintest chance of his answering them. But I know jolly well there isn't. He'd simply put me off in the way you do. He'd talk about official reticence and refer me to the Home Secretary or some other Pooh Bah with a little round button on top. Or is it the Great Panjandrum himself who had the button? Anyhow you know the kind of man I mean.'

'I can't listen to this kind of talk,' said Hartshorn. 'You must remember that the governor is my superior officer.'

'I suppose,' said Dennis, 'that you use the English Hymnal here, not the Ancient and Modern? Quite right. It's a far better book.'

'I won't give you any information about the affairs of this prison,' said Hartshorn.

'Thanks,' said Dennis. 'I've got practically all the information I want. Shall I tell it to you? A prisoner called Hill died in your hospital.' He had his eyes on Hartshorn's face as he spoke. 'And you attended him. Before he died he asked for a hymn book with tunes in it. You lent him an English Hymnal. He copied out half a tune, wrote a covering letter to his daughter, and handed the sheet, letter, and tune to you. You very rightly and properly passed it on to whoever it is who censors prisoners' letters. That's all right, so far, isn't it? Don't say no, for I can see by your face that it is. That's all you know, but I'll tell you a little

172

more. Your censor or whatever you call him saw no tendency to the objectionable in the letter or the tune. He passed them and they went to Miss Elsie Hill, the daughter I was speaking of a minute ago. Perhaps you didn't read the letter.'

'Oh, I read it,' said Hartshorn. 'As a matter of fact, Hill asked me to, though I told him that I couldn't post it on my own authority.'

'If you read the letter,' said Dennis, 'you know that Hill asked his daughter to send the tune on to Cresswood, our organist, the man she meant to marry, so that he could play it in the cathedral. That's the whole story, so far as I know at present, and you needn't blame yourself for telling me any of it. You did, but you couldn't help yourself, and you wouldn't have told me much if I hadn't known it all before. All I wanted you to do was to confirm what I knew, and you did that nicely by refusing to answer questions and looking a bit upset now and then when I asked you something you didn't expect.'

'I shall report this interview to the governor,' said Hartshorn.

He was irritated by the tone in which Dennis spoke, and still more irritated by the things he said. A threat to make a report to the governor was, in his opinion, the most awful threat that could be used. There was nothing worse than that. Dennis ought to have quailed, wilted sadly, and made a gasping apology. To Hartshorn's surprise he did nothing of the sort.

'Do. And when you're at it just ask him why that censor of his said nothing about the tune. He could hardly fail to notice it. It's such an odd thing for a prisoner to send in a letter. Ask the governor that, will you? And you might tell your governor that if he attempts to worry me in any way I'll set the archdeacon at him. You don't know our archdeacon, I dare say. Well, he's a man who has his faults – a bit fussy, and so forth – but he has very sound ideas of loyalty to the subordinate members of the cathedral staff. He may rag me a bit at times, but he won't let anyone else do it. Even if it was only a choirboy and it happened to be a mandarin who wanted to box his ears the archdeacon wouldn't have it. So just tell your governor that, however big a boss he thinks he is, there's no use his going for me. But perhaps he's not that kind of man. He may be quite sensible, though very few people in high positions ever are.'

19

THE Morris two-seater, which had behaved excellently on the way to Bassmore, displayed a nasty, vicious spirit on the way back. Ten miles from Bassmore a tyre punctured and the wheel had to be changed. This was a simple business for an energetic and experienced driver like Dennis. But it was a dusty job. His hands and his clothes were very dirty when he finished it. Twenty miles farther on the feed pipe choked. Dennis was quite equal to dealing with that trouble. He knew at once what had happened and set to work with a spanner. The result, so far as his hands and clothes were concerned, was more dirt, spots of oil on top of dust and a sprinkling of petrol, which left his fingertips clean, though smelly, and made his nails look singularly black in contrast. Then came a series of misfires, which could only be due to a defective plug. Dennis cured it, but he was still oilier when he had finished. He arrived in Carminster at about six o'clock.

He was hungry and slightly annoyed at being later than he meant to be, but he was perfectly good-tempered. Most men after a series of troubles in a car are in a condition of suppressed rage. Dennis, partly because he had no particular dislike of being dirty, and partly because he enjoyed getting the better of fractious machines, was not in the least upset by his troubles. He was a little impatient because he was very proud of his discoveries and wanted to report them to Inspector Smallways as soon as possible. But – with such repeated blows does ill luck strike us when it sets to work – there was another delay before he could get to the police station.

He found Hodson waiting for him in the narrow entrance hall of the precentor's house, seated on a hard and very uncomfortable chair. Dennis's housekeeper, who, like most other people, disliked Hodson, would not let him farther into the house, and when he said he would wait until the precentor came in allowed him to do so only in undignified discomfort.

Hodson was in a very bad temper. He was angry when he arrived. Three-quarters of an hour on the uncomfortable chair and the housekeeper's total want of respect made him angrier still.

He rose, grim and threatening, when Dennis flung open the door.

'I want to speak to you, Mr. Precentor,' he said: simple words enough, but the tone in which they were spoken suggested that he wanted to do something much more than speak – stab perhaps, or shoot.

'All right,' said Dennis. 'Come in.'

'No,' said Hodson, 'I'll stay where I am. If I wasn't considered good enough to be brought into your house for the last hour I'll not go in now.'

'Very well,' said Dennis. 'Stay where you are if you prefer it. I expect I know what you want.'

'I expect you do.'

'And I may tell you at once,' said Dennis, 'that there's no use kicking up a row about the money that Cresswood owed you. You'll get it in the end, but you won't get it a minute sooner by making yourself objectionable to me.'

'Cresswood owed me four hundred pounds,' said Hodson.

Dennis whistled softly. He had no idea that Hodson would have lent such a sum of money to a man like Cresswood.

'And I mean to have it,' said Hodson; 'every penny of it. The law is the law, Mr. Precentor, even in Carminster, though you and your dean and chapter don't think so.'

'If the matter is left to the law,' said Dennis, 'you'll get about twopence halfpenny in the pound. That's what'll come of the law being the law. But fortunately for you there's a dean and chapter as well as the law in Carminster. So you'll get your money in the end if Cresswood really owed it to you.'

Hodson, like many men, grew sulky at the thought of receiving a benefit which, in spite of his dislike of the benefactor, he didn't see his way to refuse.

'It wasn't the money I came to speak about,' he said.

'Then why on earth speak about it? Here I am, dusty, tired, hungry, thirsty, with a lot of business to do, and after you've ragged me for half an hour, driving me to the verge of exasperation over some debt that I don't believe Cresswood owes you at all, you have the nerve to tell me that you didn't come to talk about that at all. What did you come for? Get to the point at once, Hodson, and don't waste any more time. But I warn you fairly that if you say "the law is the law" or anything like that I'll throw an inkstand at you. I may tell you that this very afternoon a member of the staff of a convict prison took up that line, threatening to report me to the governor, who'd give me solitary confinement, and bread and water, and a lot more. Well, he didn't frighten me in the least, so it's not likely you can. If you didn't come here to talk about Cresswood's debts why did you bring up the subject at all?'

'I didn't,' said Hodson. 'It was you who began about the money. I wasn't thinking of it.'

'As a matter of fact, I expect you've been thinking of nothing else since poor Cresswood died. And of course there's no objection to your doing so. It may not be a very noble thing to think about, but that's your affair. All I object to is your coming here and talking about it, garrulously and nastily, as if you had a grievance, which you haven't. Do try and get it into your head, Hodson, that we're not all as interested in your miserable financial affairs as you are yourself. You may think that your money is the most important thing in the universe, but it isn't, and just because you have nothing to do, because you're a pensioner with no duties or real interests in life, because you're one of the idle rich – a detestable class – now don't say you're not, for you are. A man who has nothing to do but draw a pension is idle. And a man who says he's owed four hundred pounds is rich, at least he's a great deal richer than I shall ever be. But being that kind of man, Hodson, gives you no kind of right to sit in my hall for half a day and then waste my time when I come home more or less exhausted after a journey undertaken for the public good.'

'It's not the money, I tell you, though I mean to have that money in the end.'

'That's what I'm trying to get you to believe; but you're either unusually thick-headed or criminally obstinate. You either can't or won't take in the meaning of a simple statement.'

'I'll take in the meaning of a simple statement soon enough, when I hear one. What about my son, the boy you have in that school of yours?'

'Your boy,' said Dennis, 'isn't a bad boy at all. He's up to his neck in every mischief there is. He takes next to no interest in his singing, the thing he's paid for by that scholarship of his, and he's an utter rotter at lessons of every kind. But you've no right to complain of him, Hodson. He has one virtue, which you ought to cultivate: he doesn't sit about in chairs waiting for busy men when they come home after their day's work with a view to wasting their time.'

'I'll waste no more of your time anyway. I'll just tell you this: I'm taking an action against you and the dean and chapter for assault.'

Dennis thought this over for a moment. He supposed that Hodson must mean something by his threat, but at first sight it seemed merely ridiculous. Neither the dean nor any member of the chapter was in the least likely to have assaulted Hodson. He had done nothing of the sort himself. At last he caught a glimpse of what might be a meaning.

'If,' he said, 'the archdeacon has caned that boy of yours —'

'It's not the archdeacon, nor it wasn't a cane. The boy's been beaten something cruel. Bruised he is. I had him examined by a doctor, and I've evidence enough to convict the lot of you. There's bruises on that boy's thighs —'

'If you're suggesting that the dean put on a pair of thick-soled boots and kicked your boy round the cloisters you'll find it a little difficult to prove. I don't suppose there's a judge in England would convict the dean of a thing like that, whatever your doctor says.'

'It's not the dean – it's you.'

'Oh, go away! I quite admit that I ought to have beaten your boy, and he'd be a better boy than he is if I had. But I never touched him.'

'I never said you did.'

'You've said nothing else,' said Dennis, 'since you've stopped talking about your beastly money. You say that you can bring a doctor into court to swear that he saw me do it. Very well. Bring him. But just warn him that he'll leave the court in custody with a good long sentence hanging over him for perjury. Do try and be sensible, Hodson, if you can. It's just possible that you may be able to take an action against me for neglect of duty for not beating your boy as I should, but it's perfectly ridiculous to say that I walloped the brat when I didn't.'

'If you had,' said Hodson, 'I'd think better of you than I do. But you weren't man enough to do it yourself. What you did was to incite the rest of the boys to do it, incite them to the commission of outrage. That's what the charge against you will be, and I've witnesses enough to prove that you did that.'

Then Dennis remembered. He had agreed to allow the usual half-holiday if the boy who played the piano in the Song School were properly punished. Apparently Hodson's son had been the culprit. But Hodson's son had been the boy who proposed that way of dealing with the culprit. He had been obviously unwilling to make the suggestion. But he had made it.

'Let me tell you this, Hodson,' said Dennis. 'Your son asked for it. I intended to keep the whole school in on Saturday doing long division sums because the boy who had been guilty of a breach of rules wouldn't own up. Your boy, Hodson, who has been beaten with a cricket stump came forward – I don't say voluntarily, but he did come – and asked that the boys should be allowed to punish the culprit themselves. I said they might if they undertook to do it thoroughly. They promised they would, and apparently they kept their word. Tell me this: can your boy sit down comfortably and without pain?'

'No, he can't.'

'That's all right then. That's exactly what I told the boys to do. I'm greatly pleased with them. It isn't every day that boys do exactly what they're told. When they do it shows that there's a really good spirit in the school, the true English spirit – Trafalgar and Balaclava and everything of that sort, "England expects", "Theirs not to reason why". You know what I mean. I expect the London police force was full of that spirit in your day. You ought to be proud and pleased, Hodson, to think that your boy is being educated in a school where that spirit prevails. All I had to do was to give a hint. The boys acted on it at once, and I expect that son of yours would tell you that he jolly well prefers the hiding he's had to spending Saturday afternoon doing long division sums. It may be inconvenient not to be able to sit down when he wants to, but it's a great deal worse to have to sit down when he doesn't want to. And that was the alternative. Good evening, Hodson. I'm so glad you came round and told me all about it.'

'You've not heard the end of it yet,' said Hodson. 'If you think that just because the dean and chapter are little gods almighty in Carminster they can defy the law —'

'Drop in any time you like,' said Dennis. 'I'd offer you a drink if I thought you'd take one, but I know you wouldn't. But whenever you have a grievance – that money of yours which you lent to Cresswood, or the condition of your boy's backside, or anything else that occurs to you – just drop in and talk it over. Goodbye.'

By a series of gentle pushes he got Hodson to the door and through it. A very tiresome interview had come to a satisfactory end and he was free at last to go to the police station with his report for Smallways.

20

'NOW, SMALLWAYS,' SAID DENNIS, 'don't you think it's about time that you stopped playing for safety and started a proper hunt for the man who murdered Cresswood?'

'Was Cresswood murdered?'

'Of course he was. You've got the dean's story as good as first hand. You can have it told straight to you any day you choose to ask for it. What happened is perfectly plain. Somebody slipped up behind Cresswood while he was playing and knocked him on the back of the head, fracturing the base of his skull. A pretty hefty bash, of course, but easy enough with a heavy-headed club of any kind. Cresswood fell forward over the keyboard. He would if he was hit that way. The murderer, whoever he was, switched off the current from the bellows, pushed in the stops, and arranged the body neatly enough to give the impression that Cresswood had fallen backwards and hit his head on the edge of the oak chest.'

'That,' said Smallways, 'is a very pretty theory. But it wants a lot of support. Why should anyone do such a thing?'

'I should have thought that was plain enough even for a policeman,' said Dennis. 'The murderer, whoever he was, knocked Cresswood on the head in order to get the paper which he had, the paper which Hill sent his daughter Elsie to tell her where the jewels were hid. What do you want more in the way of a motive? Thirty thousand pounds' worth of emeralds! If a man wouldn't commit murder for thirty thousand pounds — Well, I dare say the dean wouldn't, and I wouldn't myself. Being an Irishman I know what a nasty thing murder is. But you can hardly deny that lots of people would knock a man on the head for far less than that.'

'Your idea,' said Smallways, 'is that the scrap of music you found in the Song School is a sort of cryptogram giving away the secret of the hiding place.'

'What else could it be? Hill sent a tune from his deathbed to Elsie, telling her to pass it on to Cresswood. Binder, calling himself Bently, comes here searching for a tune, and Binder knew or could guess that Hill sent the message that way. He was in the next bed to him in the hospital. Elsie came here searching for the tune. She also knows what it is. Neither of them found it. Why not? Because the murderer stole it.'

'And left it about in the Song School?' said Smallways, smiling. 'Don't you see, Dennis, that we're miles and miles away from being able to prove anything. I'm inclined to agree with you that Cresswood was murdered, and I believe you've hit on the motive. But you must see that the dean's story by itself is very little use to us. In the first place, everyone will say that the poor old man's mind is wandering. Even if you get over that, and the story is believed, it's still possible to account for what he heard without supposing a murder. Our strongest point is that Cresswood was not drunk that night. We've got plenty of evidence that he was sober when he went into the cathedral. You and I are prepared to swear that there were no empty bottles in the organ loft next morning. But there's still what the doctors said about heart failure.'

'Two heart failures, if not three,' said Dennis. 'If we believe the dean's story, he fell forward, got up, walked about, sat down on the organ stool again, had another heart failure, and fell backwards.'

'Say fainting fit instead of heart failure,' said Smallways, 'and you'll still have a possible explanation of the dean's story without dragging in murder. A man might have two fainting fits, one after the other.'

'But what about the tune?' said Dennis.

'The tune is no use to us as things stand,' said Smallways. 'We don't know, or, rather, we can't prove, that the tune came from Hill.'

'The chaplain admitted that to me.'

'No, he didn't. By your own account you inferred from what the chaplain didn't say that the tune was Hill's. If you put that chaplain into the witness box, or the officer who censored Hill's letter, or both of them, you'll get nothing out of them – nothing at all. Even if they are forced to admit that the tune came from Hill – and it will be mighty hard to make them admit anything of the sort – it's still up to them to say it was just a copy of a tune from a well-known hymn book and means nothing.'

'But it does mean something: it means where the jewels are hidden.'

'That's what you say,' said Smallways. 'And I don't mind admitting that it's what I think. But that's no use. We've got to prove it.'

'What you mean is that we've got to read Hill's cryptogram?'

'Exactly.'

'Well, let's do it.'

'I've been at it more or less all day,' said Smallways, 'and I haven't got a glimpse of sense out of it.'

'All the same,' said Dennis, 'it must be possible to read it, and what's more, it can't be very difficult. Hill expected it to be read. That's the first thing to get hold of. Therefore it can be read.

The other thing we know is that he wanted it sent to Cresswood. Now why?'

'Because Cresswood was engaged to be married to his daughter.'

'Quite so. But why send it to anyone? Why not trust Elsie to read it herself? Apparently Hill thought she couldn't, or was doubtful whether she could. But he thought Cresswood could. See that? Cresswood could. Elsie couldn't. Cresswood's a musician. Elsie isn't. So some knowledge of music is necessary, or at all events desirable, if the thing is to be read. That gives us a hint, just as it would have given Cresswood a hint how to start. Get the thing out, Smallways, and let's have a go at it at once. I absolutely refuse to believe that you and I together can't make sense out of anything which Cresswood could be expected to understand.'

Smallways unlocked a safe, built into the wall behind his chair, and took out the paper with the tune on it. He laid it on the table in front of Dennis.

'Cresswood,' said Dennis, 'wasn't what I'd call a clever man, apart from his music. If he could get the meaning out of this thing we certainly can. But it may be a stiffish job, and I've had a long day already with precious little to eat. Suppose you send out for some beer.'

'Beer!'

'Yes, say a quart for me and as much more as you think you're likely to drink. Beer stimulates the working of the brain. That's another reason why Hill sent the tune to Cresswood. Elsie might try the thing without beer, but Cresswood wouldn't. In an affair like this, Smallways, we can't afford to neglect help from any quarter. Call it two quarts of beer. Any part of your share which you don't drink I'll finish. Now for goodness' sake don't bleat about police regulations and licensing laws. Get the beer.'

'If you've had nothing to eat all day,' said Smallways, 'I'd better get some food. It'll be much better for you than beer on an empty stomach.'

'Very likely,' said Dennis. 'I don't deny for one moment that a good square meal would be better for me than beer, and more enjoyable. But I'm not considering my own health or even my own pleasure. What I'm thinking of is the public good, catching murderers, recovering stolen jewels and so on. Now, how is that to be done? By the exercise of my mental powers working at their very best. But it's a well-known law, a physico-psycholog-ical law, that the mind works best when the body is hungry. That's why all the great theologians went in for fasting, and why all first-rate artists, inventors, and so on, begin by starving in garrets. Therefore, in order to make the best use of my mind, I propose to go without a solid meal. But beer I simply must have. I wish you'd get it, Smallways, instead of arguing.'

'There you are,' said Smallways ten minutes later, setting down two jugs of beer on the table. 'I've broken the police regulations and the licensing laws, so I expect in return that you'll make short work of that cipher. If you wait a minute I'll fetch a tumbler.'

'Don't bother about a tumbler,' said Dennis. 'I rather like drinking out of jugs.'

To show that he meant this he lifted the jug nearest him and swallowed about half a pint of beer at a draught.

'Now,' he said, 'let's consider this cipher. To begin with, we see at once that Edgar Allen Poe's dodge of finding out what letter occurs oftenest and deciding that it must be E is no kind of use to us here. The first part of the thing is a simple hymn tune, copied quite correctly, out of a hymn book which is in common use.'

'Exactly,' said Smallways. 'That's been my difficulty all along. If Hill had made up a tune, or anything that looked like a tune, it might be some use searching for a meaning. But an old, well-established hymn tune like this can't contain a cipher. You might just as well expect to find the Crown Jewels which were stolen out of Dublin Castle by whistling "Annie Laurie". There's nothing wrong about the tune. I've gone over it with a hymn book in front of me. Every single note as far as the double bar is perfectly correct, accurately copied. After the double bar —'

'Leave the double bar till we come to it. Let's go at the tune first. What about the time signature? 7/8?'

'That's wrong,' said Smallways. 'You couldn't possibly play that tune in 7/8 time. You couldn't play any hymn tune I ever came across in 7/8 time. Whoever wrote in that time signature knew nothing about music.'

'I'm inclined to think,' said Dennis, 'that he knew as much as you do. He may not have known that Tchaikovsky and one or two moderns have used that rhythm, but he did know that no hymn tune was ever written in it.'

'Then what did he put it there for?'

'To attract Cresswood's attention. It might not have attracted Elsie's. It wouldn't have attracted the attention of anyone who knew nothing about music. But Cresswood being a musician was bound to notice it, just as you did and I did. It was pretty nearly the first thing we noticed. Therefore it must mean something.'

'Could it be a date?' said Smallways.

''78, that would be 1878. I don't see what that would direct Cresswood's attention to, do you? 1878 was ages before he was born. The burglary was committed in 1924, wasn't it?'

'1924, towards the end of November.'

'Not the 7th of August by any chance?' said Dennis.

'I'm sure it was in November. But I'll look it up.'

'7/8,' said Dennis. 'People often date letters that way. If the burglary was on the 7th of August, Hill might very well have hit on that way of telling Cresswood that his cipher referred to the jewels.'

But the suggestion, though ingenious, was useless. It turned out that the burglary was committed on the 23rd of November, and 23/11 cannot by any possibility be connected with 7/8.

The next suggestion came from Dennis.

'I wonder if it could be any kind of measurement. Seven feet one way, eight feet another way, or yards, or inches?'

Smallways was scornful.

'Measurements of what?' he said. 'The hymn is about the New Jerusalem, but it was pretty accurately measured in the Book of the Revelation. Hill wouldn't want to do it again; 7 and 8 have no more to do with the hymn than they have with the tune.'

Dennis jumped up from his chair.

'Smallways,' he said, 'I believe you've got it. Give me the hymn book – quick!'

He began turning over the books and papers on the table in search of what he wanted.

'Got what?' said Smallways.

'The meaning of the 7/8 time signature. Where have you put the hymn book?'

'There's no hymn book here,' said Smallways. 'The police aren't served out with hymn books as a regular issue, and my own is at home.'

'Send a man to get one. Send to my house, or your own house, or anywhere. But tell him to ask for the English Hymnal, not the Ancient and Modern.'

'I'll go myself,' said Smallways. 'One of my fellows might be half an hour getting the book from your house, and get the wrong one in the end. I know I've a copy at home.'

'Bring a chunk of bread with you,' said Dennis. 'I'm really extremely hungry, and if there's such a thing in your house as a cold ham, bring a slice or two of it, but don't stop to make sandwiches.'

'I thought you said that the mind works best when the body is half starved,' said Smallways, grinning.

'I did say that, and it's perfectly true. But it's also true that the mind won't work at all when the body is altogether starved. I'm beginning to feel that in another half hour I shall be dead unless I get something to eat.'

Perhaps to ward off total starvation Dennis finished the first jug of beer while Smallways was away. Then he lit his pipe and sat glaring at the hymn tune.

A few minutes later, setting aside half a loaf of bread and some cold beef, he opened the hymn book which Smallways brought, at Hymn 638.

'Verses 7 and 8,' he said. 'Here we are:

Thy walls are made of precious stones,
Thy bulwarks diamonds square;
Thy gates are of right orient pearl,
Exceeding rich and rare;
Thy turrets and thy pinnacles
With carbuncles do shine;
Thy very streets are paved with gold,
Surpassing rich and fine.

Now what does that suggest to you, Smallways?'

'It seems to hint at jewels.'

'Seems to hint!' said Dennis. 'It's as plain an indication as anyone could possibly give that he's going to write something about jewels. Hill writes out a tune, or enough of it for Cresswood to recognize. It's a tune that's only in one particular book.

189

That sends Cresswood to that book if he has an ounce of intelligence. Then Hill writes 7, 8, as if it were a time signature, which it can't possibly be, a thing which Cresswood would see at a glance. What can it be but a reference to two particular verses? What are those verses? A catalogue of jewels. Nothing could be plainer.'

'The Carminster jewels were emeralds,' said Smallways.

'Hill couldn't suggest emeralds,' said Dennis. 'So far as I know there isn't a single hymn in any hymn book which even mentions emeralds. He had to do the best he could with the material he had at hand. And I'm bound to say he didn't do badly. Cresswood was bound to spot the hymn at once. He's played it thousands of times. He was bound to notice that there was something queer about the time signature. Being a musician that 7/8 time jumped up and hit him between the eyes. Sooner or later, knowing that he had to puzzle the thing out, he'd hit on the idea of the number of verses. I dare say he wouldn't have got to it as quickly as we have. Cresswood wasn't a very intelligent man, whereas —'

'Whereas you are,' said Smallways. 'Don't be too modest.'

'I was going to say we are,' said Dennis. 'I don't want to deprive you of your proper share of credit, Smallways. It was you who fetched the hymn book, and I couldn't have got on without it. Very well, Cresswood finds that verses 7 and 8 are a list of jewels. Elsie had probably given him a hint that her father might be trying to smuggle out a message telling her where the Carminster emeralds were hidden. But even if she didn't tell him that, Cresswood was bound to tumble to the idea that he'd got the secret in his hand, and all he had to do was read it.'

'That's what we've got to do,' said Smallways. 'But we're no nearer doing it, so far as I can see.'

'We are nearer,' said Dennis – 'a great deal nearer. We know that the secret isn't in the first four bars of this piece of music.

They're copied straight out of the hymn book, and they're a traditional English melody. Now, the traditional English composer, whoever he was, can't have been concealing the hiding place of the Carminster emeralds in his tune, for the simple reason that he'd never heard of them. Therefore the secret must be in the last few notes which follow the double bar and are no part of the tune. You see that, I suppose?'

'Yes,' said Smallways, 'that's plain enough. But what do you make of these notes after the double bar?'

'Before we go into that I'm going to have a bit of your bread, Smallways, and a couple of slices of that beef. You didn't think of a spoonful of mustard, I suppose.'

'No,' said Smallways. 'You told me not to make sandwiches.'

'Oh, all right. I'm not the kind of man who is dependent on condiments for an appetite.'

During the next five minutes he proved by eating voraciously and very fast that the lack of mustard did not trouble him. Then he took another drink of beer and relit his pipe.

'Now,' he said, 'leaving out the hymn tune and the time signature, let's have a good look at the remaining notes.'

He and Smallways bent over the paper together.

'As they're written there,' said Dennis, 'those notes are just nothing at all. As music they're absurd. My idea is that Hill wrote them down wrong. You see the way his mind was working. By copying out a tune from a hymn book he gave us the tip that he was going to reveal the hiding place of the jewels. The next thing he was sure to do was to think of a tune set to words which would suggest to any intelligent man where to look for the jewels. For instance, if he had written out a few bars of that tune about the roses round the door making me love mother more – just the sort of song Hill would be likely to know – we'd have known that he'd hidden the jewels at the root of some rose-bush to which he'd had access before he was arrested.'

'But it's not that tune,' said Smallways.

'No, it isn't. But you see the idea. Take another example. If Hill had hidden the jewels in the works of some clock he'd think at once of a tune which used to be popular when I was a boy:

My grandfather clock was too large for the shelf,
But it stood ninety years on the floor.

Then we'd know where he'd put the jewels.'

Smallways, who knew the grandfather clock tune, whistled it, keeping his eye on the notes as he did so.

'That's not it,' he said.

'I knew that before you whistled it,' said Dennis. 'I merely mentioned that tune to give you an idea of the way Hill's mind must have been working. But it's not the slightest use guessing at tunes. What we've got to do is to get at the notes themselves. Now listen to this.'

He whistled slowly and clearly the five top notes, then the three underneath them, then the three in the bass clef.

'Is that any tune you know?' he asked.

'It's not any tune at all, or the least like any tune.'

'Quite so,' said Dennis; 'so now we come to my real point. The first tune Hill wanted – the one which was to suggest the idea of jewels to Cresswood – was a hymn tune. He borrowed a hymn book from the chaplain and copied out what he wanted. He got it right, perfectly right as far as he went. But the next tune he wanted wasn't in the hymn book. If it had been he'd have copied it out too and got it right like the other. But if it was a secular tune he couldn't have got it to copy. There was no use his asking, for instance, for the full score of the "Mikado". The chaplain wouldn't have given it to him; so if he wanted a tune out of that he'd have to trust to his memory and write it down as best he could; and he might have wanted one of the "Mikado" tunes. Suppose he'd hidden the jewels in a hole in the ground near a tree beside a river. He'd naturally think of

On a tree by a river a little tomtit
Sang "Willow, 'tit willow,"

and so on. Now, I don't know what you'd make of writing down that tune from memory without the help of an instrument.'

'I couldn't do it at all.'

'Exactly. Nor could Hill. But he tried, and my idea is that he probably got a note or two right, enough to suggest the tune he wanted.'

'That's a most ingenious idea, Dennis.'

'Hill,' said Dennis, 'was a most ingenious man. Now, just you listen while I whistle the notes, and see if you can't catch some hint of a tune.'

Once more he whistled the whole thing through. He whistled it through three times, altering the emphasis on the notes, sometimes even their length. Smallways shook his head hopelessly.

'I don't catch a hint of anything I've ever heard,' he said.

'Nor do I,' said Dennis. 'I wish to goodness Hill had been more careful. No man has a right to muddle up a tune as badly as he's muddled this one. There's only one other thing we can do: we must alter one or two of the notes and put others instead of them. Assuming that Hill made a mistake, that he had a real tune in his head but couldn't write it down correctly, what we've got to do is to go through it, changing each note into something which it might have been meant to be. You catch the idea, don't you?'

'That'll be a longish business, won't it?'

'Very long indeed,' said Dennis. 'There are eleven notes altogether; but first of all we need only deal with the five top notes. They're the most likely to give the tune, and we may assume, to start with anyhow, that Hill didn't go very far out, not perhaps more than a semi-tone either up or down. Suppose we start with that minim in the bar by itself. We make it C natural instead of C sharp and try what the thing sounds like then.'

'C sharp,' said Smallways thoughtfully.

'Yes, and when we're at it we'll flatten the two Cs in the last bar. They are sharp too. Now listen.'

'Wait a minute,' said Smallways. 'It sounds ridiculous, I know, but I've just thought of a silly old riddle which I used to be asked when I was a boy: "What musical note would you use in ordering a sentry to keep a good lookout?" The answer is C sharp. See sharp! Got it?'

'Great Scot!' said Dennis. 'I believe you've hit it, Smallways. It isn't a tune at all. It's a series of notes which spell something. See sharp, and then at the other end See sharp twice over. That is to say: "look carefully". Hill was a most ingenious scoundrel. I wonder if Cresswood would ever have found it out. Now we've only got to read off the notes between the two Cs – the notes in the middle bar. Take the first chord: B. He may be making another pun. He may mean "Be" or even "Bee", though I don't see how he could have hidden the jewels in a beehive. Still we'll keep that idea in mind. BED. That's sense so far – B e d: "bed".

The jewels are in some bed or other. A flowerbed would be a likely enough hiding place. But what flowerbed? The next chord ought to tell us that: EFA.'

'That's no good. EFA doesn't mean anything.'

'Don't be too sure of that,' said Dennis. 'We must remember that Hill had only seven letters to work with, A to G. Using this musical scale cipher of his he had to spell what he wanted without using any letter farther on in the alphabet than G. If he wanted another letter he'd have had to use one of the first seven instead of it. For instance, if he wanted P the natural thing would have been to use B. If we have to go through the rest of the alphabet letter by letter, substituting each for E, and then for G, and then for A it will take us weeks. We could do it in time, and when we had done it we'd have the word that Hill wanted to write. But I think I see a shorter way than that. EFA isn't a word, but it's very nearly two words. All we have to do is to substitute an O for the first E and we have two words.'

'"Ofa", what word's that?'

'Don't be incredibly stupid, Smallways. I told you it was two words: "of a".'

'"Of a". But of a what?' said Smallways. 'I don't see how anyone can be expected to guess a thing like that.'

'I've guessed it,' said Dennis, 'so it was evidently guessable. Now, see where we've got to so far: "Look carefully. Bed of a…" The next chord will no doubt tell us where that bed is.'

But the next chord did nothing of the sort. It read D E. Then all by itself came another D. Not even Dennis's optimistic guessing could make anything out of DE D.

'So far,' said Smallways, 'leaving out that attempt of yours to turn E F A into "of a" what we've actually got is BED E FADED. It's all very well to tell us to see sharp or look carefully; but what's the good of looking carefully at a thing like that?'

'All the same,' said Dennis, 'I'm convinced that we are on the right track. That C sharp riddle of yours, Smallways, gave us the clue. Suppose we try reading the letters from left to right instead of downwards in chords. It's quite likely that Hill wrote them that way. He'd have been thinking of the letters themselves and not of their musical connotation. How does this strike you: B E D D? That's the first line.'

'"Bed", spelled wrong. That's all.'

'E F E, that's the second line. D A, that's the third. Taken altogether, B E D D E F E D A. I've got it, Smallways! I've got it! Give me that jug if there's any beer left in it. The last four letters gave it to me.' He took a hasty drink before he spoke again. 'F E D A: "Feda". Does that mean anything to you, Smallways? Nothing. You sit in that cathedral Sunday after Sunday. You sit in the choir every Sunday evening. You sit on the Cantoris side. You stare and stare at a great, recklessly adorned Renaissance shrine with a tomb inside it, and you've never had the curiosity to ask whose tomb it is.'

But this was unjust. Smallways had asked. He had even remembered the answer to his question.

'Feda!' He said. 'Bishop Feda.'

'Exactly. Now read the thing. C sharp: "Look carefully": Supply the words "at" or "in" and "the": "Look carefully in the B-E-D, bed" – another word for tomb (see Hymns Ancient and Modern: "The grave as little as my bed", "Each within his narrow bed", and so on passim). "Look carefully in the bed (or tomb)". D E, "de", French for "of". Hill couldn't write "of" because he hadn't got the letter O. "Look carefully in the tomb of Feda".'

'Worked out that way,' said Smallways, 'it does make a kind of sense.'

'It makes exactly the sense that Hill meant it to make,' said Dennis; 'and gives us a hiding place for the jewels which in itself

196

is extremely likely; in fact, so likely that I'm amazed at nobody thinking of it before, even without the help of Hill's cipher.'

'It's the last place I'd ever think of hiding anything,' said Smallways.

'That's because you're not a cathedral verger. Hill was. He spent his days mouching about the cathedral and looking at things. Bishop Feda's tomb was being shifted from its original place in the choir to the south transept just when Hill was there. He was bound to look at it for hours every day. While that was happening he brought off his burglary, with the aid of Binder and the others. Now see how his mind worked – must have worked. Here's a good stone coffin, empty except for a few bones. He knows that it's never been touched and won't be touched again for perhaps another five hundred years. All he has to do is prise up the lid, at night, when nobody is there, and drop the emeralds in. There they'd stay till he got out of prison. What could be more probable than that? Given the conditions, I'd say that Hill's action was almost inevitable, and now here's his cipher to turn the probability into a certainty.'

21

'I'LL CALL IT A certainty when I see the jewels,' said Smallways.

'And you shall see them, touch them if you like. Let's see. I have to be at a choirmen's supper tonight. Shall we say tomorrow night at half-past ten?'

'What do you mean?'

'What I say of course. You and I, taking a crowbar with us, will go into the cathedral tomorrow night at half-past ten and open dear old Feda's stone coffin.'

'You can't open a grave,' said Smallways, 'without an order from the Home Secretary.'

'If you propose to go at the job in that spirit,' said Dennis, 'I may as well tell you that you can't touch a monument in the cathedral without getting a faculty from the Chancellor of the Diocese. I don't know how you feel about it, Smallways, but my impression is that if we have to get permission from the Home Secretary and a faculty from the Chancellor it'll take about thirty years. The Home Secretary will take the view that the Chancellor ought not to interfere with him. The Chancellor will say that the Home Secretary is a rank outsider with no authority over ecclesiastical monuments. They'll argue with each other until each has to engage two extra clerks to take charge of the correspondence. That's the way our Civil Service keeps growing and growing. In the end, if we get them to agree – the new clerks being pensionable by that time – we'll come up against the Dean and Chapter, who'll refuse permission, just to show that they don't care two hoots either for the Home Secretary or the Chancellor, and it will take us another thirty years to talk them round. That's the way things are done, Smallways, and a man with your experience of public life ought to know it.'

'That's all very well,' said Smallways; 'but we can't go breaking into tombs on our own.'

'I can and I would without bothering about your ridiculous scruples. But it's an awkward job for one. I suppose I could prise the lid off the tomb all right, but I don't care for doing it. Suppose the thing slipped and came crashing down and got smashed. The archdeacon doesn't care much for old Feda, I know. He regards him as rather a dog, more of a dog than a bishop ought to be. All the same he'll make himself very unpleasant if I smash the lid of the tomb. Besides, it would be no use doing it unless you were there. I'm quite convinced that the jewels are in the tomb, and seeing them won't convince me any more. It's you who say that you won't believe what's been demonstrated without the evidence of your own eyes. You might just as well insist on measuring the sides of a triangle after Euclid had proved to you that two of them must be longer than the third.'

'Don't you see,' said Smallways, 'that before I do anything I must be certain that you've really read that tune thing right?'

'I'm offering you certainty,' said Dennis – 'the additional certainty of seeing with your own eyes, and you won't take it.'

'What you're suggesting,' said Smallways, 'is sacrilege.'

'Rot! If we were going to root about among the bones of the Apostle Paul or any other recognised saint there might be some sense in talking about sacrilege. But old Feda! By all accounts he committed far worse sacrilege himself. Why, he wanted to have that girl of his, Chloe, or whatever he called her, buried with him in his tomb in the cathedral. Pretty dashing for a bishop, that! I don't think we need worry about disturbing his bones. If he has any feeling at all about it he'll rather like it. A bit of variety for him after lying quiet for centuries.'

'I didn't mean sacrilege in that sense,' said Smallways.

'You're thinking of an offence punishable by law. Is that it? Well, I quite admit that it would be a bit awkward for you if you're caught. But you won't be.'

'I'd much rather get an order from the Home Secretary,' said Smallways. 'But if I do that —'

'It'll take fifty years at least,' said Dennis. 'I've explained that to you.'

'If I ask for an order and it turns out that there's nothing in the tomb —'

'Oh, old Feda's bones will be there,' said Dennis; 'and I shouldn't wonder if you found Chloe's skeleton too. It'll annoy the archdeacon and Miss Grosvenor frightfully if we do.'

'I wish to goodness, Dennis, that you'd be serious if only it's for five minutes at a time. I don't think you realise what a nasty affair this is and what an infernal stink we're going to raise if we go on with it. If you're right about the damned piece of music and the jewels are in the bishop's tomb, then it follows that someone must have taken that paper from Cresswood, and it looks as if whoever took it killed Cresswood to get it. In other words, there's been a murder, and it's my job to lay my hands on the murderer. Don't you see what that means? How did that cipher of Hill's get out of the prison? There'll be an infernal row about that. What about the verdict of the coroner's court here? It will look very much as if the dean's story of what he heard in the cathedral was deliberately suppressed. We shall have the archdeacon hauled over the coals for that.'

'Jolly good for the archdeacon,' said Dennis.

'And Miss Grosvenor and Harrowby. It'll appear as if they were in the conspiracy too. They've been saying that the dean's mind has given way.'

'All right,' said Dennis. 'If you feel that way about it I'm quite willing to drop the whole matter. After all, Cresswood's dead and the jewels will be no more loss than they were six weeks ago. Nobody knows a thing and nobody even suspects anything except you and me. If we keep our mouths shut —'

'That's impossible,' said Smallways. 'We can't suppress a murder and a robbery.'

'You're the most difficult man to deal with, Smallways. First you say that if we go on we shall raise an infernal stink – your own words, my dear fellow. Personally I should rather like that, just for the sake of seeing the archdeacon hopped on by a judge or two. But I'm perfectly willing to give up my own pleasure for your sake and say nothing. When I propose that you take a tone of virtuous indignation, wrap yourself up in the shining armour of incorruptibility, truth, and justice, and all that sort of thing, making me feel like a maggot. Now what *do* you want?'

'I want to be perfectly certain that the jewels are in that tomb before I do anything more. Don't you see that we've really nothing to go on but your guess about that scrap of music, and if —'

'Guess! It's a mathematical demonstration.'

'It's a guess,' said Smallways, 'a fantastic guess. If it's wrong and the jewels aren't there and it ever comes out that we opened that tomb – well, all I can say is that I shall deserve what comes to me for starting the worst kind of row about nothing at all.'

'That brings us back to where we started,' said Dennis. 'Let's open the tomb and see.'

'All right,' said Smallways desperately, 'I'll risk it.'

'Good man!' said Dennis. 'I thought you'd agree in the end. And you'll never regret it. Just think what a hero you'll feel when you walk into the office of the insurance company with a suitcase full of emeralds and say, "Alone I did it!" And you can. I shan't claim any of the credit. Why, the very least they can do is to give you a large emerald for yourself, a great fat stone worth perhaps five hundred pounds.'

'I'm not thinking about rewards,' said Smallways, 'or the insurance company, or the jewels. I want to catch the man who murdered Cresswood.'

'Binder?'

'Well, of course one thinks of Binder first,' said Smallways, 'but I don't believe he did it. Unless both Carson and Powell were lying, Binder couldn't have been in the cathedral when Cresswood was killed. He didn't leave the Mitre when Cresswood did. But unless he went into the cathedral with Cresswood he couldn't have got in at all. The doors were all locked.'

'Then you think that Cresswood was murdered by someone who had a key of the south transept door and could get in? But there are only about a dozen people who have keys: the dean, the four canons, Cresswood, a couple of vergers, the assistant organist, and myself. I say, Smallways, you're not thinking of suggesting that the archdeacon did it? I should rather like to see him tried for his life, but I don't believe he did it. I don't believe he would. Are you thinking of Carson?'

'Carson is a possibility.'

'But Carson didn't do it. I quite admit that he could let himself into the cathedral any hour he chose. Or he might have gone in with Cresswood that night instead of saying goodbye to him as he said he did. But why should Carson steal Cresswood's key of the door? Somebody stole it, for it's disappeared. You didn't find it in his pockets. I've had the whole cathedral swept out in the hope of finding it. The archdeacon made such a fuss that I had to. But the key wasn't there. It seems pretty plain that the murderer took it when he took the tune. If he wanted to get out he'd require a key to open the door, so he took Cresswood's.

Carson wouldn't have done that. He had all the keys he could possibly want. But, I say, if the murderer hadn't the key before he took Cresswood's, how did he get in?'

'He might have strolled in during the day when the cathedral was open and simply stayed there. I don't suppose the vergers search the cathedral before they lock up. And, anyhow, there are plenty of hiding places. He might have slipped in behind Bishop Feda's tomb.'

'It would be rather funny if he did that. He'd have been leaning up against the emeralds without knowing it. Anyhow, what that suggestion comes to is that we've no sort of indication at all to show who it was. It might have been anyone, absolutely anyone. The only thing we know is that it's not likely to have been a member of the chapter or me or Carson. We all have keys. It might be anyone else.'

'It must be someone,' said Smallways, 'who knew that Cresswood had that piece of music, that is to say, someone who had heard of it from Elsie Hill, or from Binder, or had private information from one of the prison warders. That narrows things down a bit.'

'I'll tell you something which narrows them down still more,' said Dennis. 'Whoever stole the tune left it in the Song School, where I found it. There aren't so many people who have access to the Song School.'

'Unless Cresswood dropped it there himself,' said Smallways, 'in which case there was no robbery and probably no murder.'

'That's quite impossible,' said Dennis. 'If you'd seen the way Binder searched for that tune you'd know he wouldn't have missed it if it had been in the Song School when he was there. He had the place to himself for the best part of half an hour, and you may bet your last shilling that he'd have found the tune if it was there.'

Smallways rose from his chair rather wearily. He lifted first one of the two jugs, then the other. There was no beer left in either.

'There's no use talking any more tonight,' he said. 'We can't really do anything, or even decide what to do, till we're sure that the jewels are in that tomb.'

'That,' said Dennis, 'you'll know for certain tomorrow night. Call round for me at ten and don't forget the crowbar. We may not want it, but if we do we shan't be able to get on without it.'

22

MATINS HAD ENDED. THE organ, played by an assistant organist, made an appropriate noise, while the choir and clergy stepped with due reverence towards the chapter room. The boys, dismissed with a final pious wish, tramped into the Song School, and there, under the eye of Dennis, took off their surplices and cassocks. Both psalms and lessons had been short that morning. The boys had twenty-five minutes of playtime before them. They hurried along the cloisters to make the best of their opportunity, all of them except Tom Hodson. He lingered in the Song School.

'Please, sir —' he said to Dennis.

'Feeling better again?' said Dennis with a grin. 'They gave it to you pretty hot, I understand?'

'Yes, sir, please, sir. Hot and strong, please, sir, with a cricket stump.'

'So I understand from what your father said to me yesterday.'

'Please, sir, my father says, sir —'

'I've heard what your father says, Tom, and I don't in the least want to hear it again.'

'Please, sir, it's not that, sir. What my father says, sir, is that I'm to tell you that I'm sorry, and that I won't go into the Song School again.'

This surprised Dennis. Mr. Hodson had been in a very different mood the night before. It was difficult to believe that he had insisted on this message of abject apology. Sleep brings wisdom with it sometimes, and many a man who has gone to bed in a rage has wakened in a pacific mood next morning. But Dennis did not think that Hodson was that kind of man. Did you say your father told you to say you were sorry?'

'Yes, sir, please, sir. He said as how he thought I'd got what I deserved, and he hoped you'd give me more of the same if I required it. That's what he said, sir. But I hope you won't.'

'All right,' said Dennis. 'You can tell your father that it's all over and done with and nothing more will be said about the matter.'

'Yes, sir. Thank you, sir. And please, sir —'

Tom hesitated. It was evident that he had a request to make and was a little shy about making it. 'Please, sir,' he said at last, 'might I take a look for something I lost, sir – dropped it when Mr. Carson came in that day and I ran away.'

'Penknife?' said Dennis. 'Lump of toffee? Not cigarettes, I hope, Tom?'

'No, sir. Nothing like that, sir. It was a piece of music – the piece of music I was playing when Mr. Carson came in. I must have left it on the piano, sir. It may have slipped down, sir. Please, sir, may I look for it?'

'Tom,' said Dennis eagerly, 'tell me the truth. What was that piece of music?'

'A tune, sir. Not a regular tune, but wrote out on a bit of paper.'

'Where did you get it? Who gave it to you?'

But Tom, who had answered willingly enough so far, suddenly became obstinately silent. Dennis asked question after question. 'Did your father give it to you?' 'Did he tell you to come back to me and ask me to search for it?' 'When did he find out that you'd lost it?' 'Did he send you here to play it on this piano?' 'Did you play it before Carson came in?' 'Did you recognize the tune as one that you'd heard before.'

Under this shower of questions Tom remained silent. At first he seemed amazed, as he well might be, for Dennis spoke with an eagerness quite unlike anything that Tom had heard before. Gradually his face settled into a sulky scowl. It was plain that he was quite determined not to answer. At last, quite suddenly, he hung his head and began to cry bitterly.

Dennis, a tender-hearted man, and really fond of his boys, felt very sorry for him. He also realised that he was saying – indeed already had said – far too much. He felt sure that he knew now who had stolen the tune and – he shivered slightly at the thought – who had killed Cresswood. He realised that it would not do to put Hodson on his guard, perhaps give him a chance of escaping, by saying things to the boy which he would certainly report to his father.

'Very well, Tom,' he said, speaking as quietly as he could. 'You may search for your piece of music. I have to go away, and must leave you here by yourself. Don't do any mischief.'

'Please, sir' – Tom had stopped crying – 'please, sir, if Mr. Carson comes in —'

'Tell him I said you may stay here. But I dare say he wouldn't believe you if you said that. I'll tell Carson myself as I go out that he's not to interfere with you. Find your piece of music and take it home with you to your father, but don't ever come to the Song School again to play tunes on this piano.'

'Thank you, sir. No, sir. I won't be long, sir. Thank you very much, sir.'

Dennis hurried out. Regardless of what the archdeacon's feelings might be he ran through the cloisters. He ran even faster – ran at the top of his speed – across the close, taking forbidden shortcuts across the grass. He was on his way to the police station to tell Smallways what seemed very important news. After leaving the close he had to stop running. It was market day in Carminster, and the streets, all of them very narrow, were crowded. The best Dennis could do was to walk fast, jostling everyone who got in his way. In spite of his determination to get on he was stopped before he reached the police station. A taxi cab had pulled up outside the Mitre Inn. A lady got out. Dennis recognised her at once. It was Miss Elsie Hill. She also recognised him.

'It's the precentor,' she said. 'Now I do call that lucky! You're the very man I want to talk to.'

'I'm sorry,' said Dennis, 'but you can't talk to me now. I'm in a desperate hurry.'

But Elsie, as he might have known, was not an easy person to shake off. She grasped him firmly by the arm, holding it with both her hands. The taxi driver, who, like everyone else in Carminster, respected the cathedral clergy, stared in astonishment. Powell coming out to welcome an arriving guest, also stared, grinning.

'Now, precentor,' said Elsie, 'don't go saying things like that. Nobody could be in a hurry in a place like Carminster. Anyhow a cocktail won't hurt you. Come in and have one with me.'

'Can't possibly,' said Dennis, struggling to free his arm.

'Now, now,' said Elsie, 'that's what I call naughty temper.'

She looked round at the taxi driver and winked. She looked at Powell and winked again. A small crowd was gathering on the pavement. Elsie took them into her confidence with a third wink. Many young men, and perhaps most clergymen, would have been embarrassed. Dennis was not afflicted in that way. The smiles of the onlookers did not affect him at all. But he realised that it would not be very easy to get away from a determined young woman who held him firmly.

'Come along with me,' he said. 'We can talk as we go. You can tell me what you want and I'll do it at once if I can. If it's anything serious Inspector Smallways will help. I'm on my way to the police station.'

Elsie dropped his arm at once.

'No police station for me,' she said. 'If that's where you're going you can go without me.'

Dennis, his arm released, pushed his way through the gathering crowd. Before he passed altogether out of earshot Elsie's voice came to him.

'See you later then, unless the police keep you when they get you there.'

A grave hush fell upon the people who heard her. The grins faded from the faces of Powell and the taxi driver. Elsewhere – in London, in Manchester, in Liverpool, anywhere – a crowd would have shouted merrily at a joke well suited to the popular mind. In Carminster people were shocked, as if by very blasphemous words. Indeed, the suggestion that the police might imprison one of the cathedral clergy was very like blasphemy.

Dennis reached the police station and burst into the inspector's office.

'Smallways,' he said, 'I've got your man for you. I've found out how the tune got into the Song School and who brought it there. You can arrest Hodson, and you'd better do it at once before he makes a bolt for it.'

'Ah,' said Smallways, 'I had a feeling that it might be Hodson.'

It cannot be pleasant to arrest a man suspected of murder, and Smallways, whose heart was kindly, greatly disliked the duty. Yet there was a certain satisfaction in the thought that Hodson was to be his victim. Long ago, at the time when Hodson came down to investigate the Carminster jewel robbery, Smallways had suffered snubs and indignities. Only a few days before, when Binder paid his first visit to Carminster, Smallways had been snubbed again, for the business of watching the convict was entrusted to Hodson and not to him. Moreover, Hodson had been objectionable, steadily and continuously objectionable, to everyone in Carminster – that is to say, to everyone who held office or position in church or town. If an arrest had to be made and a dreadful charge brought, better Hodson than anyone else.

Smallways listened to Dennis's story, and together they went over the evidence against Hodson, building up a case little by little.

Hodson knew that the stolen jewels had never been recovered. Every one else knew that too, but Hodson was not likely to forget it, for he had been engaged in searching for them.

Hodson knew that Hill, and only Hill, had the secret of the hiding place.

Hodson knew that Hill had been given the opportunity of telling his secret before he died.

Hodson might have – there was nothing unlikely in supposing that he had – some friend on the prison staff at Bassmoor. He might have been told about the letter to Elsie and the tune.

'The case is weak there,' said Smallways. 'It isn't enough to say "possible" and "might" when a man is being tried for his life.'

'Hodson' – it was Dennis who spoke – 'was mighty keen on trying to prove at the inquest that Cresswood was drunk. I thought at the time that it was just general nastiness of disposition that made him do it. But I can see now that what he really wanted was to make it quite clear that an accident was likely. That was what we all believed, but we'd have believed it more if it had been shown that Cresswood was drunk.'

'Then there's the dean's story,' said Smallways. 'That knocks the accident theory on the head.'

'And now there's the tune,' said Dennis. 'What evidently happened was this: he had it but he couldn't make it out. He sent that boy of his to play it on the piano in the Song School, where nobody would hear him, in order to find out what it was. I suppose Hodson hasn't got a piano of his own?'

'No, he hasn't. I happen to know that.'

'Well, that seems to me to prove – pretty completely prove – that Hodson did it.'

'If we find that the jewels are really in that tomb —'

'We'll find that tonight.'

'If we do,' said Smallways, 'it'll be a great help to us. To tell you the truth, nothing that we have got so far will bring the thing home to Hodson unless we find the jewels in the tomb. No jury will believe in that music cryptogram of yours unless it turns out that the jewels are really there. It'll be precious hard to make a jury believe a thing like that, even if the jewels are there.'

'Do you mean to say you are not going to arrest Hodson?'

'I'll arrest him all right,' said Smallways, 'after I've found the jewels. I don't suppose I could even get a warrant against him unless I do. But I'll take care that he doesn't slip away in the meanwhile.'

'But he did it,' said Dennis. 'Surely you believe that?'

'I believe it,' said Smallways. 'But believing isn't proving. There are plenty of men arrested who are never hanged, and no jury would find him guilty on the evidence we've got unless we can connect that tune of his with the jewels.'

23

'I THINK,' SAID THE dean, 'that I shall go straight to my study. I have a little work to do and I should like to get on with it.'

There was a hint of apology in his tone and a hint of doubt-fulness, such as a man might feel who is not sure that his apology will be accepted or his excuse believed.

Dinner was over. The dean was holding the door of the room open for Sybil. His manners, even when alone with his daughter, were formally correct. He rose when she left the room and opened the door for her as courteously as if a whole procession of ladies were to precede her.

'Don't do too much, father dear,' said Sybil. 'Remember what the doctor said.'

'Oh, it's nothing very exacting,' said the dean. 'Just that little poem addressed *ad Paulum Diaconum. Hinc celer egrediens facili*. You remember it, don't you?'

Sybil remembered it. She also remembered something else.

'You won't forget, will you, father, dear, that the archdeacon is to be here at half-past nine? I asked him to dinner, but he had some engagement and couldn't be with us till nine-thirty.'

The dean had been trying, without success, to forget this visit of the archdeacon's ever since he first heard of it at luncheon-time.

'Ah, yes,' he said meekly. 'I remember. Something about poor Cresswood, wasn't it?'

'About that unfortunate man's debts,' said Sybil. 'The archdeacon thinks —'

'Yes, yes. They ought to be paid. Must be paid. Very well, Sybil, send me word when the archdeacon arrives. In the meanwhile —'

The dean slipped quietly past Sybil and into his study. He had nearly an hour before him. He had waiting for him the poem in which Paul the Deacon no doubt once rejoiced. He set to work on one of the most delightful lines of it: *Pax pia, mens humilis, pulchra et concordia fratrum.*

Religious peacefulness and humble mood

And fair agreement of the brotherhood

But that was not good, not good at all. The dean ran his pen through the words and tried again:

All pious peace, all lowliness, all fair

Affection of the brotherhood, are there.

That was no better. The dean took a fresh sheet of paper. '*Pax pia.*' Is there any English rendering of '*Pax pia*' which is adequate? Miss Waddell – the dean respected her work; but here she had shirked the difficulty. '*Pax pia*?' She had left out the '*pia*' altogether.

Quiet and brother's love and humbleness.

That was her rendering. It was quite good, excellent for '*Pax*' But what about the '*pia*'? The dean felt that '*pia*' should mean something. It ought to mean much, perhaps everything.

'Miss Grosvenor wishes me to say, sir, that the Archdeacon has arrived.'

It was Redington, surely long before his time, with this horrible announcement. The dean glanced at his watch. It was twenty-five past nine. So swiftly time seems to fly when we are pleasantly busy. The archdeacon was no more than five minutes too early, a mere nothing for a man who specially prides himself on never being late. The dean gave one last sad glance at the poem. '*Pax pia.*' How little there is of it in life! How little too of the *pulchra concordia fratrum*! The dean, no matter how he tried, could never feel that way in the archdeacon's company.

He greeted the archdeacon with a sigh which he did not attempt to stifle.

'An unpleasant business, I fear,' he said; 'very unpleasant.'

The paying of debts for someone else is always very unpleasant. No gratitude can be expected from the creditors who, after all, receive nothing but what is due to them. It is foolish to look for gratitude from the debtor, who feels humiliated by the investigation of his affairs, and in Cresswood's case even insincere expressions of thanks cannot be expected, because the man was dead. No public recognition of generosity is to be looked for, because such matters must always be carried through privately. Indeed, of all forms of giving, this is the least satisfactory to the giver.

But this time, disagreeable as the business was, it was not dull. The archdeacon had a most surprising announcement to make.

'I thought it best,' he began, 'to ask my solicitors to investigate Cresswood's affairs thoroughly, and to prepare for us a detailed list of his debts.'

'Quite so,' said the dean. 'Very wise of you.'

'And the result?' said Sybil.

She too, since she had a little money of her own meant to bear her share of the burden. She was naturally anxious to know the amount of the liability.

Then the archdeacon made his amazing announcement.

All Cresswood's debts, with one or two trifling exceptions, had been paid. Carson was still owed a few pounds. Powell had an unsatisfied claim. Every one else had been paid in full.

'How very remarkable,' said the dean, 'and how very satisfactory!'

But the archdeacon had more to say. His solicitors had done their work thoroughly, and had discovered the curious fact that the money for the payment of the debts had been received by Cresswood only two days before his death. It had been given to him, or lent to him, by Hodson.

'I cannot imagine,' said the archdeacon, 'that Hodson, an aggressive Dissenter, invariably hostile to the cathedral – I cannot imagine that he would have given such a sum to Cresswood out of simple goodwill. But the money was certainly received and the debts were certainly paid. My solicitors have no doubt about the facts.'

'Hodson must have lent it to him,' said Sybil.

'In that case,' said the archdeacon, 'Hodson must be paid, and our liability remains unchanged. Indeed, it is all the more necessary to pay at once since the creditor is Hodson.'

Even the dean understood that. Sybil was quite clear about it.

'The odd thing,' said the archdeacon, 'is that Hodson has made no claim. My solicitors invited all Cresswood's creditors to send statements of the amounts owed to them. They made individual requests to those whom they knew or thought likely to be creditors. When they became aware of the facts, that is to say, of the payment of the debts, they wrote to Hodson asking him to make his claim. No answer has been received from him.'

'Perhaps,' said the dean, who was a man of charitable mind, inclined to think well of his neighbours, 'perhaps Hodson meant to give the money. He may have been a friend of poor Cresswood's.'

'Father, dear,' said Sybil, 'don't talk nonsense.'

There was a frown of perplexity on her forehead, and Sybil hated being perplexed. She liked to understand everything, and generally did understand everything quite clearly. Being puzzled was a novel experience to her, and she did not like it. Her father's suggestion irritated her. It also irritated the archdeacon.

'Hodson,' he said, 'is quite incapable of such generosity.'

Then Redington, coughing discreetly as he opened the door, came into the room.

'A young person,' he said, 'has called and wishes to see the dean.'

'I can't possibly see any young person now,' said the dean.

'Tell her to call tomorrow,' said Sybil.

Redington drew himself up with a slightly offended air. He was a butler who knew his business and did not like to be told how to do it, even by his employers.

'I have already informed the young person,' he said, 'that the dean is busy, and I requested her to call tomorrow. I regret to say that she declines to go away.'

'If necessary,' said the archdeacon, 'you must telephone the police to remove her.'

But that seemed to the dean an unduly harsh way of dealing with a visitor who might have some legitimate reason for calling.

'I wonder,' he said, 'if I ought to see her.'

'Certainly not,' said Sybil. 'If anyone sees her I shall.'

'Or perhaps if I spoke to her —' said the archdeacon.

But, so it happened, they were all to see her.

Redington, who was standing in the doorway, was taken by the shoulders, turned round and pushed out of the room. Miss Elsie Hill stood in his place.

'Hullo, dean!' she said. 'Going strong? That's right.'

The dean rose to his feet. He remembered Elsie distinctly. Indeed it would have been hard for him to forget her. He had never in his life, until she first called on him, come across a girl like Elsie Hill. He meant to say a word of gentle protest, but the archdeacon was too quick for him.

'May I ask,' he said, 'the reason of this intrusion?'

'Are you a bishop?' said Elsie.

'An archdeacon,' said the dean mildly. 'Not a bishop – an archdeacon.'

'More of a boss than a dean, I suppose?' said Elsie.

Now that is a difficult thing to decide. Even Sybil, deeply skilled in ecclesiastical precedence, could not have said, without explanation and many qualifying clauses, whether an archdeacon ranks before a dean.

'Anyhow,' said Elsie, 'he's more of a boss than a precentor.'

'Oh, yes,' said the dean. 'Certainly.'

'A precentor,' said Sybil, 'ranks among the minor canons.'

She spoke with chilling severity. She would not have spoken at all to this ill-mannered intruder if she had not been goaded into saying something by Elsie's unpardonable ignorance of clerical rank.

Elsie, who had not noticed Sybil before, turned towards her and took a long look at her.

'And I expect,' she said, 'that you boss the lot. So that's all right.'

'I cannot understand,' said Sybil, 'how Redington came to admit you to this room.'

'He didn't,' said Elsie. 'If Redington is your old pet of a butler he did his best to keep me out, but he couldn't. I just watched where he went and walked after him. I'm glad I did, for I want you all to help me. The dean will, I know; and I expect the deacon will too.'

'Arch,' said the dean. 'Archdeacon. A deacon is quite a different thing.'

'And you'll help me too,' said Elsie to Sybil. 'You look as if you don't want to, but that may be only dignity. I expect you'll be quite keen to help me when you know what I want.'

What do you want?' said the archdeacon.

'I want you to make your precentor give me back my tune,' said Elsie. He's got it. He must have, for I don't believe old Carson ever saw it. And Hodson hasn't got it. Binder told me that Hodson paid poor Ben hundreds for it – hundreds and hundreds – but Ben wouldn't give it up. He told me so himself. That's why I say that your precentor must have it.'

'Your tune!' said the dean, who was beginning to feel confused. 'But – but last time you came here you said you wanted some letters. I sent you to the precentor. Didn't he get them for you?'

'I was taken in by that young man,' said Elsie. 'He pretended to be ever so pi and quite shocked that I offered to kiss him, just as if nobody ever kissed a precentor before. Ridiculous, wasn't it?'

She turned to Sybil, as if expecting support from her, almost as if the kissing of precentors were a thing which Sybil was sure to know all about.

'Really,' said Sybil, 'this is outrageous! I must insist. Archdeacon, will you —'

'Oh, but I didn't do it,' said Elsie. 'I wouldn't when he pretended to be innocent and shocked at the very idea. But I might have known that he wasn't – not really. No young man could be. It wouldn't be natural, would it?'

Again she appealed to Sybil. But Sybil, though she had several things to say, could not manage to speak. She was so angry and so profoundly shocked that she lost all command of words – a thing which had never happened to her before.

'I think,' said the dean feebly, 'that if you'll excuse me I'll slip away to my study. I'm not feeling very well. Oh, nothing serious – just a little upset.'

He rose and tottered towards the door. As he went he grasped for support the backs of such chairs as he could reach. There was no doubt that he was feeling 'a little upset'. Indeed the words were a very mild description of his condition.

Sybil was upset too, and more than a little. So was the archdeacon. But they were braver and more determined than the dean. Neither of them thought of running away from Elsie Hill.

'The telephone,' said the archdeacon. 'May I use your telephone, Miss Grosvenor?'

'That's right,' said Elsie. 'Ring up the precentor, and tell him he's jolly well got to give up that tune at once. He'll do it for you, because you're an archdeacon. He wouldn't do it for me this afternoon though I spent hours and hours begging him to. You ask him too.' She turned to Sybil. 'He'll do it if you tell him to. You're his fiancée, I suppose?'

'Certainly not,' said Sybil. 'The suggestion is outrageous.'

She was years older than Dennis; but even if she had been of a more suitable age she would still have regarded it an outrageous suggestion that she should marry one of the inferior clergy.

'Oh, all right,' said Elsie. 'Don't get ratty. I only thought you might be, because I could see you were furious when I talked about kissing him; but I didn't, so you needn't mind even if he is your young man.'

Sybil, once more too angry for words, pointed to the telephone, which was on the table in a corner of the room. The archdeacon took up the receiver.

'Give me the police station,' said he; 'at once, please. I've forgotten the number, but the call is urgent.'

'Did you say the police station?' said Elsie.

'Yes,' said the archdeacon. 'I am summoning the police.'

'Then I'm off,' said Elsie. 'I can't bear the police. Never could. I told that precentor of yours at the very start that I wouldn't have the police mixed up with my affairs.'

'Is that the police station?' The archdeacon's call had gone through with remarkable swiftness. 'I want Inspector Small-ways. Yes, I want to speak to him. Out? Did you say out? Then please send a man, or two men, to the Deanery at once. No, not exactly burglary. It's —'

'Good night,' said Elsie, 'I'm off. Say good night to the dean for me, won't you? When your silly old policemen come tell them to arrest your precentor for stealing my tune. They can't arrest me. I haven't stolen anything.'

She waved her hand gaily to Sybil. She patted the archdeacon on the back in a friendly way. Then she vanished.

'Mad!' said the archdeacon. 'Quite mad!'

'Vicious,' said Sybil. 'I've never come across a more aban-doned woman.'

'For her own sake,' said the archdeacon, 'she ought to be put under restraint.'

'And I'm very much afraid,' said Sybil, 'that the precentor is as bad as she is.'

'I don't think,' said the archdeacon, 'that he can have stolen – she said tune. Why should the precentor steal a tune? She's evidently suffering from a delusion.'

'I wasn't thinking of the tune,' said Sybil. 'I was thinking —'

But though a member of a committee for preserving social purity, Sybil was still a modest woman. She shrank from saying the word 'kiss' out loud. Fortunately the archdeacon under-stood her.

'But,' he said, 'she assured us that she didn't.'

'I've always been uncertain about the precentor,' said Sybil. 'An erratic young man; not sufficiently conscious of the dignity of his office in the cathedral.'

'In a country parish,' said the archdeacon – 'a remote country parish – Mr. Dennis might do well enough.'

'In a place like Fishpond Canonicorum,' said Sybil, 'yes, quite possibly. He would at all events be less noticeable than he is here.'

The parish of Fishpond Canonicorum is in the gift of the dean and chapter of Carminster. It was, just then, vacant, owing to the death of a very aged vicar. It is a small parish. It is a long way from anywhere, especially from Carminster. It does not matter to anyone whether the vicar of Fishpond Canonicorum is conscious of his dignity or not. Indeed, the vicars of such places have very little dignity to be conscious of.

The archdeacon nodded.

'There will be a chapter meeting next week,' he said, 'to appoint a new vicar.'

Sybil nodded.

In this way Sybil and the archdeacon arranged for the future of Dennis and for the cure of souls (about 200 of them) in Fishpond Canonicorum. Dennis was to have very little say in the matter. The parishioners of Fishpond Canonicorum were to have none.

24

IT WAS ABOUT HALF-PAST ten when Dennis and Inspector Smallways reached the cathedral. They entered through the south transept door, using Dennis's key.

Inspector Smallways carried a crowbar. Dennis had a screwdriver, a small hammer, one or two other tools, and an electric torch in his pockets.

They closed the door behind them and stood for a while listening intently for any sound. The great building was perfectly silent and very dark. Even Smallways, who was pitifully nervous, was satisfied at last that they were alone in the cathedral. His nervousness was excusable. It would have been very awkward for him if he were found breaking into an ancient tomb in a cathedral late at night.

'Come on,' said Dennis. 'There's nothing to be afraid of.'

He led the way along the south transept, through the screen, up the choir to the shrine of Bishop Feda. He switched on his electric torch. The ray of light ran round the upper part of the bishop's tomb. The stone lid fitted closely to the great coffin, but the line of junction was discernible enough.

'Slip in the crowbar,' said Dennis. 'Gently, now, gently. We mustn't chip the stone.'

Smallways was a careful man and deft when handling tools. He pushed in the sharp edge of the crowbar end. He pushed it farther and the lid stirred slightly.

'Prise it up,' said Dennis.

The lid rose slowly.

'Hold on,' said Dennis. 'It won't do to let it slip off altogether. I'll go round to the far side and steady it while you raise it until you are able to see in. Here, take the torch.'

Dennis, at the far side of the tomb, gripped the edge of the lid firmly, letting it rest on his hands and steadying it by pressing his chest against it. Smallways depressed the end of the crowbar with his right hand. The lid rose slowly. Smallways pushed the electric torch into the cavity, leaned forward, and peered into it. Save for some bones the tomb was empty!

'There's nothing in it,' he said, and then added bitterly, 'I never thought there would be.'

'Nonsense!' said Dennis. 'The jewels must be there.'

'Come and see for yourself, if you don't believe me.'

The change of places and functions was a troublesome business and took some time; but in the end Dennis held the crowbar and the torch while Smallways, at the far side, steadied the lid.

'Well,' said Smallways, 'found the emeralds?'

'No,' said Dennis. 'But I say, Smallways, there are a lot of bones.'

'What does it matter about the bones?' said Smallways. 'Let's get out of this as quick as we can.'

'All these bones can't possibly belong to the old bishop,' said Dennis. 'No one could have so many, not even if he was a cardinal, and Feda wasn't that.'

He had raised the lid so high that he could thrust his head into the coffin. Smallways had to exert his full strength to prevent the stone slab from slipping and crashing to the ground.

'Let down the lid at once,' he said. 'I can't hold it.'

'But, I say, Smallways,' said Dennis, 'this is almost better than finding the jewels. The bishop must have managed somehow to have that Chloe of his buried with him. What an old boy!'

'I can't hold on,' said Smallways, gasping.

'One minute,' said Dennis. 'If I could only make sure that there are two skulls. Just think of what the archdeacon's feelings will be when I tell him.'

But Smallways' next appeal for relief was too anguished to be ignored. Dennis, in spite of his anxiety to examine the bones, felt bound to let the lid slip into its place.

'And now,' said Smallways, 'let's get out of this before anybody comes.'

Ten minutes later they were sitting together in Dennis's study.

'That,' said Smallways, 'destroys our case against Hodson.'

'I don't really much mind if it does,' said Dennis. 'What I'm thinking of is the archdeacon, and how to make the most of this scandal about Chloe and the old bishop. The archdeacon does hate scandal of any sort so heartily.'

But Smallways was totally uninterested in the morals of Bishop Feda, and found no special pleasure in outraging the archdeacon's feelings.

'I believe he did it,' he said. 'But what's the use of believing a thing if you can't prove it?'

'Of course he did it,' said Dennis, 'and it ought not to be impossible to prove whether the bones belonged to a man or woman.'

'Oh, damn the bones!' said Smallways. 'What I want is the jewels, and they're not to be found.'

'Does it matter so much about the jewels?' said Dennis. 'You've got a fairly complete case against Hodson, haven't you?'

'I've got no case at all,' said Smallways; 'no case that a lawyer couldn't tear to flitters.'

'The dean's story,' said Dennis. 'That seems to me pretty strong evidence that Cresswood was murdered.'

'It's no evidence at all that Hodson murdered him.'

'Hodson's boy,' said Dennis, 'dropped that tune in the Song School. How did he get it if Hodson didn't give it to him, and how could Hodson have had it if he didn't steal it from Cresswood?'

'There's no proof that the boy left it there. There's no proof that Hodson gave it to him. And now there's no proof that the tune meant anything.'

'Hang it all,' said Dennis, 'there is proof of that. I demonstrated that the thing was an ingenious Cryptogram, giving the hiding place of the jewels.'

'If the jewels had been there,' said Smallways, 'you might have persuaded the jury to believe in the cryptogram. But they weren't there.'

'That does not alter the conclusiveness of my demonstration,' said Dennis. 'Hill hid the jewels in the old bishop's tomb. What happened to them afterwards I don't know, but I expect that Hodson went and got them.'

'Hodson didn't,' said Smallways. 'I've had that man watched for the last four days, and he hasn't been near the cathedral day or night. As for your demonstration, as you call it —'

'It is a demonstration.'

'It may be. I think myself that it is. But how are we going to persuade a jury of it? We can't put Elsie Hill into the witness box, or Binder. Even if we did no one would believe a word they said. The prison people won't give themselves away. All we have to go on is a scrap of paper which might have come from anywhere. Fancy going into court with that C sharp theory of yours!'

'It was you who suggested the explanation of C sharp.'

'Whoever suggested it, it's no good. Even a judge would snigger at it.'

'What do you make of Hodson's paying Cresswood's debts for him? If he wasn't trying to buy that tune from him why did he hand over all that money?'

'Pure goodness of heart,' said Smallways.

'Goodness of heart! Hodson!'

'Oh, I don't believe it,' said Smallways. But it's what he'll say, and, what's more, a jury will believe him.'

'Oh, well,' said Dennis, 'if you can't hang Hodson you can't. It's a disappointment to you, but apparently it can't be helped. But it's some consolation to think of the state of agonised fury the archdeacon will be in over Chloe's bones.'

'I wish,' said Smallways, 'I knew where those damned emeralds are. Hodson didn't get them, that's one comfort. I don't believe Binder could. I don't see how Elsie Hill could have managed it. The only thing certain is that they're not in the tomb.'

'I rather hope,' said Dennis, 'that Elsie has pulled it off somehow. She's not a girl that I'd actually care to marry, but she seems to have more right to those jewels than anyone else.'

'The insurance company,' said Smallways, 'are the only people with any rights at all.'

In the end, to Smallways' satisfaction, the insurance company got them.

25

LETTER FROM T. SMALLWAYS, Inspector of Police, to the Rev. John Dennis, Vicar of Fishpond Canonicorum, dated October 9th 1930:

MY DEAR DENNIS,

I wonder if you hear any Carminster news nowadays. If not, it will interest you to know that Carson, the dean's verger, died on Tuesday – a stroke, after matins in the cathedral. He was carried home but never recovered consciousness. You remember his wife, a tall, rather silent woman who lived with him, not much of a woman any way you take her, but, as it turned out, honest. She came to me yesterday and asked me to go round to Carson's house. She had been going over the old boy's things and had opened a tin box, like a lawyer's deed box, which he kept under his bed. It had been there, so she said, for over three years, and she'd never seen it open. Naturally enough she was a bit curious, and as soon as she got hold of the old man's keys she opened it. It was that box, or rather the contents, which she wanted me to see. I went with her, opened the box, and found the Carminster emeralds. What do you think of that?

The insurance company is delighted, of course. I made a point of telling Hodson, and he's in a state of black sulks, but it's really a very mild punishment, considering that he murdered Cresswood. I expect Binder and your pet Elsie are pretty furious too, but of course I haven't seen them. Neither of them have shown up in Carminster since you left.

I wonder how Carson got them. He might have had a look at the tune in the Song School before you found it; but I doubt it. If his wife's right, about the box being under his bed unopened for the last three years, he must have had the jewels long before Hill wrote the cryptogram.

Anyway, if he'd been using the tune he wouldn't have left it there for you to find. My own idea is that he'd all along kept a pretty close eye on Hill. It came out at the trial that he disliked the man and always resented his being made a verger. He may have had good reason to suspect that Hill hid the jewels somewhere in the cathedral. The old Bishop's tomb was being moved at the time. Carson may have guessed that that was a likely hiding place, or he may simply have gone on searching systematically till he found the things.

If his wife's story is true he had them tucked away safe in that tin box of his for the last three years. What do you think about it?

'Ever yours sincerely

'T. SMALLWAYS'

Telegram from the Rev. John Dennis, Vicar of Fishpond Canonicorum to T. Smallways, Inspector of Police, Carminster:

'Be sure to publish the facts. This scandal will be more than the archdeacon can stand. It ought to finish him off.'

THE END

Head over to Oleander to see the books in the series so far and to sign up to our infrequent Newsletter to be told of our latest titles before anyone else?

www.oleanderpress.com/golden-age-crime

Made in United States
Orlando, FL
20 February 2023

30210344R00140